CW00539905

MURDER IN THE DRAWING ROOM

ROOM

A CLEOPATRA FOX MYSTERY, BOOK 3

C.J. ARCHER

WWW.CJARCHER.COM

CHAPTER 1

LONDON, FEBRUARY 1900

I had been expecting a visit from Harry Armitage ever since the newspapers reported his detective agency solved the murder of the Piccadilly Playhouse actress. The fact that he had not called on me at the Mayfair Hotel was a source of both disappointment and regret. Disappointment because I'd assumed he'd be gentlemanly enough to thank me properly for giving his name to the journalists, and regret that I hadn't taken the glory for myself and set up my own agency on the back of the publicity instead. The regret, however, was fleeting.

My friend Harmony's irritation was not. She made it very clear she thought I was a fool for letting the world think Mr. Armitage had solved the crime. She wouldn't speak to me for two days, although she continued to clean my rooms of a morning as part of her maid's duties. I left her half my breakfast, as usual, but she didn't touch it. It took an order of French pastries for the frostiness to thaw, and even then she made it sound as if she were doing me a favor by sharing them.

"I wouldn't want you getting fat," she said right before she bit into a buttery *pain au chocolat*.

"You're such a sweet friend."

She stopped chewing to stare at me.

"Yes, we're friends," I said, taking the other *pain au*

chocolat from the plate. "We must be or we wouldn't be able to tell the other what we truly think."

"I'm just your maid."

"You are not *just* anything. You are marvelous to protect me as you do, and to want me to succeed. But you must allow me to explain my decision." I had already explained it to her, but it seemed we needed to revisit it. "Mr. Armitage's new business needed a helping hand, and I was in a position to give it."

"He can take care of himself. He's a man. You've got to take care of you."

"And I will, in due course. Mr. Armitage may be a man but he must fend for himself. I have this lovely hotel to live in and no financial burdens. One day, I'll make my own way in the world, and move out of here, but until then, I must abide my uncle's wish that I shouldn't work. Giving Mr. Armitage the glory was a way of killing two birds with one stone. I don't anger my uncle and Mr. Armitage reaps the benefits of the publicity."

She licked each of her fingers, taking her time to savor the chocolatey goodness. Or to think about what she wanted to say next. "It wouldn't have anything to do with him being handsome, would it?"

I barked a laugh. "Good lord, no! Do you think I would be taken in by a strong set of cheekbones, warm eyes and an athletic physique? I'm hardly a giddy schoolgirl."

By the way she eyed me, I suspected she thought I protested too vehemently. "Then did you help him because you felt guilty for getting him dismissed from his position here?"

I shot to my feet. "No. Shall we do my hair?"

I avoided her gaze in the mirror as I sat at my dressing table. She picked up the brush and stroked it through my hair with surprising gentleness. She must know I was lying about feeling guilty and feel sorry for me.

"Are you surprised he hasn't thanked me?" I asked. "I'm surprised."

She abruptly stopped brushing. "About that…"

I spun around to face her. "Harmony? What is it?"

2

She reached into her apron pocket and pulled out a letter. "This arrived for you from Mr. Armitage."

I unfolded it and read. It was dated two days prior. "Harmony! Why did you withhold it?"

"He's not deserving of your generosity."

"I don't see what that has to do with you not giving me this. Please don't withhold my mail from me again."

The letter was very brief. It simply stated:

Miss Fox,

I suppose you are responsible for the surge in new clients coming through my door.

Sincerely,

Harry Armitage.

I turned the letter over, but there was nothing written on the reverse. It was hardly the gratitude I'd hoped for.

"You're disappointed," Harmony said carefully.

I forced myself to smile at her reflection. "Not at all."

"That man's not worth the trouble of your thoughts, let alone your kind actions. You should put that letter where it deserves to go—in the waste basket."

I didn't need to be a detective to know she'd read the letter earlier and had kept it from me to spare my feelings. She'd known I'd be disappointed with Mr. Armitage's lack of appreciation.

She put down the brush and I caught her hand as she let it go. "Thank you, Harmony. But I would rather be informed than not." I rose. "Now, to write a response."

She hurried into the sitting room ahead of me, pulled the chair out from the writing desk, and plucked a blank sheet of hotel stationery from the top of the small stack on the silver tray.

I sat and wrote:

Mr. Armitage,

You're welcome.

Sincerely,

Cleopatra Fox

Another week passed before a second letter arrived from Mr. Armitage, inviting me to a meeting at his office. He wished to discuss a business proposition with me that would be to our mutual benefit.

Finally! He must be so busy that he needed a partner to help with the load. While I hoped to one day have my name on his agency's door, I was willing to bide my time and be more of a silent partner for now. That would not ruffle Uncle Ronald's feathers. He might be able to accept that I'd solved two murders, but he could not accept me investigating professionally, for money. For now, while I needed his financial support, I would be Mr. Armitage's business partner in secret. Painting my name on the door would come later.

The following morning, armed with a notepad, pencil, and a smart new hat covered in dark gray satin, trimmed with a brass buckle on one side and a cluster of silk leaves on the other, I left the hotel. I got no further than the building next door where my cousin Floyd and Uncle Ronald stood with two other men, both of whom sported mutton chop whiskers. I'd been avoiding my uncle ever since the last murder had been solved, but it was too late to cross the road; he'd already seen me and beckoned me to join them. At least, with others present, he wouldn't lecture me on forming an inappropriate friendship with Harry Armitage. Ever since the previous assistant manager, Mr. Hirst, had informed my uncle of my frequent meetings with Mr. Armitage, I'd known a confrontation would come. I was ready for it. But I wanted to put it off for as long as possible.

"Cleo, come and join us. You always have good insight into the hotel's business."

"I do?" I looked to Floyd, but he merely pursed his lips. I suspected his father had never heaped such praise on him.

Uncle Ronald introduced the two men, an architect and the hotel's accountant, who both worked for large firms in the city. "Tell them what you said a few weeks ago, Cleo." At my blank look, he elaborated. "About how the hotel should open a restaurant to attract the public as well as service guests, and convert the current dining room to a ballroom." I'd never seen him so enthused. The flushed cheeks weren't entirely the result of the chilly air. Usually he looked like a bulldog who'd lost his favorite chew toy, but now he looked like he'd spied a new, better one.

I didn't want to disappoint him, but I could hardly recall what I'd said to him weeks ago. I would have to make it up.

"I hear all the luxury hotels have restaurants that can be accessed by the public from the pavement nowadays, rather than reserved for hotel guests and positioned at the back. If the Mayfair is to compete with them, it ought to have one too."

The architect gave me a polite if somewhat condescending smile. "Well said, Miss Fox. We are all in agreement, except for Mr. Dreyfuss."

The accountant indicated the door to the hotel where Frank the doorman welcomed new guests and Goliath the porter piled luggage onto a trolley. "You have a perfectly good restaurant already."

"At the back," Uncle Ronald pointed out.

"Does it matter where it is? If you advertise to the public, they will soon discover it, if that's the sort of diner you wish to attract."

"Precisely the point, Dreyfuss. I don't wish to advertise." Uncle Ronald made a sound of disgust in the back of his throat. "The very notion goes against everything the Mayfair stands for. Exclusivity, luxury, and above all, discretion. An advertisement splashed all over the newspapers says the opposite."

The accountant might have been taller than my barrel-shaped uncle, but he was as slender as a lamp post. At Uncle Ronald's darkening face, he swallowed hard. He held his ground, however. "You may have to advertise if you want to go ahead with this."

"We'll see."

"The Mayfair can't compete with its larger rivals."

Uncle Ronald bristled. "We *have* to compete. The bank has approved the loan so I say we go ahead and lease the entire ground floor." He turned to me. "Do you think it will be large enough?"

"Is what large enough?" I asked.

He swept his hand from side to side to indicate the tea room, photographic studio, and chemist shop housed on the ground floor of the building neighboring the hotel. On their own, none were very large, but combined, it would make an excellent space for a restaurant befitting a luxury hotel. The Savoy's was larger, but they also had many more guest

5

rooms. This would be perfect for the Mayfair, a smaller, family-owned hotel. Being located beside the Mayfair meant the hotel's suites wouldn't be impacted and capacity wouldn't need to be reduced during renovations.

"I think it's marvelous," I said. "The size of the senior staff offices could be reduced, and the one currently occupied by Mr. Hobart could be opened up and knocked through. Then you'd have a lovely wide thoroughfare leading from the foyer to the new restaurant so guests don't have to leave the hotel, but access from the pavement will mean the public can arrive via a separate front entrance."

Uncle Ronald beamed. "I told you she has a good sense for business."

Floyd's lips pursed tighter.

"The wide street frontage has four windows." I nodded at Floyd. "My cousin once told me his friends like to be seen when they dine out together."

Floyd came to life, roused from his self-pitying strop, and grasped the olive branch I held out to him. "Indeed they do, and it's vital to the success of an exclusive restaurant that it attract the young, fast set. Believe me, they'll flock to such a favorable setting, and they'll bring actresses and opera singers with them. The windows are perfect."

"I would say food is also important," Mr. Dreyfuss muttered.

"We have an excellent chef," my uncle said. "He's French."

"I suppose he approves of expansion."

Uncle Ronald's smile froze. "Of course. Do *you* approve of the idea?"

"You don't need my approval. I advise you, and you make your decisions anyway."

Uncle Ronald chuckled and clapped the accountant on the shoulder. "Prepare the paperwork and we'll go to the bank together at your earliest convenience." He put out his hand and Mr. Dreyfuss shook it.

The accountant did not immediately let go, however. He took a step closer to Uncle Ronald and lowered his voice. "If it doesn't work, you could lose everything."

"Let me worry about that." Uncle Ronald didn't look

worried in the least, which, from what I'd learned of his nature in the month since arriving at the hotel, was unlike him. He seemed to carry the weight of the hotel on his broad shoulders. He pored over ledgers during the day and charmed guests in the evening. He worried over details, great and small, and rarely delegated to Floyd. He seemed to have no true friends, only guests, potential guests, business associates, and important people he felt he ought to cultivate relationships with. When he spent time with his wife and children, it was in full view of guests as if to remind them that the Mayfair was a family hotel.

Perhaps I was being unfair. He had taken me in when he didn't have to, welcoming me to the hotel and the family with open arms and a generous allowance. He was neither the snob nor the brute my grandparents had led me to believe. Any harsh words I'd heard him speak were said under the pressures of dire circumstances.

I resolved to be fairer towards him. I did not, however, plan to tarry and endure his lecture about Mr. Armitage. As the architect and accountant bade us farewell, I made to leave too.

"Cleo, come by my office later," Uncle Ronald called out to me. "There's something I need to speak to you about."

I gave a little wave and hurried off. Later, when I failed to show up at his office, I would claim I never heard him over the rumble of carriage wheels and shouts of passing hawkers. The traffic on Piccadilly was truly atrocious.

"Cleo! Wait!" Floyd caught up to me and I worried I would be given a lecture by proxy.

"Not now, Floyd. I have an appointment with a...dentist."

"Toothache?"

I rubbed my jaw. "See you later."

He lightly caught my elbow. "I just wanted to say thanks for what you did back there. But it's not necessary. I can fight my own battles."

"What battle?" I called over my shoulder as I walked off. "I have no idea what you're talking about."

He tilted his head to the side and watched me go. I hurried off, somewhat annoyed at his masculine pride. Why couldn't he accept a little help? It was a small thing I'd done for him, hardly even worth mentioning. At least he thanked me, proving masculine pride may be hard to swallow, but not impossible.

I quickened my step and reached Broadwick Street in Soho a short while later. The street was damp from recent rain, the gutters clogged with mud and horse deposits that had been swept aside. At least the pavement was clean. I entered the Roma Café and greeted the two elderly men sitting on the stools by the counter. My limited Italian earned me nods of appreciation in return. They were always in the café, along with Luigi the owner. Like barnacles on a sea rock, I doubted even a storm could pry them off their stools.

"*Bella*, what a pleasant surprise!" Luigi's Cockney accent was at odds with his tanned skin and the occasional Italian word he threw into conversation. He beamed and indicated I should take a seat. "We ain't seen you in so long."

"Almost two weeks," I said, pulling over a third stool. Another two men sat at a table by the window, speaking quietly over small coffee cups. The café was busier than I'd ever seen it.

Luigi jerked his thumb at the ceiling. "He's upstairs."

"May I have two coffees to take up, please?"

He poured beans into the grinder and turned the handle, intensifying the delicious aroma already filling the café. "Lucky Harry."

"In what way?"

"To have a beautiful woman bring him coffee." He flashed me a grin as he poured boiling water from a kettle into the bottom of a metal siphon pot. "And for his flourishing business."

"He has new clients?"

He nodded. "A steady stream has passed my café going up to his office. Some even come in. It's been good for business. Thank you."

I blinked. "Oh?"

"Harry tells me you are responsible for the newspaper article that named his agency in the solving of the actress's murder." He set two cups on the counter in front of me then returned to the stove and peered into the top of the siphon pot. Satisfied, he poured in the ground coffee and stirred it with a wooden spoon. "He also told me he didn't deserve the publicity, and that *you* were the one who solved it. I should warn you that he ain't happy about it."

"He's being childish."

"Can I be there when you tell him that?" Once the coffee was brewed, he stirred it again. After allowing it to steep for a couple of minutes, he poured coffee from the bottom section of the siphon pot into the cups. "These are free."

"You don't have to do that. I was helping Harry, not you, although I am glad the café has benefited too."

"They're not free because you sent customers my way. It's because you're a beautiful lady."

I laughed and thanked him. He rounded the counter and opened the door for me then opened the door to the stairs that led up to Mr. Armitage's office. Just as I suspected, the elderly customers remained glued to their stools.

In the past, I'd opened the door to Mr. Armitage's office at the top of the stairs without knocking. But our relationship had changed again and I didn't feel comfortable entering unannounced. Besides, my hands were full. I tapped the door with the toe of my boot.

He opened it, smiling. The smile slipped a little upon seeing me, but not entirely. That was a good start.

"Peace offering," I said, holding out the coffee. "No need to pay me back."

"Since Luigi gave them to you for free, I wasn't going to offer."

"How did you know?"

He accepted the coffee and returned to his seat behind the desk. "I'm a good detective."

"And Luigi is a terrible flirt whose business benefited from my actions? You don't need to be Sherlock Holmes to guess that he'll thank me in the only way he knows how— with a wink, a smile and free coffee."

He gave me one of those wry smiles he liked to give, the sort that filled his handsome face with character and warned of an intelligence lurking behind the warm eyes and charming manner. Not that he turned the warmth and charm on for me these days. In the beginning, when he worked at the hotel, he treated me as an assistant manager should treat

9

his employer's niece. But ever since he lost his job because of me, he'd shown his truer self, the one where he was occasionally annoyed, somewhat brusque, and rarely charming.

I liked this Harry Armitage better. He was more real, and far more interesting.

I found it difficult to suppress my smile. I was simply glad to have this opportunity to speak to him about our future partnership after almost two weeks of silence.

I glanced around the office and took in the decorative touches I'd suggested on a prior visit—a photograph of Mr. Armitage with his adopted parents and another of a woman alone, most likely his birth mother, a framed sketch of Tower Bridge, and the velvet cushion on the armchair. I was glad to see he'd kept the worn, brown leather armchair. Along with the secondhand desk, it gave the office a welcoming, lived-in feel which could help establish his authenticity and calm agitated clients.

He drained the cup and set it to one side, then sat forward. "I'll begin by saying something I should have said days ago. Thank you for mentioning my agency to the journalists. I appreciate it."

"Then why do you sound like you're choking on the words?"

"I do not."

"You do."

He leaned back in the chair and rubbed his jaw. "Fine. I'm sorry. It's just that...I didn't deserve to benefit from that case. I did very little to catch the killer. You did it all. I'm happy to accept publicity for something I did, but it feels like cheating to receive it for something I didn't do."

When he put it like that, it actually made sense. I would feel unworthy too. But on the other hand, I would also accept the assistance with grace. "So it doesn't have anything to do with the fact a woman was the one to help you?"

"I'm equally dismissive of the assistance afforded me by men *and* women."

I laughed. "I'll be sure to tell Harmony. She'll be pleased to hear it, although she might not forgive you for the brusque tone in your letter."

"Harmony? You speak to her about me? I mean, this?" He indicated both of us turn. "Our...whatever this is?"

"Yes. She's my friend. A friend who kept your letter from me." I explained why it had taken me two days to reply, including that she did it to protect my feelings.

"She thought your feelings needed protecting from my letter?"

"To be fair, it was rather curt."

"It was brief. And that's not the point. Why did she think your feelings needed protecting? Did the letter injure you in some way?"

"Of course not. I can cope with a little brusqueness in written correspondence from an acquaintance."

"Then why—?"

"Can we change the subject? We're going around in circles and I have work to do."

"Work?"

"Isn't that why I'm here? To work with you on a case since you're too inundated to do it all?"

"Hardly inundated, but you're right. Let's get started." He removed some folders from a stack on the corner of the desk and spun them around to face me. "Ever since my agency's name became associated with the Piccadilly Playhouse murder, I've had several inquiries from people wishing to engage my services." He tapped the stack of files. "I would like to give these ones to you."

I flipped open the first folder and scanned the single page inside. The details were written in a neat if tight hand, beginning with the client's personal information and concluding with a description of the problem he needed investigating. The client was a man who wanted to determine if his wife was committing adultery so he could divorce her. I closed the folder and opened the next.

"You mean you'd like me to *join* your agency as your partner to solve these cases," I said as I read.

"That's why I like you. You're an optimist."

I looked up from the file of yet another husband wanting to engage Mr. Armitage's services to discover if his wife was involved with another man. "You want me to *assist* you," I said flatly. "Mr. Armitage, is that fair considering my experience?"

"Not assist either."

I frowned. "I don't understand. Why are you showing me these if you don't want me to assist you or work alongside you?"

"I'm *giving* you those cases. I don't want them. You can set up your own agency and work on them officially, or you can continue in an unofficial capacity. Either way, I'm sure you can negotiate a fair rate for yourself." He sat back, arms crossed, looking rather satisfied with himself.

It took me a moment to gather my wits. "Is this your way of thanking me?"

"No. I truly don't want them. If you don't either then I'll inform the clients and they can go to another agency. I don't expect a commission, if that's causing your hesitation."

"It's not. I...I'm not sure what to say." I studied one of the files again, at a loss for words. It was a disappointment not to be asked to join him, even as an assistant, but not altogether surprising. "You don't want any of these cases? Not a single one?"

"No."

"Why not?"

"My agency isn't going to investigate adultery."

"But if you're being paid, what does it matter?"

His jaw firmed. "I'll wait for more challenging cases."

I opened my mouth to continue protesting, but shut it again. He looked as though he'd made up his mind, and I knew from experience that once he made up his mind, he rarely changed it.

I scanned each of the files again. There were five in total. By the look of the depleted stack of folders on his desk, there were not many more cases. Indeed, there was only one. He wasn't giving these up because he had too much work on. He was giving them up because he honestly didn't want them. I admired his conviction. Associating his agency name to the sordid business of catching unfaithful spouses could narrow his focus too early and stop more interesting cases coming his way.

And then it struck me. There was another reason he was

giving these away. I checked each folder again, to be sure. "They're all the same. They are all husbands investigating their wives. Except this one, where it's a wife investigating a husband's infidelity." I looked up at him and smiled. He scowled back. "However, she suspects her husband of having a liaison with a man, so it's not completely dissimilar."

"What of it?"

I tapped the final line on the document I'd been reading. It had appeared in each of the files. "The husbands—and the one wife—want you to 'use your masculine ingenuity' if no lover can be unearthed through the usual investigation methods. Does that mean what I think it means?"

He snatched the folders off me and shuffled them into a stack. His jaw had firmed even more and his shoulders were quite rigid. "It does."

"They want you to seduce their wives to ensure their guilt?" And the one husband, I almost added.

"Only if I've exhausted all investigative leads to find their lover."

My smile widened.

"It's not amusing."

"It is a little."

He looked at me over the files he held in his hands. "You find it amusing that husbands want to pay another man to seduce their wives so they can use that in divorce proceedings as evidence of her adultery?"

My smile vanished. When he put it like that, it wasn't amusing at all. "You're right. I don't blame you for not taking those cases and I don't want them either."

He nodded as if he agreed with me, but I could see he wasn't convinced. "Are you sure? If you're prepared to investigate them privately, without starting an agency, then you can keep your name out of it while being paid. Also, there'll be no misunderstandings over the techniques you employ. As a woman, you can't seduce the wives. And that one husband wouldn't look twice at you if the information in that file is correct."

He made some good points. Excellent ones, in fact. Besides which, the fee would be helpful. If I took on one or two of these cases, I could begin to build a financial cushion

13

for myself for when I moved out of the hotel. And as Harry said, there would be no attempts at seduction. I would not be trapping anyone, or risking my reputation.

"Are these the only cases that have come your way?" I indicated the sole folder he hadn't given me. "And that one?"

He nodded. "It's not uncommon. My father has encountered several private detectives in his time and they claim marital infidelity makes up more than three-quarters of their case load."

"It's going to limit you if you exclude them."

He merely lifted his shoulders in a shrug. "So you'll take them?"

I put out my hand and he passed back the files. I read through them again. "I will. Thank you. I'll call on each of these gentlemen, and the woman, this afternoon and see which of them wishes to hire me, if any."

Mr. Armitage offered to write a letter to each of the five explaining that his "esteemed and very experienced colleague" was willing to investigate since he couldn't.

I tucked each of the letters into the relevant folders and headed for the door.

Mr. Armitage was quick and beat me to it. He smiled down at me as he opened it. "So you thought I was going to offer you a partnership here?"

"It crossed my mind."

"I told you, I don't want a partner."

"You don't want a partner *yet*."

"Your faith in my business acumen is refreshing. I hope to one day have so much work on that I do need to employ other investigators. But I won't be taking on a partner. Nor would I ask you to work for me."

I sighed. "Because you don't wish to anger my uncle. Yes, I know."

He shrugged an apology, although by the way his lips quirked I suspected he wasn't at all sorry.

I slipped past him through the doorway, getting closer than a woman should to a man who wasn't a relative. It was hardly my fault since he was partially blocking the exit. Well, it was somewhat my fault. I found I couldn't stop myself brushing up against him. "I won't tell him if you won't."

His eyes were bright with humor even though his lips were set into a flat line. "Good day, Miss Fox."

I trotted down the stairs with my bag in one hand and the files under my arm, feeling lighter than I had in two weeks. Mr. Armitage had not only thanked me for getting his name into the newspapers, despite it not being what he wanted, he had also given me something to do. I preferred to have an occupation than sit around the hotel all day drinking tea.

And, for once, he bade me good *day*, not goodbye.

CHAPTER 2

$\mathcal{I}$ spent the next few hours in the heart of the city's financial district having doors slammed in my face, metaphorically speaking and, in one instance, quite literally. The men had only given Mr. Armitage an address for their places of work, not their homes, to keep the investigations a secret from their wives. The first three potential clients expressed either regret or anger that Mr. Armitage wasn't willing to help, and none wanted a woman taking their case. A fourth, the only woman, refused to hire me too, on the grounds that I wasn't "suitable."

That left only one gentleman on the list, and it was not as easy to gain an audience with him. He'd given Mr. Armitage the Savile Row address of his club. Since Mr. Armitage was not a member, he could only be admitted as a guest. As a woman, I couldn't even do that. I had to suffer through the disdainful sneer of the manager on duty before he finally agreed to give Mr. Warrington my written message along with Mr. Armitage's letter of recommendation.

Mr. Warrington's response arrived a full ten minutes later. He refused to see me.

The manager attempted to close the door on me, but I wedged myself into the gap before he could. "Kindly take another message to Mr. Warrington, if you please." I took out my pencil and notepad and scrawled a second note. I tore it out and handed the paper to the manager.

His nostrils flared. "Mr. Warrington has made his position clear. He doesn't wish to speak to you."

"He will once he reads that. I promise you, if he refuses to see me a second time, I'll leave without a fuss. But he *must* read it."

Unlike the first four cases, I wasn't giving up on Mr. Warrington. I knew something about him. Something that gave me leverage.

The manager returned after mere moments. "Mr. Warrington will see you now. This way, Miss Fox."

He led me across the black and white tiled entrance hall to an adjoining room with barely enough space for two leather armchairs and a wall of shelved books. A large painting of a snow-capped mountain range took up almost the entirety of another wall. With no fireplace, it must only be used in summertime. It was freezing inside, and smelled faintly of cigar smoke and leather-bound covers.

I remained standing and only had to wait a few minutes before a slim man of medium build entered. I guessed him to be aged in his late thirties, with a luxurious black mustache speckled with gray, thick hair that fell in waves to his nape, and a set of clear blue eyes. The scent of sandalwood and musk followed him into the room and quickly overwhelmed even the cigar smoke.

"How did you know I was receiving threatening letters?" he asked after we exchanged greetings.

He had not invited me to sit, but I sat anyway and indicated he should take the other armchair. After a moment's hesitation, he did.

"I'm afraid I can't reveal my sources," I said.

"Nobody knows except a few close colleagues and the police."

Having a good memory for names and an ear for gossip had proved fruitful for once. Uncle Ronald often tried to get Floyd interested in politics, but Floyd usually found the topic dull. To pique his interest, my uncle had mentioned an interesting piece of news he'd heard about a politician who'd recently received threatening letters because of a controversial bill his party was trying to block in parliament. Uncle Ronald hadn't divulged where he'd heard the information, but I suspected it was in a club such as this.

"It seems at least one of your colleagues isn't as discreet as you thought," I said.

He studied me for a long moment. "What does any of this have to do with my wife's adultery?"

"Nothing."

"You wanted me to see how good an investigator you are. Is that it?"

I simply smiled.

"Very well. Consider me convinced. You're hired."

I was taken aback by the speed of it all. I'd expected his refusal, and had prepared an explanation as to why a woman would be suitable for the task of discovering the movements of another woman.

Mr. Warrington grunted humorlessly at my surprise. "I am not particular as to whom I hire, as long as they are good and discreet. You've proved you're good, and Mr. Armitage's letter also vouches for you. Now you must prove to me that you can be discreet."

"A promise isn't enough?"

"No." I wondered if his no-nonsense manner worked in parliament. Given the theatrics the newspapers often reported, I expected he was an exception, but that didn't mean his approach wasn't effective.

"My uncle is Sir Ronald Bainbridge, owner of the Mayfair Hotel."

His brows rose. "I see. And you don't wish him to find out about your little investigative enterprise."

"Precisely. So I will promise to be discreet if you are."

He hesitated then thrust out his hand. "I'll give you five pounds."

I swallowed. Was that a good amount? It sounded good, but given I didn't know how long this case would take to solve, it might be either too generous or not enough. "Half up front, to cover expenses."

He extended his hand further. "You are a good negotiator, Miss Fox. I'll have my man of business send you the payment before the end of the day."

"He can find me at the Mayfair." I shook his hand and sat

back. "Tell me why you think your wife is having a liaison with another man."

"At first, it was just a feeling I had. She was always going out, according to my butler, and came home empty-handed or with only a few items even though she claimed to have been shopping all day. So I had her followed. She met with a man in the park and went to a hotel with him."

"The Mayfair?" I asked, thinking that was why he'd readily agreed to hire me.

"The Midland Grand at St Pancras Station."

I noted the name in my book. "What day was this?"

"Friday."

That was only three days ago. I wrote that down too. "Do you have a description of the man?"

"He had the physique and bearing of a youngish fellow. He may have been early middle age, but certainly wasn't old. He was only seen from a distance so I cannot tell you more."

"And did the person who followed them to the hotel make inquiries of the staff?"

"Certainly not." He smoothed his hand down the front of his waistcoat, stopping to finger the gold watch-chain threaded through one of the buttonholes and ending in a T-bar.

I suspected he'd been the one to follow them and hadn't wanted anyone to know, including me. "What evidence do you require for the court to grant you a divorce?"

"Anything that proves her adultery beyond doubt. I suggest you start by questioning the staff at the Midland Grand and finding one who can identify her."

I wasn't sure a matching description from a single witness would be enough. Divorces were difficult to obtain and required absolute proof of either adultery or violence. Unhappiness or dissatisfaction was not enough. Proceedings were often lengthy and therefore expensive, and because of their rarity, they almost always ended in scandal and shame.

"May I question your household staff?" I asked.

"Only the butler. Go to the service entrance and ask for Henderson."

I wrote the name down. "May I ask him to let me into Mrs. Warrington's private rooms?"

"Certainly not."

I looked up from the notebook. "There could be personal correspondence between Mrs. Warrington and her lover. All the evidence you need may be there."

"It isn't. I've looked. Henderson has looked. She's not a fool, my wife, and does not keep correspondence lying about where the staff can read it."

I wasn't suggesting she left it lying about, but somewhere hidden. I didn't say as much, however. That was a battle for another day. I would start with learning more about Mrs. Warrington's movements.

"You can begin by speaking to Henderson today," he said. "I'll tell him to expect you."

"Tomorrow." I closed the notebook and tucked it into my bag. "I have other avenues to try today."

"The Midland Grand. Yes, of course. You may need this." He pulled out a photograph from his inside jacket pocket and handed it to me. It was a head-only image of a woman in middle-age wearing a hat decorated with a whole bird nesting on one side of the wide brim. It was difficult to tell the specific bird in the black and white photo, but it looked to be some kind of parrot. "Her name is Isobel."

The photograph would help with my inquiries at the railway hotel, although that wouldn't be the only lead I'd follow today. I planned to make my way back to the Mayfair, where I would learn more about my client and his wife using the oldest of investigative techniques—gossip.

* * *

THE MIDLAND GRAND Hotel was as impressive as its name suggested. Positioned alongside St Pancras Station, it was a monolithic tribute to the booming railway industry of decades past. The Mayfair was a small cousin by comparison, but not a poorer one. Indeed, from what I'd heard, the Midland Grand was somewhat dated now, not having ensuite bathrooms and other modern amenities that newer luxury hotels enjoyed.

It was glorious, however. The gothic confection of the façade was echoed in the *porte-cochère* entrance to the hotel.

After navigating the revolving door, I found myself tipping my head back to take it all in. My first impression was of overwhelming opulence. The walls and ceiling were painted with intricate designs in vivid blues, greens, yellows, golds, and pinks, the moldings decorated with gilded carvings of peacocks and foliage. There was a Medieval cathedral quality to the place that had gone out of style decades ago, but was uniquely fascinating.

As I waited to be served at the busy front desk, I caught a glimpse of the famed staircase at the end of the curved entrance hall and would have gone to admire it if I hadn't been called up by the clerk. I schooled my features, pulled out a handkerchief and some coins from my bag, and put on the saddest face I could manage.

I introduced myself with a false name. "I have an unusual request, and rather a distressing one," I said.

The clerk maintained his professionally bland expression. "How may I help you, Madam?"

"My cousin has run away from home. We think she has fallen victim to a no-good snake who fed her lies and promised her a better life. We're very worried about her."

My sordid tale brought a spark to his eye, as sordid tales had a tendency to do for most people. "I am sorry to hear that, Madam."

"Ever since we read her note, we've been searching for her, and our search has led us here, to this hotel. We believe she stayed here on Friday. Is it too much trouble for you to look through your reservation book to either confirm or deny?"

He shook his head. "That goes against our hotel policy."

"Oh please, please, help me." I dabbed at the corner of my eye with the handkerchief. "My poor dear cousin could be in grave danger."

The clerk looked past me to the waiting guests.

"It will only take a moment and then I'll leave you be," I added. "I'd be ever so grateful." To show him how grateful, I discreetly passed the coins across the counter.

He scooped them up and pocketed them. "What name?"

"Isobel Warrington."

He flipped back through the reservations ledger and ran

his finger down the column. "No one here by that name. What about the fellow?"

I waved my handkerchief in dismissal. "He wouldn't have used his real name so there is no point looking. Were you on duty on Friday?" At his nod, I showed him the photograph of Isobel. "Does she look familiar?"

He studied it then shook his head. "I'm afraid not. A lot of people pass through this hotel."

"What about your colleague?"

The second clerk studied the photograph, but shook his head too. I thanked them and spoke to the porters and doorman next, but received the same response. As I expected, the lead had led nowhere. A place like the Midland Grand had a lot more guests than the Mayfair Hotel, and Isobel would have been one face among many on Friday. Without any remarkable features, the desk clerks would not have paid her much attention, particularly if her lover was the one to check in.

I returned to the Mayfair where Frank greeted me at the front door with a warning. "Lady Bainbridge is looking for you."

"That sounds ominous. What does she want?"

"How would I know?"

"Don't you know everything that goes on in this hotel, Frank?"

He puffed out his chest. "True enough. But not this time."

"How did she seem?"

"Who can tell with her ladyship?" He realized too late how that sounded and apologized. "I didn't mean to be so familiar, Miss Fox. It's just that your aunt doesn't let on what's on her mind. Not like Sir Ronald. His moods are easy to guess."

I patted his arm. "It's quite all right, Frank. You don't need to be as formal with me as you are with my Bainbridge relatives. I'm more like you than them."

From the skeptical way he eyed me, I suspected he didn't think of me that way at all. I sighed as I entered the hotel through the door he held open for me. My attempts at making friends among the staff had worked to a point, but not to the extent I wanted.

In truth, I was not like them and never could be while I was their employer's niece, even though I felt an affinity with them. Living with my grandparents in Cambridge, we could afford only one maid, so I'd helped her with all the household duties. I preferred to roll up my sleeves and contribute than live the idle life that my aunt and Flossy enjoyed. While the occasional long luncheon or free afternoon to explore the city was certainly more appealing than scrubbing floors for hours, it became dull after a while.

It would seem I was yet to find the happy medium between the two worlds of staff and employer. Sometimes I wondered if I'd ever find it, or if the staff would ever treat me as an equal. For now, I would take any level of friendship they were prepared to offer. I was sorely lacking in friends here in London.

There was often a lull in the middle of the day for the front of house staff. Guests scheduled to check out had already done so and new arrivals were not yet due to check in. The maids would be preparing the rooms and the cooks and waiting staff would be busy cooking and serving luncheon, but the foyer itself was quiet.

Goliath stood by the front desk, one hip leaning against the counter. Peter the clerk rested both elbows on the counter, chatting quietly to him. Goliath yawned as I approached.

"Cover your mouth," Peter said as I joined them. "And don't let Mr. Hobart see you yawning."

"Mr. Hobart's in his office," Goliath said. "He's too busy to come out here these days. And there's no one else about, so I'm going to yawn as much as I like." To hammer home his point, he yawned again.

I leaned against the counter too and looked up at Goliath. The dark circles under his eyes amid his pale face made him look like a giant ghoul. "You need to tell Mr. Hobart that you can no longer perform the duties of both night and day porter. You're exhausted."

"I'm all right. It's double the pay, so I'll do it as long as Mr. Hobart needs."

Ever since one of the previous night porters had been dismissed after it was revealed he and the new assistant manager were letting in prostitutes in exchange for money, we'd been short staffed. Goliath filled in as the second night porter and Mr. Hobart was still looking for another assistant manager. Harry Armitage's shoes were proving difficult to fill, but they needed to be filled soon. The hotel's busiest season was just around the corner.

"You're making mistakes, too," Peter said to Goliath. He turned to me. "Just yesterday he took some luggage to the wrong room. All three porters spent an age looking for it and Mr. Hobart had to use all his diplomatic skills to calm the guests down."

Goliath stifled another yawn.

Peter rolled his eyes. "Lady Bainbridge asked me where you were earlier."

"I heard she was looking for me."

"You should tell me when you'll be back each time you go out so I can pass it on if any of your family asks."

"That seems fraught with problems. For one thing, what if I'm late? They'll worry. And for another, what if I don't want them knowing where I am?"

He put up his hands in surrender. "Fair enough, Miss Fox."

"You've got a new case, haven't you?" Goliath said, proving his mind was still sharp despite exhaustion.

"I do." I showed them the photograph of Isobel Warrington. "Do either of you recognize her?"

They both shook their heads.

"Was she murdered?" Peter asked.

"No. I'm afraid I can't give you any details of this case just yet."

Goliath crossed his arms and pouted, looking like a very large toddler on the cusp of a tantrum.

Peter sighed. "Pity." He straightened and his gaze shifted to my right. "Good afternoon, Mr. Hobart."

The manager joined us and I tucked the photograph back into my bag. He looked tired too, although not quite as exhausted as Goliath. His usually bright, friendly eyes were dull, his smile strained as he greeted me. "Have you seen your aunt yet, Miss Fox?"

"I'm on my way to her now."

"She's playing bridge with friends in the small sitting room."

"How did she seem?"

"Quite well today. There was no sign of her illness."

My aunt's illness had been diagnosed as melancholy by her doctor. He'd prescribed a tonic that lifted her spirits for a few hours, but gave her dreadful headaches once it wore off. The more she took it, the more often she needed to take it. Flossy and I tried to encourage her to take it only when necessary, and sparingly at that, but she didn't always heed our advice.

As a guest approached the desk, I signaled to Mr. Hobart to move to the side with me. He smiled at the guest and greeted him by name then allowed Peter to answer his question.

"Is something the matter, Miss Fox?" he asked with the greatest concern.

"No, nothing really. When I asked you how my aunt was, I meant how was her temper? Did she seem annoyed that she couldn't find me? Or that she needed to speak to me in the first place?"

He shook his head, accompanying it with a small shrug. "Not particularly." He lowered his voice. "I know it's none of my business, but have you two had a falling out?"

"No. At least, I don't think so. It's just that…" I looked around the foyer and not seeing any of my family, stepped closer to Mr. Hobart. "The thing is, before he left, Mr. Hirst told my uncle something about me as a means of punishing me for my role in his dismissal."

At the mention of Mr. Hirst's name, Mr. Hobart's mouth set into a grim line. "I wish I'd never hired him."

"It wasn't your fault. He duped you. He duped us all, including my uncle. But his fit of pique has left me in a bit of a pickle where my uncle and aunt are concerned. You see, he told Uncle Ronald that I have called on your nephew a few times."

"When you say called on, you mean…"

"I mean in a professional capacity. We worked together to solve the Piccadilly Playhouse murder."

He tugged on the front hem of his tailcoat. "I see. Then

what's the problem? Your uncle and aunt surely wouldn't want you to conduct an investigation alone, without a man at your side."

I bit down on the instinct to point out that I didn't need a man at my side. Mr. Hobart, like most men, wasn't interested in women's suffrage and a snide response from me wasn't going to educate him.

It turned out that I wasn't being fair to him. Upon seeing me bristle at his words, he added, "I meant only when you met with an undesirable character during the course of your investigation. You don't need a man at your side at other times. I can see very clearly that you are an independent and capable woman."

"Thank you for elaborating. But the problem isn't my role in that investigation. The problem is that they think Mr. Armitage and I, er, have intentions."

He clasped his hands together behind him. "Ah."

"Not that we do have any of those kinds of intentions. I assure you, by the way Mr. Armitage talks to me you'd think I was the enemy. Or, at best, an annoying acquaintance whose company he must politely endure."

He laughed softly.

"My relationship with Mr. Armitage is purely a business one. He helped me with the Piccadilly Playhouse murder, and now I am investigating a case that he didn't want to take on."

He frowned, nodding thoughtfully. "So the problem is, you cannot avoid one another."

"It would seem so."

"And you don't want to tell your uncle and aunt that you are a private detective."

"Correct. They would only forbid me from continuing." I winced. "I am sorry if telling you this puts you in a bind. I shouldn't have said anything, except I need to ask you something."

"About the new case? Then I am happy to help. As to the matter of your aunt and uncle finding out, I do not involve myself in Bainbridge family matters. Sir Ronald and Lady Bainbridge know this and respect it. The topic of your investigative activities won't come up, and therefore your relationship with Harry won't either, since you only see each other in a professional capacity."

I breathed out a relieved breath. "Thank you, Mr. Hobart."

"Now tell me about your case and how I may help."

"I've been hired by a gentleman by the name of Warrington who believes his wife is seeing another man. He wishes me to prove it so he can divorce her."

None of what I said made much of an impact on Mr. Hobart. As hotel manager, he saw and heard things that would make me blush. The Mayfair may attract an elite clientele, but the wealthy and important weren't immune to carrying out sordid affairs. Indeed, they seemed to be more likely to live outside the rules of society than regular folk. My life in Cambridge had been a sheltered one. I'd learned more about human nature in the Mayfair than I had in the lecture halls of the university or the tearooms nearby.

"Warrington rings bells," Mr. Hobart said. "He hasn't been a guest here, I can assure you of that, but his name is familiar."

"He's a member of parliament."

"That must be it."

"He has a townhouse of his own so wouldn't stay here. His wife's name is Isobel and she was seen entering the Midland Grand last Friday with a man." I showed him the photograph. "Peter and Goliath don't recognize her, but do you? Do you think she has ever been here?"

He shook his head. "I've never seen her."

I tucked the photograph away and glanced across the foyer in the direction of the two sitting rooms. My aunt and her bridge partners awaited me in the small one. If I went to her now, she wouldn't chastise me in front of them. She would avoid all mention of Harry Armitage altogether so as not to associate my name with his in their eyes. It made sense to see her now and get this meeting over with so that I didn't have to call on her later when she was alone.

Mr. Hobart sighed, drawing my attention back to him. His gaze had fallen on a stiff-backed man standing a little to the side, waiting for Mr. Hobart to finish speaking with me. He must think me a guest and was politely waiting his turn.

"Is everything all right?" I asked. "Is that guest troublesome?"

"He's not a guest, he's another candidate for the position of assistant manager. This will be my second interviewee for the day, the fifth in a week. None have been up to the standards I expect of an assistant manager and I already don't like the look of this fellow. His beard is unkempt and his tie is loose."

Poor Mr. Hobart. I suspected the reason he didn't like the man was because he compared him to Mr. Armitage. The disappointing outcome of Mr. Hirst's appointment had made him even more negatively inclined toward anyone who wasn't his nephew.

"May I make a suggestion?" I asked.

"Of course."

"Have you looked internally to fill the position? One of the current staff could step into the role. Since they already know the hotel very well, it wouldn't be a steep learning curve." I eyed the front desk where Peter was cheerfully greeting another guest with his usual welcoming smile.

Mr. Hobart followed my gaze. "Peter would be the perfect candidate, but there is just one problem."

"Oh?"

"He's too familiar with the other staff. They wouldn't respect him as their superior and he would be too friendly with them. To be frank, he's just too nice. The assistant manager must exude authority and not be afraid to give orders to those beneath him. He needs to command respect."

I thought it might come to Peter in time, but didn't say so. It was not my place.

Mr. Hobart excused himself and approached the interviewee. I headed off towards the sitting rooms, greeting John, the lift operator, as I passed. Situated beside each other, the smaller of the two sitting rooms was accessed off a short corridor. Where the large sitting room was used for afternoon tea by guests and members of the public, the small one was for private use, usually by the family and their friends for more intimate gatherings.

Compared to its grander neighbor, the small sitting room was exactly as the name suggested. But that didn't mean it wasn't considerable in size. I'd recently been in the drawing room of a Mayfair townhouse owned by a wealthy lord, and it was about the same size as the hotel's small sitting room. It was large enough to separate into three distinct areas, each with its own cluster of sofa, two matching armchairs, and at least two occasional tables. The most expensive furniture, decor, and paintings were kept here—there was even a Whistler hanging over the fireplace—and more personal items were dotted around the room, including photographs of the family.

Two sets of sofas and armchairs had been pushed aside and two card tables put in their place. Eight women, each holding a hand of cards, sat at the tables. None looked up upon my entry, so I went to my aunt's side.

"Cleo, dear, how lovely to see you," she said as she studied her cards. "I've been looking for you all morning."

"I was at the museum."

"Again?" She played an ace, earning groans of resignation from her opponents.

"Your niece is an intellectual, Lilian," said a woman with copper red hair and freckles. While she spoke with a smile, there was a hint of derision in her tone.

Aunt Lilian gathered up the played cards and placed them beside her in a neat pile. Her movements were quick, but her fingers were bone-thin and, when she finally looked up at me, I noticed her pupils were dilated. She smiled and there was no pain in it, no worry or sorrow. Her tonic was working, for now. "Cleo is very clever, and there is nothing wrong with that these days. She is an excellent conversationalist on a broad manner of topics."

A sudden panic gripped my heart and squeezed. I glanced around the room as all eight sets of eyes settled on me with varying degrees of curiosity. Oh lord. I'd walked into a den of vipers. I hadn't been summoned to this room to be chastised about my friendship with Harry Armitage. I'd been summoned here to be put on show, paraded in front of my aunt's friends. I'd wager my entire savings that these women were all mothers of eligible sons.

"She is indeed," said the woman jotting down the score on a notepad. I recognized her as Lady Caldicott, husband to

Uncle Ronald's banker. "Good afternoon, Miss Fox. Will you sit with me?" She signaled to the footman I'd failed to notice standing by the sideboard. He brought over a spare chair. The women shuffled around and he placed the chair beside Lady Caldicott.

"I'm afraid I can't stay," I said. "I have to meet Flossy."

My aunt frowned. "Flossy is having luncheon with the Druitt-Poores. Are you sure you're supposed to meet her?"

"Perhaps I've got my days mixed up," I muttered as I sat.

Lady Caldicott smiled. "Do you know how to play bridge?"

"Yes, but I don't want to intrude on your game. We can't play with five."

"Then you can help me. I could do with some assistance."

The woman shuffling the cards to my right huffed out a breath. "Don't believe her, Miss Fox. She plays perfectly well and wins often, just not today." She stopped shuffling and put out her hand to me. "I'm Mrs. Helen Digby."

Aunt Lilian introduced me to all of the ladies at both tables before play resumed. I observed, which meant I quickly became bored. Bridge was only interesting if one had stakes in the game. I couldn't see any purses close at hand, but that didn't mean they played only for the glory of winning.

"It's been an age since I've had friends here for a bridge party," my aunt said after the second round. "The winter has felt particularly long this year." Several women nodded or murmured their agreement. "Some of my friends are filtering back into the city now, which is absolutely marvelous. I've been desperate for a day of cards with them all. We have so much to talk about."

Mrs. Digby's smile was sly as she dealt. "So much gossip to impart, you mean."

A light round of laughter drifted up from both tables. I laughed with them then angled my chair closer to the table. I might not enjoy the game, but I could get something out of this party and it wasn't a husband. These women were precisely the sort I needed to speak to. Isobel Warrington might move in the same social circles as my aunt's friends. Perhaps one of them knew her.

CHAPTER 3

ady Caldicott leaned closer and showed me her cards. After the dealer declared diamonds as the trump suit, Lady Caldicott asked me what she should do.

It was an easy decision based on her abundance of spades. "Pass."

The other players made their calls and the round was played. Lady Caldicott asked my opinion before each of her turns and between her and her partner, we won more tricks than we lost.

I gathered up the cards and shuffled as Lady Caldicott jotted down the score.

"My son, Edward, mentioned you recently, Miss Fox," she said as she wrote. "You made quite an impression on him."

Edward was the younger of the Caldicott sons. I'd been strategically seated beside him at dinner one evening, the elder brother having been earmarked for Flossy. I'd enjoyed our conversation, but only after steering him away from financial topics. Unfortunately he always steered the conversation back to the business of economics, or tuned into the conversation between my uncle and his father, seated at the other end of the table. I was surprised to hear he thought of me at all.

"How are his travel plans coming along?" I asked, recalling that he was going on a tour of the continent.

"Well enough, but his departure may be delayed."

"What a shame. He must be disappointed."

"Not at all. It was his decision." She exchanged small smiles with my aunt.

My panic returned. I needed to leave this room and these grasping, matrimonial-minded mothers, or I might get sucked into conversations I didn't want to have. But I needed to find out what they knew about the Warringtons before leaving. Unfortunately, I couldn't think of a smooth way to introduce the topic and in my panic, I blurted out the first thing that came to mind.

"What a nasty business for Mr. Warrington, receiving those threatening letters."

The players from both tables stared at me as if I had two heads.

It was too late to take it back. I'd have to brazen it out and follow through with my awkward attempts at information gathering. "Oh, did you not hear about the letters?" I asked, innocently. "Do any of you know him? Or his wife?"

The ladies continued to stare, one even wrinkled her nose. It was left to my aunt to come to my rescue, if that's what it could be called. She gave me a sympathetic look. "Dear Cleo, always concerned for the welfare of others. I heard about those letters too. You don't need to worry about Mr. Warrington. Politicians have thick skins and are used to people disagreeing with their views."

"So you know him?" I pressed. "Or Mrs. Warrington? How is she faring in all of this? She must be worried for her husband."

"I don't know her."

"I do," Mrs. Digby said. She shuffled the cards slowly, as if it were an unconscious motion of her hands. Her attention was focused on the gossip. Going by the spark in her eyes, she was enjoying this change of topic.

"And how is she coping?" I prompted.

"Rather well, I suspect."

"Does she not know about the letters? Is she not in London perhaps?"

"She's here. I saw her only last week. She was very happy. Very happy indeed." The phrase seemed to be some sort of code, understood by the other women. Some smiled coyly, others pursed their lips disapprovingly, but none looked confused.

It wasn't difficult to decipher the meaning of the code, given what I knew of Mrs. Warrington. It was confirmation that Mr. Warrington had not lied to me, something that had crossed my mind. He could have wanted me to find a liaison that wasn't there to provide him with a reason to divorce his wife. Given that he had initially hinted that Mr. Armitage ought to trap her using whatever means available to him, it was an obvious assumption to make.

"She ought to be careful her husband doesn't find out just how happy she is," one of the ladies at the other table piped up.

"Perhaps that's what she wants," Mrs. Digby said. At the shocked gasps of her friends, she merely shrugged. "Perhaps she wants him to divorce her."

"And endure the humiliation? Don't be ridiculous, Helen. Why not simply agree to live separate lives? Many couples do. Even if he refused to give her an allowance, she's independently wealthy. She came to the marriage with property and money."

"Divorce won't see her lose any of that," Mrs. Digby pointed out. "Not since the law changed in the eighties." This elicited another round of knowing nods from her friends.

"As to why she would prefer a divorce and not a separation, the answer is simple," Lady Caldicott said. "She wants to remarry."

The benefits or otherwise of divorce were debated with spirit from both sides of the argument, although my aunt didn't join in. She looked as though she was flagging. The effects of the tonic must be wearing off. I was about to ask her if she wanted to retire when the doors opened and a procession of waiters entered pushing trolleys laden with plates of sandwiches, tarts, scones, and small cakes. The women rose to help themselves while the waiters poured glasses of wine.

By the time I looked up from the impressive array of choices, my aunt had slipped out of the room. She returned ten minutes later with diluted pupils, a bright smile, and her daughter.

"It seems Florence wasn't having luncheon with the

Druitt-Poores today, after all," Aunt Lilian said with a lilting laugh. "I'm so forgetful sometimes."

I intercepted Flossy after she piled up a plate for herself and before she sat. "Is your mother all right?" I whispered.

"She insisted on taking another measure of that tonic, so I thought I'd join her in here for a while to make sure she doesn't take more later."

I squeezed her arm in sympathy. "Surely their game won't go on much longer."

"It'll go on for some time yet." She glanced at the gold and onyx clock on the mantelpiece. "They'll resume after lunch, play until six then stop for a drive in the park, weather permitting, then return for dinner and finally resume playing. Their bridge parties go well into the evening."

"Your mother won't last that long. Not without her tonic. And if she takes more, she'll need all of tomorrow to recover."

"And the day after." Flossy emitted a resigned sigh. "I'll try to cut the party short."

"I'll help."

She kissed my cheek. "I'm pleased to see you, actually." Her eyes suddenly brightened, as if she'd switched on an electric light to cast out the darkness of her mother's ailment. "I have a plan. Come and sit with me and I'll tell you all about it."

I allowed her to steer me to the sofa positioned furthest from the card tables. "A plan for what?" I asked before taking a bite of cucumber sandwich.

"I've been thinking about your debut."

I choked on the sandwich. "My what?" I spluttered when I'd recovered.

"Your debut."

"Flossy, I'm twenty-three, not eighteen."

"It doesn't matter how old you are. There are no rules about age." She put down her half-eaten sandwich and turned fully to me. "Please listen and try not to interrupt. Can you do that?"

"Only if you don't say anything foolish, like suggest I be presented at court."

She tucked a strand of strawberry blonde hair behind her

ear. "And what's wrong with that? I was presented last year. Mother sponsored me and she'll sponsor you too."

"Of course I will," Aunt Lilian said from behind us. I hadn't noticed her draw closer. "How wonderful it will be for you, Cleo. One's debut is so special."

"Better than one's wedding day," Mrs. Digby agreed.

"And wedding night," another said, before remembering two unwed women were in their company. She blushed and muttered an apology to Aunt Lilian.

My aunt hadn't heard her. She sat on the armchair opposite Flossy and me, her plate of food forgotten as it balanced precariously on her lap. "It would be my honor to present you to the queen, Cleo dear."

"It would most likely be the Princess of Wales these days," Mrs. Digby said. "The queen is far too old to sit for hours on end to greet all the girls."

"That's because the Lord Chamberlain allows too many girls to participate," said a thin-faced woman with slightly protruding front teeth. "In our day, only girls from the best families could be presented at court. Now they let in anyone."

At Mrs. Digby's censorial glare, the woman's face paled as she remembered that I was not from one of the *best* families, by strict definition. My father had been an academic with a middle-class upbringing.

My mother, however, had been presented, as had her sister, Aunt Lilian. Although their father hadn't been noble born, he'd been wealthy enough to be accepted by those who mattered, despite making his fortune in trade. He paid an impoverished dowager countess to sponsor both his daughters and they'd been presented in the same year. That was the story my paternal grandmother had once told me. She'd made it sound like an outdated ordeal that served no purpose in the modern world. Given what I now knew about her prejudices towards my mother's family, it was possible she'd embellished the story to make them look bad.

"Do say you'll do it, Cleo," Flossy begged.

"No. Absolutely not."

"Cleo," my aunt chided. "Don't dismiss the idea just yet. You have time before you must decide."

Lady Caldicott approached the sofa, a palm-sized diary in

hand. "Not all that long actually. There are usually two presentations before easter and two after. Easter this year is in mid-April. Invitations from the palace will be sent out three weeks prior…" She flipped back through the pages of the diary. "You'll need to get your application in soon, Lilian."

Aunt Lilian clapped her hands, dislodging the plate on her lap. I managed to leap up and catch it, but not before the sandwiches slid off onto the rug. The footman approached to clean it up, but I held up my hand to stay him. I picked up the sandwiches and returned them to the plate and set the plate on the table.

Aunt Lilian grasped my hand, seemingly unaware that she'd dropped food on the floor. "What fun it will be, Cleo. There'll be balls, parties and dinners every night for weeks afterward."

"That sounds exhausting."

"You'll be having too much fun to be tired."

Flossy took my other hand. "Just think of all the new dresses you'll have. Father will pay for them, of course, and I have enough jewelry for both of us."

Aunt Lilian agreed. "You shall have a different dress for each event."

"You both forget that I'm in mourning. I'll still be wearing half-mourning by easter."

"Six months will have passed by then, won't it?" Flossy counted on her fingers and realized she'd miscalculated. "Anyway, you'll be so close to the end that no one will mind."

We'd been through this before when it had been time for the hotel's New Year's Eve ball. I'd not wanted to attend but had changed my mind at the last moment in order to catch a killer.

My aunt and cousin watched me like two puppies eager for me to throw them a bone. I was very aware of everyone in the room straining to hear our conversation, perhaps sensing an argument about to erupt between Aunt Lilian and the niece she'd generously taken in. I wouldn't give them the satisfaction.

"Thank you, Aunt. It's so good of you to offer to sponsor me. We'll talk about it later."

The response satisfied my aunt, Flossy, and some of the

other women in the room, but I knew not all realized that wasn't acquiescence.

"Well played," Lady Caldicott said as she joined me at the sandwich trolley where I made up another plate for my aunt. "But it's going to be a tough battle for you to win. Lilian seems to have her heart set on you having your debut. She won't give up easily."

I remained silent as I added a macaron to the plate at the next trolley.

"If you do go through with it, it will open up a lot of doors for you," she said quietly as another lady joined us. "You'll have a wider choice."

"If you're referring to finding a husband, I don't plan to marry."

"So I recall you saying. But you may change your mind. If you insist on avoiding a court presentation, however, I want you to know there are some gentlemen who will overlook it."

Did she not hear how that sounded? Or was she deaf to the inference? I turned to her with a tight smile. "Perhaps I don't want a husband who will consider it something that needs to be *overlooked*." I marched off across the room and handed the plate to Aunt Lilian.

She thanked me and proceeded to eat with passionate endeavor, as if she'd not eaten all day. When finished, she asked for more.

The conversation over lunch didn't stray far from the upcoming social season, and the girls who were expected to be this year's most dazzling debutantes. Apparently the main requirement was that she be exceedingly pretty. The secondary requirements were in no particular order of importance, but consisted of being demure but not shy, small-waisted, well-mannered, not too tall, an excellent conversationalist but not to the point where she dominated, witty, sensible, and well-read.

"But not too intelligent as to bore the young men," one of the ladies said with a laugh.

Not a single gaze fell on me, but they might as well have. The laugh suddenly died and the resulting silence was rather stifling until finally my aunt broke it by mentioning the downfall of one young lady in last year's crop whose feather plumes drooped forward as she curtsied to the princess. When she rose, the plumes did not right themselves and continued to veil her eyes. She cried for an hour afterwards.

I managed to endure the rest of the afternoon as the card playing resumed. As six o'clock approached, Aunt Lilian was clearly flagging again. She slumped further in the chair with each passing hour, and pressed her fingers into her temple after each round. She lost often until Flossy took over playing for her.

"Why don't you retire for the day?" I gently suggested as I handed her a glass of water.

"I can't abandon my guests, Cleo. It's much too early. A drive around Hyde Park will wake me up."

"It'll drown you in this weather," Lady Caldicott said. She signaled to Mrs. Digby with a small nod and both women claimed it was time to leave.

Aunt Lilian pouted. "Already?"

"You're not well, Lilian," Lady Caldicott said gently.

Aunt Lilian pressed both hands to the table and heaved herself to her feet. "I'll be fine after I take my tonic."

"No, Mother," Flossy urged in a whisper. "You've had enough."

Lady Caldicott glanced at me, one eyebrow raised. I shook my head. "Come along, Ladies," she said, rising. "Lilian needs her rest. Doctor's orders."

Aunt Lilian opened her mouth as if to protest again, but thought better of it. Protesting further would sound desperate, and she didn't want that. She accepted their thanks for an enjoyable afternoon and watched as they filed out of the door.

Lady Caldicott was last to leave. She took my aunt's arm and walked with her across the room. "Listen to your daughter and niece and *rest*, Lilian."

Aunt Lilian smiled as her friend left the room. Then she turned on Flossy and me, eyes flashing and nostrils flaring. "The tonic would have worked," she snapped. "You ruined my party. Both of you. Kindly stay out of my affairs in future. My health is *my* concern, not yours, and if I say I am well, then I am well. I don't need you two treating me like an elderly invalid."

Flossy took a step towards her, her eyes filled with tears,

but her mother hurried away, a hand pressed to the side of her head.

I put my arm around Flossy's shoulders. "Pay her no heed. You know how irritable she is when the tonic initially wears off. She'll regret her words in the morning."

Flossy gave a shuddery sigh. "I know."

"Now, are we dining in the dining room tonight or in your room?"

"The dining room. I feel like being seen." She caught my hand, the tears already gone. "Shall we go for a drive on our own? Mother won't mind if we're together."

"All right."

She lightly clapped her hands as she bounced on her toes. "Marvelous. We can talk about your gown for the presentation, and what gowns you ought to have made for all the balls. Your debut will be such *fun*, Cleo."

I silently groaned and allowed her to drag me out of the sitting room.

* * *

I'D HOPED to find an ally in Harmony, but she proved to be as deaf to my refusals as Flossy. She was convinced that being a debutante and having a court presentation was something I ought to do.

"It's customary for ladies like you," she said as she removed the lid covering our breakfast tray.

I glared at her over my coffee cup but she was too intent on distributing the sausages onto our plates to notice. "I am nobody, Harmony. My cousin is somebody; I am not. That suits me quite well, thank you."

"Why do you keep saying that you're nobody? Look around you. Look where you live."

My suite was elegant but thankfully not opulent. The furniture was well made, the room well-appointed with all the modern amenities I could wish for, including an ensuite bathroom. The bed was far too large for one person, and I had hotel staff at my beck and call. It was easy to see how Harmony would think me wealthy or important. But none of the luxuries I lived amongst were paid for by me.

I decided not to quarrel with her about it, however. Compared to her, I *was* fortunate. "My meeting with Mr. Armitage went well yesterday."

She *humphed.*

"I know you don't like him, although I'm not sure why."

"I don't *dislike* him. He's just too sure of himself and that note he wrote to you was quite curt. He didn't thank you for your help."

I accepted the plate she offered and attacked the sausage with the knife and fork. "He thanked me in person and explained that he didn't like accepting all of the accolades when he did nothing to deserve them."

She rolled her eyes. "That's another thing. He's too proud."

"Perhaps this will make you more inclined to like him. He offered me some cases to investigate on my own."

She paused with a forkful of sausage near her lips. "Will he let you have any of the glory of solving them or will he take it all himself?"

"The cases are all mine. He gave them to me. I won't be working for him."

"Oh. Well then." She concentrated on slicing up the sausage and not looking at me. I suspected that was the kindest words I'd hear from her mouth where Harry Armitage was concerned.

"I approached four of the five potential clients, but none wanted to work with me," I went on.

She looked up. "Because you're a woman?" When I nodded, she rolled her eyes. "And the fifth?"

"He paid me half up front. I started yesterday."

"Congratulations! That deserves another sausage."

"I'd prefer an egg."

She passed me one of the boiled eggs and an eggcup then refilled my coffee cup, and I told her all about the Warrington case. I had to explain how divorces worked, and that Mrs. Warrington would not be left impoverished, as long as she was married after the law changed. "She brought property and wealth to the union, which she'll keep."

"So he doesn't get to keep all her money if they married *after* the new law, but he does if they married before?"

I nodded.

She considered this for some time as she sipped her coffee. I waited for her to speak, but she remained silent. She simply watched me over the rim of her cup with those dark eyes until I felt as though I was being swallowed by them.

"I know what you're thinking," I blurted out. "You're thinking that if they married before the law changed, I will be a willing participant in making her an impoverished woman."

She blinked. "No. I was wondering why he would divorce her at all."

"Oh." I cleared my throat. "I suppose he's doing it because his wife is unfaithful."

"But only he knows that. If he goes through with a divorce, everyone will know. I thought politicians hated scandal."

She had a point, but the fact was, he wanted a divorce. "I'm going to call at their house today and speak to the butler. Hopefully he can tell me what her movements were and I can follow them up. If I can get the name of her lover, it'll help the case."

"You need to speak to her lady's maid."

"Lady's maids are not likely to gossip about their mistress's whereabouts to a stranger. She knows who her employer is, and it's not Mr. Warrington."

"Have you asked Mr. Hobart if Mrs. Warrington ever came here with her lover? Sometimes women like that do. Not many, not nearly in the same number as their husbands, but some."

"I showed him a photograph Mr. Warrington gave me. He didn't recognize her. Nor did Peter or Goliath, but I didn't ask Frank."

"I'll do it. I'll ask the other staff too." She sliced the top off her egg and scooped out the hard-boiled yolk. "I could ask Victor when he comes in. I don't *want* to ask him, mind, but I'll do it for you and your investigation."

I sipped my coffee to hide my smile. Once my features were schooled, I set the cup down. "No need to go to any bother."

"Speaking to him is a bother, I agree, but I'm prepared to

do it. Someone must, and better me than you. You have no reason to be in the kitchen."

She was making it very hard for me to keep a straight face. Thankfully she was concentrating on her egg and not looking at me. "But what could Victor tell you? The cooks never see the guests."

"They like to gossip as much as the rest of us. Probably more. It's all that heat and spices. It loosens the tongue."

Unable to hold it anymore, I chuckled into my coffee cup.

Harmony sniffed. "It's true. Men gossip just as much as women."

"Indeed. Have you finished with breakfast? I want to get on and interview the Warringtons' butler."

She followed me into the bedroom and quickly worked to arrange my hair in a simple yet elegant style, a Harmony specialty. She always managed to make me look good and I told her so.

She rolled her eyes. "You have easy hair. Unlike mine." She wrinkled her nose at her reflection in the mirror and teased out one of the tight black springs that framed her pretty face.

"Your hair is beautiful," I said. "One of these days I want to see what it looks like when its loose."

I gave her the photograph of Mrs. Warrington to show around to the other staff members then together we made the bed. She left carrying the breakfast tray. A few minutes later, I left too.

I met Flossy and Floyd in the corridor, waiting for the lift to arrive. It was early for both of them. Floyd had been out with friends the previous night, which usually meant he got out of bed late the following morning. Flossy was just generally a late starter.

"Do you have plans together?" I asked as I waited with them.

Brother and sister looked appalled at the idea of spending time with one another. "I've got a meeting with a man from a motor car company," Floyd said.

Flossy gasped. "You're not getting one! Mother will have an attack of hysteria if you do, and Father will grumble about the cost."

"I have my own money to do with as I please. Anyway, I'm not buying one. The engineering is still in its infancy and the traffic in London is horrendous. A motor car could never reach its top speed going down Piccadilly, and if it can't go fast, what's the point? I'm considering investing in this fellow's company. Motor cars are the way of the future."

Flossy shook her head. "Smelly, noisy, death traps if you ask me."

Floyd sighed theatrically. "I was going to ask you to join me, but if you feel that way about them you obviously won't want to come."

The door to the lift opened and John's smiling face greeted us. He bade us each good morning and we piled in.

The slow descent was smooth, if a little crowded, and silent except for the whirring of the mechanisms.

"What are you up to this morning, Flossy?" I asked to fill the silence.

"I'm heading downstairs for breakfast. I forgot to put my order in last night."

"You should put in a standing order," I told her.

"I tried that and the kitchen kept forgetting. You must be special." She nudged me with her elbow and grinned. "Where are you off to anyway?"

"The museum," I said, without skipping a beat. It was the only place I could think of where I knew she wouldn't ask to come with me.

"Again? Honestly, Cleo, haven't you absorbed enough knowledge yet? You've been so many times I've lost count. In fact, you were there just yesterday."

"I thought you went to the dentist," Floyd said to me with a smug look on his face.

"I did both."

"Perhaps she meets someone at the museum," Floyd said to his sister.

I scowled at him and the rascal winked back.

Two could play at this game. If he wanted to tease me, I would tease him right back. "Perhaps you're meeting one of your lady friends this morning, instead of a motor car manufacturer, and that's why you're up early."

"If he is, she's hardly a lady if he has to lie about seeing her," Flossy pointed out.

Floyd crossed his arms. "Come with me and see."

"All right," Flossy said.

His face fell. "You just said motor cars are noisy, smelly and dangerous and you want nothing to do with them."

"I didn't say I wanted nothing to do with them. Will the fellow let you drive one?"

"He says he'll take me for a drive."

"Excellent." The door slid open on the ground floor but Flossy didn't get out with Floyd and me. "I'll fetch my coat and gloves and meet you back here in a jiffy. Cleo, will you come too? It will be much more fun than the museum. We can each take turns."

Floyd thrust his hands on his hips. "You are *not* coming with me."

"We have nothing better to do. Cleo?"

"I prefer the museum," I said.

"Suit yourself." She asked John to take her back up to the fourth floor. As the door slid closed, she pointed at her brother. "If you don't wait for me, I'll tell Father something that will get you into trouble."

The door closed before he could retort. He turned to me with a bemused expression. "I can't believe I let her talk me into taking her. She'll hate every minute of it."

"She must be bored."

"Entertaining her is your department, not mine." He clasped my elbow and gave me the most desperate look. "Take her to the museum with you. Please, Cleo. I'll pay for your entry."

"It's free."

"Really?"

I patted his shoulder. "Enjoy your day."

He groaned. "You two are conspiring against me. I'm convinced of it. I thought having one sister was bad enough, but it's double the irritation with two."

I walked off, unable to hide my grin. Floyd thought of me like a sister. It was more than I'd let myself hope for.

* * *

THE WARRINGTONS' Kensington house was identical to its neighbors on either side, except for its green front door. All three were covered only half way in white stucco with a bay window protruding from what must be the drawing rooms. The two levels above were unclad, and the exposed cream brick made the houses look handsome rather than pretty. The only difference between the houses were the door colors. The neighboring ones were black and blue.

Following Mr. Warrington's instructions, I headed down the steps to the basement and knocked on the service entrance. The housekeeper answered but refused to fetch the butler upon my request.

"Mr. Henderson is busy," she snapped. She screwed up her eyes and squinted at me. The closer scrutiny must have helped her see that I was dressed as a lady, not a maid or shopkeeper because her tone softened to a more deferential one. "Can I help you, Mrs..."

"Miss Fox. I have an appointment with Mr. Henderson this morning. He's expecting me."

She opened the door wider and asked me to go through to the office at the end of the corridor. "I'll fetch him for you."

The butler's office was little bigger than a larder. When Mr. Henderson arrived, he could hardly fit around the gap between the desk and cabinet to take his seat. Despite the lack of space, there were three cabinets squeezed into the room. That must be where the best silver and wine were kept, under lock and key.

Mr. Henderson was a tall, straight-backed man of about forty, with a square jaw and broad shoulders. His face would be considered handsome if it wasn't set into a scowl. He regarded me down his nose with a look which could only be described as disdainful.

"Thank you for meeting—"

"Mr. Warrington told me to co-operate fully with your inquiries," he said, cutting me off. He opened the top drawer of his desk and pulled out a piece of paper. "I took the liberty of collating a list of places Mrs. Warrington visited in recent days. You may take it and leave."

I scanned the column of addresses. He might be bad-tempered, but at least he was helpful. "Is this a complete list or just the places you know about?"

His lips thinned. "I have complete authority in this house. The staff cooperated fully with my request."

"Even Mrs. Warrington's lady's maid?"

"Even her." He drew a cloth-covered ledger from the corner of the desk closer to him. "If you don't mind, I have work to do."

"Actually I do mind. I have some questions for you."

He opened the ledger and picked out a pen resting in the stand. "Be as brief as possible."

I sucked in a breath between gritted teeth. So much for being cooperative. "How long have you known Mrs. Warrington?"

"I've worked for Mr. Warrington since before they married, and met her on their wedding day. I was a footman in those days."

I opened my notebook. "When was that?"

"June 1883."

I penciled the date into my notebook. "And have you personally seen her alone with other men, either here or away from the house?"

"What a waste of a question."

My grip tightened on the pencil. "Has Mr. Warrington given a limit as to how many I may ask?" I kept my tone light, feminine, in the hope he'd respond to that tactic.

Mr. Henderson shifted in the chair. "Of course not."

I smiled. "Excellent. Then I have a few more."

"Your kind always do."

I bristled. "You mean women?"

"Private detectives."

Good lord, if it wasn't one thing, it was another. I couldn't win with people like Mr. Henderson, so there was no point wasting breath to try. "Has Mrs. Warrington's behavior changed in recent times?"

"In what way?"

"Does she take greater care in her appearance, for example? Does she go out more frequently? Does she seem…happier?"

"I cannot comment on her state of mind, or her appearance." Going by his tone, he considered me a fool to ask such a thing. "She does not go out more frequently than she used to, but she has always had a busy social calendar, no matter the season."

I closed my notepad and held up the list he'd given me. "How did you obtain this information?"

"Those are the places she told me she was going, or where the coachman took her."

"But if she met with a man, she would hardly inform you where she was meeting him, would she?"

He merely met my gaze.

I folded up the paper and placed it with the notepad and pencil in my bag. "I can see you don't like what I'm doing, Mr. Henderson, but if you have a problem with me investigating your mistress, you should take it up with Mr. Warrington."

"Their business is none of my affair. He is entitled to hire you, if he wishes. It is neither here nor there what I think of your investigation."

Yet he had no qualms throwing me disdainful looks. Perhaps it wasn't the investigation he found undignified, but my profession. Or perhaps it was both, and he couldn't make his disgust known to his employer so he made it known to me instead.

I rose and opened the door, catching a woman listening in. She gasped, then picked up her skirts and hurried away up a narrow flight of stairs.

"Mrs. Warrington's lady's maid," Mr. Henderson said from behind the desk.

"You're not worried she'll tell your mistress about our meeting?"

He opened the ledger again and dipped the pen into the inkwell. I was dismissed.

"Is Mrs. Warrington at home?"

"She is," he intoned without looking up.

I left the house, but instead of heading to the address on the top of the list, I positioned myself near a lamp post a few doors down and waited for Mrs. Warrington to leave. As I expected, I was rewarded only a short time later.

CHAPTER 4

*H*aving Mrs. Warrington's maid overhear my interview with the butler wasn't the complete disaster I thought it would be when I first saw her scurrying away from his office door. She had immediately alerted her mistress, and Mrs. Warrington was most likely now on her way to warn her lover, or to send him a letter from the post office.

The light rain, while annoying, worked in my favor. I was able to use the umbrella to partially shield my face while hurrying after my target. Being dressed in black was an equally helpful disguise—I blended in with the dozens of other women on the street. If the maid had given Mrs. Warrington my description, she wouldn't be able to pick me out of the crowd.

My fears were further allayed as we turned onto Kensington High Street where the numerous shoppers strolling along the pavement provided some cover. I almost lost her, however, when two men carrying a large buffet out of a furniture shop blocked the pavement. I couldn't peer over it and had to wait for them to pass before dashing after Mrs. Warrington. Thank goodness she wore a hat covered in distinctive speckled brown feathers or I wouldn't have spotted her.

I followed her past the western edge of Kensington Palace gardens then headed north into Bayswater. She didn't stop there, however, and continued on to Paddington. Mrs. Warrington's brisk pace left me quite breathless, so I was pleased when we turned the corner and the imposing structure of the Great Western Hotel came into view. Mrs. Warrington must be meeting her lover there, just as she'd met him last Friday at another great railway hotel, the Midland Grand.

But she continued past the entrance to the hotel and Paddington Station, and left Praed Street altogether. After a few more turns, she suddenly stopped at the front door to a photographic studio. I held the umbrella low as I continued past. When I glanced back, the door was closing on Mrs. Warrington and her feathered hat.

I waited in the rain and was rewarded when a mere fifteen minutes later she exited the studio and hurried on her way. I decided not to follow. The photographic studio must be important to her or why make it her first stop after learning from her maid that I was making inquiries about her whereabouts?

According to the sign painted on the bay window, the photographer was D.B. Sharp. I entered and a youth sitting at the desk looked up from a photograph he'd been studying. He couldn't have been more than eighteen. He smiled toothily as he rose. "May I help you, madam?"

I took a moment to admire the photographs on the desk, and the larger ones displayed on easels around the shopfront. The space was very small, with a door positioned at the back that must lead to the studio.

"I hope you can, Mr. Sharp."

"Oh, I'm not he. Jeffrey Deacon, at your service." He thrust out his hand and I shook it. "I'm assistant operator and photograph retoucher."

"How fascinating." He looked much too young to be having a liaison with a middle-aged woman, but I needed to be absolutely certain. "I just saw my friend, Mrs. Warrington, leave. Is she a friend of yours too?"

His smile froze and his gaze slid to the door through which she'd just left. "She's a customer." If she were merely a customer, why did he suddenly look worried?

A bout of feminine giggles came from the room beyond

the door. Mr. Deacon's face flushed and he looked down at the floor. How very odd.

"Perhaps I made a mistake," I said. "Mrs. Warrington told me she has a particular friend at this photographic studio who will take good care of me. I thought she meant you."

"No!" The youth's voice cracked. I hadn't thought it possible, but his face went even redder.

"So she's referring to Mr. Sharp then?"

"No! Yes. Perhaps." He glanced at the door again as the woman's giggle continued. This time a man joined in with a loud guffaw.

"Which is it, Mr. Deacon? Is Mr. Sharp her *particular* friend?" I gave up trying to be subtle and dug into my bag for some money.

He backed away, hands in the air, as I tried to offer it to him. He knocked over an easel, sending the large photograph to the floor. The frame broke in two places.

The studio door opened and a wizened man with a bent back and stooped shoulders appeared. "What the—?" He stopped upon seeing me, and apologized, but reserved a fierce glare for his assistant. "Mr. Deacon, kindly tidy up then see to the customer while I finish in here. And try do it without breaking anything," he added in a mutter.

He smiled at me and shuffled back into the studio. The door closed on him, but not before I'd seen something that made *me* blush. I'd caught a glimpse of the couple having their photograph taken. They were about my age and kissing passionately in front of a tropical beach scene painted on a large cloth backdrop.

They were completely naked.

I turned away and studied another photograph on an easel while Mr. Deacon picked up the broken frame. The awkward silence stretched, but I was now convinced that neither Mr. Deacon nor Mr. Sharp were Mrs. Warrington's lover. The former was too young, the latter too old. Mr. Warrington would have noticed if his wife's lover had the gangly limbs of a youth or a stoop the day he spotted them entering the Midland Grand.

That left one reasonable explanation for her coming here in such a hurry after she learned her husband had sent a private detective to look into her adulterous affairs. She'd had a photograph taken with her lover in this studio. Not only would it identify him, it would also be absolute proof that she was committing adultery, particularly if the photographs were taken of them both naked.

I cursed myself for not following her when she left the studio. She could have easily thrown the photographs away or destroyed them by now. All that evidence, gone.

Or was it?

I turned to Mr. Deacon. "What do you do with the glass plate negatives after a customer picks up their photographs? Are they destroyed?"

He swallowed and glanced at the door to the studio. "If you could wait for Mr. Sharp. He will answer your questions."

No doubt Mr. Sharp would lie to suit his own ends if he thought I was a detective rather than a customer. If I wanted answers, I had to press on the weakest point.

I joined Mr. Deacon at the desk where he was attempting to piece together the frame. "It's just that if I have some photographs taken with my husband, I'd like to know they'll be in safe hands. I don't want them lying about here where anyone can see them. Do you understand?"

Mr. Deacon moved so that the desk was between us. Did he think I was going to accost him? He cleared his throat. "Mr. Sharp can tell you all about that side of the business. I'm not allowed."

"But you know the answer, and it's just a simple question. I don't want to wait for Mr. Sharp. I don't want to see that couple, you see." I touched my hat brim to demurely hide my face behind my arm.

Mr. Deacon cleared his throat again. "The negatives are kept under lock and key."

"Not destroyed?"

"No, but the customer is welcome to buy them. It costs extra, but some prefer it."

"Did Mrs. Warrington purchase her negatives just now?"

"I, um, I cannot say."

The door burst open and the couple spilled into the shop, laughing. Both were fully clothed. The man wore the well-cut suit of a gentleman, but the woman was more gaudily dressed with her petticoat showing and her cheeks and lips painted pink. At a guess, I would say she was his mistress, but not the discreet sort who sometimes stayed at the Mayfair with their benefactors. She was more like the ones who stole in and out in the middle of the night. She was also quite drunk and could barely walk. The man wrapped his arm around her, propping her up.

Mr. Sharp opened the front door for them, smiling. "The photographs will be ready tomorrow afternoon. If I am unavailable, my assistant can serve you."

"Lucky boy," the woman said, winking at Mr. Deacon.

Mr. Deacon made a strangled sound in his throat.

The gentleman glanced at me and blushed. His mistress tapped the end of his nose and laughed as he pushed open the door and steered her out.

Mr. Sharp shuffled towards me and bobbed his head. "I do apologize for that, madam. It was the first time the lady has been photographed and she found the process amusing."

I wasn't going to get answers from these two about Mrs. Warrington. They must be very discreet or they wouldn't remain in business for long. I gave up and left.

The rain had stopped but the dark clouds hung low and expectant. I looked up and down the street then hurried after the couple who'd just had their photograph taken.

"Excuse me!" I called out. "Excuse me, sir, madam!"

The man turned around but the woman appeared not to hear me. She kicked a puddle of water, splashing the apron of a matronly shopkeeper standing in the doorway of the grocer's. She scowled at the whore who laughingly apologized.

"Yes?" the gentleman prompted me.

"I wondered if I could ask you some questions about the photographic studio." I pointed back the way we'd come. "I'm considering engaging Mr. Sharp's services to take some photographs of my husband and me. I saw you leave and I wondered if you could tell me whether he's good."

"You can see the quality for yourself. There are some pictures on display that you couldn't have failed to notice."

The man touched the brim of his hat and headed off with the woman clinging to his arm.

I hurried past and stepped in their way. The gentleman clicked his tongue, but his companion suddenly grasped my hands. She spun me around in an awkward sort of dance. The closed umbrella I'd tucked under my arm almost smacked a pedestrian passing by.

"Clara," the gentleman growled. He grabbed her by the elbow. There was no sign of his jovial mood anymore. He had remembered himself now that he was in the public eye with a drunken mistress at his side. She was embarrassing him, and there's one thing an English gentleman loathes, it's to be humiliated in public.

I would have to tread carefully and not embarrass him further if I wanted his cooperation. I leaned in a little and lowered my voice. "I want to have some...private photographs taken of my husband and me, and I was given Mr. Sharp's name. But the person who gave me that information hadn't personally used Mr. Sharp's services."

The gentleman gave an irritated huff and eyed the pavement ahead with longing. "I'm sorry, but we must get going."

The woman kissed the gentleman's cheek and giggled in his ear. "Aye, got a train to catch."

He gently pushed her to put some distance between them, but folded his hand over hers resting on his arm. She pouted.

"Is Mr. Sharp discreet?" I pressed. "It's just that I would hate for someone to approach him and try to buy the negative plates off him. Can you imagine?"

"He's discreet. Excuse us." He pushed past me.

The woman glanced over her shoulder at me. "You must have your photograph taken. It's a lot of fun. Your husband will be ever so grateful to have a memory of you as you are now, before you get old and fat. Ain't that right, Felix?"

The gentleman hissed at her to be quiet, but it was no use. She threw her head back and laughed.

I sighed. I wasn't sure what I'd expected to learn from them, but I'd hoped for something more.

"I'd steer clear of Sharp, if I were you," said the shopkeeper standing in her doorway, arms crossed beneath an ample chest.

My face heated. I hadn't expected my little ruse to be over-heard. My hastily uttered lie about wanting to have a risqué photograph taken had just begun to sink in. Ordinarily I'd be far too conservative to suggest such a thing, even as a joke, but the lie had served a purposed. Now it hung like the ominous clouds above, ready to burst over my head in a storm of regret.

Earlier, I'd touched my hat brim to hide my face as part of my act. Now I did it because I wished to actually hide. "I'll keep that in mind," I muttered.

The shopkeeper thrust her broad chin in the direction of the studio. "We're respectable folk around here with honest businesses. But that man Sharp brings us all into disrepute with his shameful actions. We know what goes on there. He can't pretend all is clean as a whistle."

"I see," I said weakly. "I am sorry. I won't come back. I've changed my mind anyway."

"Good for you." She moved her hands to her hips so that she now completely filled the doorway, elbow to elbow. "I didn't think you were the type to go in for *that*. I can tell. I've got a good nose for bad eggs, but you seem like a respectable girl. Most who go to Sharp's studio are more like them." She jerked her head in the direction of the retreating couple. "Some are just bored, looking for a little amusement. I reckon they'd run the other way if they found out where their photographs end up."

I lowered my hand to look at her. "What do you mean? Where do they end up?"

She glanced behind her then beckoned me closer. "According to my husband, Mr. Sharp makes cards of the naughty photographs and sells them. Some men collect them —dock workers and sailors, mostly. So my husband says. The people in the pictures never even know."

"Do the police know?"

She merely shrugged. "You're wise not to come back. You don't want to end up on a card in the pocket of a sailor, do you?"

"Thank you for the warning. I've abandoned the idea alto-gether, now."

"Good girl." She pressed her lips together and shook her

head. "That Mr. Sharp is rotten to the core, if you ask me, and he's taking that boy down into the den of iniquity with him. He should be ashamed of himself for corrupting the lad."

I caught an omnibus back to the hotel where I handed my umbrella to Frank. He opened the door for me and deposited the umbrella into the stand where it was the sole occupant. Today's rain had made them a popular item to borrow.

The foyer hummed with activity and conversation. Newly arrived guests waited to be checked in by Peter at the front desk, their luggage piled up on trolleys, ready to be steered away to their rooms by Goliath and the other two porters on duty. Two ladies sat on the comfortable chairs, chatting. A third joined them and they departed, umbrellas and tourist maps in hand. At the end of the corridor, one of the double doors to the main sitting room opened and a gentleman emerged, a book tucked under his arm. He must have come from the hotel's library, situated at the back of the sitting room. Before the door closed I could see the staff setting the tables for afternoon tea.

The maids should have finished cleaning rooms for the day, and I hoped to find Harmony waiting for me in the staff parlor with a warm pot of tea. I was waylaid by Mr. Hobart, however. He peeled away from the group of guests he'd been talking to beneath the central chandelier and hurried towards me.

"I was hoping to catch you, Miss Fox." He could barely contain his excitement as he checked to see that no one was in the vicinity. He smiled at a guest passing by then when she was out of earshot, turned to me. "After you told me about your new case, I decided to do some investigation of my own."

"That wasn't necessary, Mr. Hobart, but thank you."

He waved off my gratitude. "It's my pleasure to assist. You are working with my nephew, after all."

"Not quite."

"I know you said he gave you the case, but his own reputation is still associated with it, in a way. Besides, I'm glad to help you where I can. And there are some parts to sleuthing that I am excellent at."

"Such as?"

"Such as gaining information by talking to guests." He glanced at the cluster of dour looking gentlemen he'd been chatting to. "Two of them are politicians. Since your Mr. Warrington is a politician, I thought I'd find out what I could about him, in a discreet manner, of course. I found out something most unexpected, which one of them was very happy to impart, thanks to Mr. Warrington being for the opposition party."

"Does that mean the information is scandalous?"

"It could be damaging if it got into the newspapers, although not altogether ruinous."

"I am on tenterhooks, Mr. Hobart. What did you learn?"

He leaned closer. "Mrs. Warrington has an illegitimate half-brother. It seems her father's mistress had a son thirty-odd years ago. The rumor is that he made sure his son never lacked for anything. The boy was sent to a good school and was given a comfortable allowance. He was even given his father's name, which is almost as good as being brought up in the father's household."

Almost, but not quite. "Mrs. Warrington was the only legitimate child?" I asked.

He nodded. "She inherited some or all of her father's fortune upon his death."

"That must have galled the son."

"That depends on how much he inherited, I suppose."

Mr. Hobart was right to say the information was scandalous but not ruinous for Mr. Warrington's career. Some gentlemen had illegitimate children scattered all over the country so it wasn't unusual. It was, however, a distraction. If journalists got wind of it, they would delight in reporting it and the public would revel in it, lapping up the salacious details. Considering Mr. Warrington was not a particularly important figure in his party, and the scandal belonged to his wife's family, not his, it wouldn't bring down either the government or Mr. Warrington. It was a mere side-act, at worst.

I glanced at the politicians, now heading towards the front door. "How did they know about Mrs. Warrington's brother?"

"It's an open secret amongst the gentry, apparently. But

that's not all I need to tell you." Mr. Hobart's eyes sparkled as brightly as the crystals in the chandelier. "I asked them the name of Mrs. Warrington's father. It's Trickelbank."

I shook my head. "I don't know it."

"But I do."

"Has he stayed here?"

"Not him. He died a few years ago and this Trickelbank is a recent guest. Very recent, in fact."

"Do you think it's Mrs. Warrington's half-brother?"

"It's such an unusual name that he must be related to Mrs. Warrington's father, but if Mrs. Warrington inherited her father's money because there were no *legitimate* heirs, then she has no brothers or male cousins on that side. So this Trickelbank must be her half-brother."

I wasn't sure how Mr. Trickelbank could help in my investigation to prove Mrs. Warrington was seeing another man. Unless she confided in her half-brother and I could somehow extract the information from him.

"Did your sources say whether Mrs. Warrington is close to Mr. Trickelbank?" I asked.

He shook his head. "It's unlikely, since he stays here and not with the Warringtons. Although there is a possibility that her husband forbade it and she is seeing her half-brother in secret."

It occurred to me that Mr. Trickelbank might be the man Mr. Warrington had seen entering the Midland Grand with Mrs. Warrington. If that were the case and they were meeting there in secret to avoid Mr. Warrington's detection, then she wasn't an adulteress at all. She was merely a woman wanting to spend some time with her half-brother.

"I haven't told you the best part yet." Mr. Hobart looked positively youthful as he tried to contain his excitement. "Mr. Trickelbank is checking into the hotel today."

"The Mayfair?" I blurted out.

He gave me a smug grin. "Isn't that a coincidence?"

"It certainly is." I tried to think how I could use it to my advantage. "Is he staying alone?"

"He is, and for one night only. He has one of the fifth floor traditional rooms."

"Traditional" was the name given to the rooms on the

top floor of the hotel that didn't overlook Green Park. Before the lift had been installed, several years before, the top floor was used by the staff who lived on-site. It was too high for guests to traipse up all those stairs. After the lift was installed and the staff moved to a nearby residence hall, walls separating the smaller rooms with the park view were knocked down to make larger rooms suitable for guests. They weren't as large as the suites on the fourth floor, but they were sought after for the spectacular views they sported.

The traditional rooms, however, did not have the park view. They were located on the other side of the corridor and their windows looked over gray rooftops and brick chimneys. They were smaller and did not have ensuite bathrooms. They were the hotel's cheapest rooms, according to Flossy, who'd told me all of this with a sympathetic note in her voice as if she felt sorry for those who couldn't afford one of the better rooms.

"Does Mr. Trickelbank have a dinner reservation?" I asked.

"I'm not sure. I'll check with Mr. Chapman."

"I'll do it. You've done enough, and I can see you are very busy."

Mr. Hobart smiled at a guest who waited nearby to speak to him. It was times like this he must miss having an assistant, particularly one as competent as Mr. Armitage who could share the burden of answering the guests' numerous questions and requests.

I went in search of Mr. Chapman the steward, but he was not in his office or the dining room. He was probably discussing the wine with the sommelier in the cellar or the food with the chef in the kitchen.

I didn't need to speak to him anyway. The restaurant's reservations book was on the stand near the entrance to the dining room. I glanced around to make sure I was alone then opened it to tonight's listings. Mr. Trickelbank was scheduled to dine alone eight.

"What are you doing?" The waspish voice made me jump.

I turned to see Mr. Chapman standing behind me. The steward's usually handsome features were as thunderous as the clouds outside. He reached past me and snatched the book off the stand. He clutched it to his chest.

"Good afternoon, Mr. Chapman. Please don't be alarmed."

"I'm not *alarmed*, Miss Fox."

"Oh? Then why are you holding that book as if you have something to hide?"

He returned the book to the stand and opened it to the page listing tonight's bookings to make his point. "If you have a question about the reservations, kindly ask me and I can check for you. It's no trouble."

"I would have asked you, but you weren't here."

"Is there a particular guest you hope to see in here tonight?" Mr. Chapman was a notorious busybody. I'd caught him listening at doors and hovering near tables. I wasn't sure if he did anything with the information he learned, but I wasn't going to risk my investigation on him keeping secrets. I wouldn't inform him of anything.

"I found what I wanted. Thank you, Mr. Chapman."

He stiffened but there was nothing he could say to make me confide in him. As a member of the family, I was outside his authority. I'd wager that galled him.

I headed to the staff parlor, located behind the lift. Behind the parlor was a warren of store rooms and service rooms used by the maids and footmen. All manner of doors and stairs led to other parts of the hotel that only the staff accessed. It was here that a narrow flight of stairs led down to the basement kitchen, larders, laundry and steam room.

Harmony was waiting for me in the parlor, along with Victor. She looked annoyed, but I wasn't sure whether she was annoyed with him or me. It was most likely Victor. The poor fellow couldn't seem to do anything right in her eyes. Fortunately it didn't seem to bother him. Indeed, sometimes I suspected he said contrary things just to get a rise out of her.

They sat a little apart from another group of maids occupying the corner near the teapot. Harmony got up to pour me a cup. "Goliath said you got in a while ago." She indicated my coat and gloves, which I still wore. "You haven't been up to your room, so where have you been?"

I removed my coat and folded it over the back of a chair before sitting beside Victor. He cradled a teacup between both his hands like a bowl. The tea steamed, so the cup must be hot, but he didn't seem to notice. His hands were scarred from mishaps in the kitchen. Or perhaps mishaps in the streets. Before he worked as a cook at the Mayfair, he'd been a delinquent, although I didn't know the extent of his crimes. He'd certainly never been caught, because no one with a criminal record was employed by my uncle—I'd learned that the hard way with Mr. Armitage.

"Miss Fox," he said in greeting.

"Victor," I said, matching his tone. "What were you two discussing before I entered?"

Harmony pulled a face. "We weren't talking. We were waiting for you."

And yet they were sitting separately from the others. I arched my brows at Victor.

He sipped his tea. His eyes crinkled at the corners as if he were smiling.

"So where were you?" Harmony asked.

"You're nosier than my cousin," I said. "I spoke to Mr. Hobart then went to the dining room to look in the reservation book. I wanted to see if a particular guest is dining in the restaurant this evening."

Harmony leaned forward and lowered her voice. "Is it Mrs. Warrington's lover? Do you know his name already? Is he staying here?"

I held up my hand to slow her down. She really was a curious woman with a passion for detecting. So much so that she might be better suited to investigative work than me. Most likely her passion was helped along by being dreadfully bored with her work as a maid. I certainly couldn't blame her for seeking a distraction.

"So I can assume you've told Victor all about the case?" I asked.

Harmony nodded. "And we've discussed it with Peter, Goliath and Frank. Sometimes they're helpful at finding things out."

"And sometimes they're helpful for opening doors that are locked." I winked at Victor.

His baby-faced features remained passive except for a slight uptick on one side of his mouth.

Harmony clicked her tongue. "You shouldn't encourage his nefarious activities, Miss Fox."

"You're right. We don't want him getting caught and losing his position here. Which is why I'd like you to teach me how to pick locks, Victor. That way I won't have to rely on you."

"Miss Fox!" Harmony gawped at me. "You can't go about breaking and entering! It's not seemly for a lady like you."

If she didn't like that then she wasn't going to like what I was about to tell her. "I think I have moved well past seemly and landed in the sordid. Today, I followed Mrs. Warrington to a photography studio in Paddington. It so happens that this studio doesn't limit itself to portraiture of the kind seen in parlors and drawing rooms."

She frowned. "They do landscapes too?"

Victor chuckled quietly, earning himself a frosty glare from Harmony. He knew what I was inferring.

I lowered my voice further. "They photograph couples with no clothes on and—"

Harmony emitted a squeak. She slapped her hand over her mouth and glanced at the other maids, but they paid us no mind.

"—and apparently the photographer sells copies of the pictures without the subjects' knowledge."

"Why would anyone want to pose naked for a photograph?" she asked.

"Money," Victor said in that matter-of-fact way he had.

"Surely Mrs. Warrington isn't short of a quid."

"She isn't," I said. "She might have had her photograph taken as a memento for her lover to keep. Apparently some couples do that."

Harmony and I both looked at Victor, but he merely shrugged. "Toffs are strange," he said.

Harmony nodded sagely.

"The photographs will likely prove that Mrs. Warrington has a lover," I went on. "I need to get my hands on them or the negatives."

"Did she collect the negatives from the studio today or just the photographs?" Victor asked.

"I don't know for certain, but I suspect she bought all of

the proof of her adultery then destroyed it. That's what I would do if I knew my husband had hired a private detective to find evidence of my adultery. Of course, she might not have thought about the negatives and simply collected the photographs..."

"You are *not* breaking into the studio to look for the negatives," Harmony hissed. "Neither of you."

I sipped my tea as I gathered my thoughts.

"Miss Fox, don't do it. It's one thing to break into a hotel room owned by your uncle, but quite another to break into a shop. Please, I'm begging you not to. And you, Victor, should not encourage her." She wagged her finger at him. "If I find out you have, I'll tell Chef you've been taking leftovers and giving them to the maids."

Victor caught her finger and enveloped it in his hand. "Would it be so terrible for me to give you food?"

She snatched her hand away. "I didn't say me."

"No, but when you said maids, all I could think about was you."

Her jaw slackened and her lips parted with her sharp intake of breath.

He sat back with a smile. "You were the only one in my line of sight and shaking your finger at me, so naturally I thought of you."

She clamped her jaw shut and shot him a withering glare. "So." She cleared her throat. "You won't do anything dangerous tonight, will you, Miss Fox?"

"You have my word."

Victor glanced at the clock and got to his feet. He adjusted the belt knife strapped at his hips and straightened his chef's hat. "I have to go. You won't tell Chef any lies about me, will you, Harmony?"

She crossed her arms.

"It's just that everything makes him angry, right now. Things in the kitchen are tense all the time. No one dares get on his bad side."

"Why is he angry?" I asked.

Victor shrugged then left the parlor.

Harmony and I finished our tea then rose too. "You

wouldn't get him into trouble with the chef, would you?" I asked.

She gave me a rare smile. "Of course not. But it won't hurt for him to worry, will it? Sometimes I think he doesn't worry nearly enough about himself or his future."

I squeezed her hand. "That's almost sweet."

Out in the foyer, Goliath cut me off as I headed for the main stairs. "You had a meeting with Harmony without us, didn't you?"

"You were very busy, Goliath. You, Peter and Frank. In fact, you still look busy."

"It's not so bad for me and Frank, but Peter's doing extra on account of there being no assistant for Mr. Hobart." He pulled out a folded letter from his pocket. "Terence asked me to give this to you. It arrived at the post desk just a few minutes ago."

I thanked him and headed up the stairs where I sat at my desk and read the note. It was from Mr. Armitage, wishing me luck with my investigation. His uncle had informed him last night that I was working on the Warrington divorce.

I smiled as I folded it and dropped it into the top drawer then dashed off a response, updating him on my progress. I even put in the scandalous detail about the studio taking naked photographs of customers, and therefore probably also of Mrs. Warrington and her lover. Thankfully no one was around to witness my blushes.

How odd that I could tell Harmony and Victor about the naked photographs without my face heating, but I couldn't even write a letter to Mr. Armitage without my cheeks burning.

CHAPTER 5

*D*inner in the hotel dining room with my family was not the casual affair most families enjoyed in the privacy of their own homes. For one thing, we dined in full view of dozens of guests and for another, my uncle used the opportunity to play the friendly host. Some nights he hardly ate; he was too busy flitting from table to table like a butterfly in a spring garden, spoiled for choice. He encouraged us all to get up and speak with the guests, or invite them to our table. As one of the last family-owned luxury hotels left in London, he wanted to show off his family as much as possible.

It could be exhausting, however. I looked forward to the evenings when he ate elsewhere. I usually dined alone in my room on those occasions, or with Flossy and my aunt. Floyd never joined us. If his father was out, then he took the opportunity to meet his friends.

I glanced at the table where Mr. Trickelbank should be seated, according to the reservations book. He had not yet arrived.

"What are you going to order tonight, Cleo?" Flossy asked as she took her seat beside me.

Floyd sat opposite and waved away the waiter offering him a menu. "Never mind that. What I want to know is, who are you looking for?" He arched his brows at me.

"I was just taking in the room," I said. "Tell me how your day went. Did you get to ride in a motor car, Flossy?"

She clapped her hands lightly. "It was absolutely thrilling! The driver took us on a special track so he could make it go as fast as it was able. You should have seen it take off. He took me around three times and Floyd twice."

Floyd crossed his arms. "I'm not taking you with me next time. You were a distraction and we couldn't talk business with you there."

"Tosh. Of course you could. And I will certainly go again." She clasped my arm. "Cleo will come too, won't you?"

"Perhaps."

Flossy touched her hair, arranged into a swept-up style and kept in place with a blue enamel comb. "My hair was a mess afterwards. I had to remove my hat to save it from being blown away. No amount of pins could keep it in place. Next time I'll wear a headscarf and tie it tightly under my chin. That's the only problem with motor cars, that I can see. The lack of protection for the driver and passenger. The wind plays havoc with one's outfit and hair."

"That's not the *only* problem with motor cars," Floyd said with a roll of his eyes. "But the engineers are making great strides so it won't be long before they're more efficient. We'll be swapping horse-drawn vehicles for motor cars in no time, just wait and see."

"So you're going to invest in the company?" I asked.

Floyd's gaze focused on something behind me. I turned to see Uncle Ronald storming towards us like an out of control barrel rolling down a hill. He must have learned that I'd taken on the Warrington case.

"Hell," Floyd muttered. "Did you tell him where we went today, Flossy?"

"No! I swear. I haven't even told Mother."

Uncle Ronald yanked the chair out before the waiter could do it for him. "I'll have the soup then the duck. And wine."

The waiter seemed to shrink a little more with every barked word. Usually Richard, the head waiter, served the family table, but Uncle Ronald had ordered so quickly that he hadn't had a chance to join us. He was tied up with other diners at a nearby table. He glanced anxiously at the hapless junior waiter, still hovering uncertainly at my uncle's side.

"Uh, what sort of wine would you like, sir?" he asked.

"Anything. I don't care."

The waiter sent an appealing glance at Richard, but Richard was once again speaking to other diners. "Very well, sir." The junior waiter bowed and went to walk off.

"I'll also have the soup and duck," Floyd called after him.

The waiter hurried back, recollecting himself. "Very good, sir. And for Miss Bainbridge and Miss Fox?" The poor fellow had gone quite pale and the hand that held the menus shook. I worried he wouldn't remember our orders if we made them too complicated.

"I'll have the soup and duck too," I said. "And so will Miss Bainbridge."

Flossy blinked at me. "But—"

I kicked her lightly under the table and she thankfully kept her mouth shut. "And please ask the sommelier for a wine that goes well with duck," I added.

The waiter backed away, looking relieved that he only had to remember a simple order and he didn't need to take responsibility for the wine choice.

My two cousins sat in silence while my uncle continued to fume like an active volcano. I waited for one of his children to speak up, but neither seemed too keen to probe.

I could stand the tension no longer, however. "Is something the matter, Uncle?"

"It's the bloody chef." Not apologizing for swearing in the presence of Flossy and me was a testament to his fury. "He's too self-important. He forgets that he doesn't own this hotel; I do. He takes his orders from *me*."

Floyd shot me a warning glare but I forged on.

"What has he done?"

"I called him up to my office and told him about the plans for the new restaurant. He threw a tantrum, saying he won't work in it. He wants to keep this restaurant for the guests only and not expand to serve the public."

"Did you explain the benefits of expansion?" Floyd asked, suddenly taking an interest.

"Of course I bloody well did."

The guests at the nearby table looked up at the sound of his angry voice. Uncle Ronald collected himself and greeted them warmly. When he turned back to us, he appeared some-what calmer.

"If the chef doesn't come around, you'll have to dismiss him," Floyd said.

"I know," Uncle Ronald snarled through an unmoving jaw.

Floyd sucked in a breath and stared straight ahead. Beside me, Flossy picked at the tablecloth's edge. This was going to be a very long dinner.

"Is Aunt Lilian joining us this evening?" I asked.

"She's unwell," Uncle Ronald said. "She overdid it yesterday at her bridge party. It's time I put a stop to them if she's like this the next day."

That wasn't going to solve the problem, just cover it up. But I kept my mouth shut. It was a battle for another day when he wasn't in such a foul mood.

Mr. Chapman showed a gentleman to the table reserved for Mr. Trickelbank. Mrs. Warrington's half-brother was an unremarkable looking man in his late thirties with a neat gray beard and brown hair, receding a little at the front. Mr. Chapman called over a waiter who handed him a menu then proceeded to talk Mr. Trickelbank through it. Mr. Trickelbank dismissed him mid-sentence with a flick of his fingers. The waiter bowed and walked off while Mr. Trickelbank read the menu.

Despite the poor start to our evening, I wasn't giving up on the task I'd set myself. "Uncle, shall we ask a guest to dine with us tonight? Perhaps someone dining alone."

Floyd arched a brow at me.

Uncle Ronald tapped a finger on the table between us. "I almost forgot, Cleo. Why did you steal the reservations book from Mr. Chapman?"

A bubble of laughter escaped my lips. His insinuation was absurd. "I didn't steal anything from Mr. Chapman."

"I didn't think you would, but those were his words."

"Chapman is a turd," Floyd said.

"He's a good steward."

"How hard can it be to write down names in a book and show guests to their table?"

"He does more than that and you know it."

"I was simply looking through it," I said quickly, before the conversation descended into an argument. It seemed such an unlikely topic for them to argue about, but I got the feeling that anything was possible given the tension in the air. "I didn't even remove the book from the dining room."

"Well?" Uncle Ronald asked. "Why were you looking through it?"

I should have taken the small window of opportunity to think of a suitable answer. Indeed, I should have thought of one while I'd been dressing for dinner in my room. Harmony would have helped. But I didn't think Mr. Chapman would tattle to my uncle. He *was* a turd.

Flossy came to my rescue, bless her. "Cleo doesn't like to say, but there's a particular gentleman she wishes to acquaint herself with."

Oh dear. This could make everything worse.

"A guest?" Uncle Ronald looked around. "Who?"

"A friend of a guest," I said. "I thought he might dine here tonight with Mr. Trickelbank, but my hopes were dashed after I looked through the reservation book. Mr. Trickelbank dines alone."

Uncle Ronald followed my gaze then signaled to a passing waiter. He asked the waiter to invite Mr. Trickelbank to join us for dinner.

Uncle Ronald's mood seemed to instantly lift. He even smiled at me. "I'm glad to see you taking an interest, Cleo. Your aunt will be pleased. She's determined to find you a husband before the year is out."

I sighed.

Floyd pressed his lips together to suppress his smile. At least someone found my situation amusing.

Mr. Trickelbank listened to the waiter then glanced our way. With a nod and a self-conscious brush of his fingers along his sleeve, he rose.

"Please don't mention the friend to him," I begged my uncle and cousins. "The thing is, I hardly know him and it would be terribly gauche to claim an acquaintance when there isn't one."

Uncle Ronald patted my arm. "We'll use tonight as an opportunity to get to know this Trickelbank. If he's a good man then I'm sure his friend will be too, and we can orchestrate a proper meeting between you."

I breathed a sigh of relief. Hopefully that had averted a disaster.

"Thank you for inviting me to dine with you, Sir Ronald," Mr. Trickelbank said as he joined us. "I'm honored."

"We are the ones who are honored, my good man." My uncle introduced us then Mr. Trickelbank gave his order to the waiter.

"Do you personally dine with all your guests?" he asked as the waiter walked off.

"Not as many as I'd like."

"Then I am fortunate indeed."

He spoke in the cultured accent of the upper class and sported an air of confidence that my uncle responded to. Indeed, the two of them got along splendidly as they discussed all manner of topics. We learned that Mr. Trickelbank had gone to Oxford then went into law. He was now a barrister in Birmingham. It seemed being illegitimate had not held him back.

I listened attentively, biding my time before I asked him about his family.

"And are you in London for business of pleasure?" my uncle asked as our soup bowls were taken away.

Mr. Trickelbank plucked up his wine glass and sipped. If I weren't mistaken, he was stretching out the pause before he answered. Was he considering how much to reveal? If he were here to see his sister, it could lead to uncomfortable questions. Mr. Trickelbank might be reluctant to open that can of worms.

"Business," he eventually said. There was a finality in his tone that invited no further questions.

"I hope you have an opportunity to visit our many museums while you're here," Uncle Ronald said.

"I hope so too."

"My niece, Cleo, is a great patron of museums."

"She goes *all* the time," Flossy added. "Perhaps you saw her there."

"Where?"

"At the British Museum, of course. She went today."

"I just arrived in London today and have not yet had the pleasure. I'm not sure I'll have the opportunity before I leave either. I'm a busy man. You know how it is, Sir Ronald. We gentlemen of business don't have the benefit of endless time like gentlemen of leisure."

Considering Uncle Ronald was descended from nobility and had only gone into the hotel business out of necessity, I thought he might feel slighted, but he bore it with only a moderate tightening of the corners of his eyes.

Flossy didn't notice a thing. She seemed intent on following her own thread of the conversation. "If you have friends who enjoy museums, you should ask them to go too. Museums are more bearable with friends. Oh, I've just had an excellent idea! You and your friend could meet Cleo there. I could attend too, and Floyd and Mother. We can make it a party. What do you say?"

She seemed to have decided that I'd met Mr. Trickelbank's friend at the museum. I supposed it made sense since, as far as she was aware, I frequented the British Museum often.

Mr. Trickelbank blinked at her. "I don't quite follow. Which friend?"

"The one who likes museums, like Cleo. Perhaps he went today too."

"I'm not sure I have such a friend as you describe. Not here in London anyway."

Flossy frowned. My uncle did too, but Floyd sported a curious expression. He was skeptical of my motives for inviting Mr. Trickelbank to our table.

It was time to focus on what I needed to achieve from tonight. "Do you have family in London?" I kept my tone pleasant. Hopefully he thought it merely a polite question one asked a stranger.

"No."

That one-word lie ended my hopes of learning more about his relationship with his half-sister. If they were close, he wasn't going to admit it if he couldn't even admit that he had a sibling here. It would seem I couldn't rely on Mr. Trickelbank to feed me information about Mrs. Warrington's affair.

Finding Mrs. Warrington's photographs or the negatives was not only my best option for obtaining the proof Mr.

Warrington needed, it had just become my only option. I might have to break into the photographic studio, after all.

* * *

I AWOKE with a start the following morning to bright light streaming through the curtains that Harmony unceremoniously pushed open.

"Get up, Cleo! There's something you have to see."

I sat up and rubbed my eyes. "Are you calling me by my first name now?"

She held out my dressing gown to me. "Only in private. Is that all right?"

"Of course. I'm glad you feel comfortable enough with me to do it."

I must have been taking too long for her liking because she peeled back the covers and shoved the dressing gown at me. "There's been a murder. It's all over the front pages of the morning editions."

"How awful. But I can't just approach the victim's family and offer my detection services. The police investigation will have to run its course, and if that fails to find the murderer then Harry Armitage can—"

"Do *not* give this case back to him. If the situation has developed in a direction he didn't expect, that's his misfortune, not yours."

I stared at her as her words sank in. A heavy weight settled in my stomach. "Harmony, what's happened? Who died?"

"Mrs. Warrington. Last night. She was stabbed in the throat in the drawing room of her Kensington home."

CHAPTER 6

$\mathcal{T}$he newspaper had very few details, but it did suggest that Scotland Yard was speaking to a suspect and an arrest was imminent. It didn't mention which detective was assigned to the case. I hoped it was Detective Inspector Hobart, Mr. Armitage's father.

Harmony took the newspaper from my hand and replaced it with a piece of buttered toast. "Eat this and drink your coffee. You've got work to do."

"Actually, now I have no work because I have no case. Mrs. Warrington's death means Mr. Warrington no longer needs a divorce."

"Your divorce case just became a murder case."

"Not quite. We're missing one key ingredient—a client. Mr. Warrington will have no reason to hire me. Unless he's arrested for the murder, of course." I gasped. "What if he did it? No, wait. He wouldn't bother attempting to divorce her if he planned to murder her."

"What if he didn't plan to kill her but lashed out in anger?"

I nibbled on the toast as Harmony poured coffee into two cups. She was right. Mr. Warrington clearly disliked his wife enough to divorce her. Perhaps they'd argued last night and jealousy and anger had driven him to kill her.

"If she was stabbed with a kitchen knife then it would indicate the murder was planned ahead."

"Because no one carries a kitchen knife around with them?"

"Certainly not into drawing rooms. But if her throat was stabbed with something close to hand then it could have been unplanned and that would certainly put Mr. Warrington in the picture. Something like a pocket-sized blade or sharp letter opener, perhaps."

"Or fire poker." Harmony set the cup down on the table in front of me. "Or a hat pin. The ones used to keep large hats in place are as long as a kitchen blade."

"You're right. I should inform the detective in charge that all was not well in the Warrington marriage."

"At the very least you have information that may help." At my blank look, she added, "The naked photographs."

"How do they help?"

"Well, I don't know, do I? You're the experienced detective."

"Hardly."

She passed me the cup. "You'll feel more awake once you get this into you."

I accepted the cup and sipped thoughtfully. "Whether Mr. Warrington did it or not, one thing won't change. I won't be getting paid now. Thank goodness I asked for half up front."

I studied Harmony over the rim of the cup. She wasn't dressed in her maid's uniform. "Is it your day off?"

"Yes."

"Then why are you at the hotel?"

"To give you the newspaper, of course. I still wake up early on my day off and read the paper. I came as soon as I saw the article." She picked up a piece of bacon from the plate. "You also get better a breakfast than me."

I drained my coffee then rose. "Eat up quickly."

"You want me to do your hair?"

"Never mind that. I can do it myself while you finish breakfast. I want you to hurry because you're coming with me to the Warrington house. We're going to speak to the detective in charge."

She stared at me. "You want me there?"

"Yes, why not? Have you got anything better to do?"

She shoved the bacon into her mouth and drained her

73

coffee while still chewing. She waved me off to the bedroom, urging me to hurry.

* * *

To my great disappointment, Detective Inspector Hobart was not assigned to the investigation. According to the constable stationed at the front door of the Warrington house, the detective in charge was not present. The constable was the only policeman on duty, and he was there merely to keep onlookers away. He eyed the small cluster of journalists on the pavement nearby, hunched into their coats and stomping their feet to stave off the cold.

"You don't look like a journalist," he said to me.

"I'm not. Mr. Warrington is my client. Is he in?"

The constable's eyes widened. "You're his lawyer?"

"I'm a private detective and this is my associate." I indicated Harmony. "Does Mr. Warrington need a lawyer? Is he a suspect?"

He shook his head. "A vagrant was arrested early this morning. They found Mrs. Warrington's jewels amongst his things."

"What was the murder weapon?"

"A small knife." He crossed his arms and looked me up and down as if I were a statue in a museum. "Private detective, eh? Well, well."

Harmony thrust a hand on her hip. "Don't 'well, well' her. She's Cleopatra Fox. She solved both the Christmas Eve murder at the Mayfair Hotel *and* the murder of Pearl Westwood. You ought to treat her with respect."

The constable swallowed heavily. "Sorry, ma'am."

"Now let us in so we can speak to our client. Mr. Warrington will be furious if he learns you blocked our entry."

The constable couldn't knock on the door fast enough.

"I knew I brought you along for a reason," I whispered to Harmony.

The door was opened by Mr. Henderson the butler. He hesitated upon seeing me, and I thought we'd have to go through the spiel again about his employer being my client, but then he stepped aside and allowed us in.

"Wait here," he said. "I'll see if Mr. Warrington is receiving."

He returned a few minutes later and escorted us up the stairs. We passed the entrance to the drawing room where a large carpet had been rolled back. The housekeeper and another woman were on hands and knees, scrubbing the floor. The bloodstain on the chair looked as though it would be harder to remove.

"Was Mrs. Warrington sitting on the chair when she was attacked?" I asked.

"This way, Miss Fox." Mr. Henderson continued up the stairs and knocked lightly on a door off the landing. Upon Mr. Warrington's command he let us in then closed the door behind us.

I introduced Harmony as my associate and offered my condolences to Mr. Warrington. He did not look upset, but I didn't expect him to, considering he was attempting to divorce his wife. Still, his face was gaunt and his eyes troubled. He was not the same poised gentleman who'd engaged my services to find evidence of his wife's adultery.

He opened the drawer and removed an envelope. "This is the remainder of what I owe you."

I put up my hand. "You don't owe me anything. I hadn't finished my investigation. What you've already paid is enough."

He frowned. "Then why are you here?"

"To see that the police have the investigation in hand. I've found that sometimes they can be a little hasty in leaping to conclusions."

"In this instance, it's quite clear they have the right man. He was caught with my wife's jewels."

"The constable at the door said he was a vagrant. Where was he found?"

"In a cul-de-sac not far from here. The police did an early morning search of the surrounding streets and stumbled across him. He'd made a camp for himself of old blankets and newspapers. Isobel's jewels were found amongst his possessions."

"How odd to stay near the scene of the crime."

He shrugged. "Not odd, merely foolish."

Precisely, I thought but did not say. "May I ask who discovered your wife's body?"

"Her lady's maid. Poor thing is distressed, so I hear."

"You haven't spoken to her?" Harmony asked.

Mr. Warrington looked at her askance. "I have nothing to do with my wife's maid."

"What time did she find the body?" I asked.

He rubbed his forehead with his thumb and forefinger. "It was around midnight. She was waiting up to undress Isobel, but when Isobel didn't return to her room, she went looking for her."

"Did anyone hear the intruder?" I asked.

He shook his head. "I was out at my club, and I suppose the rest of the servants were asleep too at that time. I don't know."

"Has Mr. Trickelbank been informed of his sister's demise?"

Mr. Warrington's lips parted. "How do you know about him?"

"He's staying at the Mayfair Hotel. I dined with him last night in the hope he could tell me about Mrs. Warrington's relationships."

"And what did he say?"

"He said he doesn't have family here."

Mr. Warrington stared absently at a framed map of western Europe with blue pins stuck into it, hanging on the far wall. His eyes briefly fluttered closed before they reopened. He rose and headed for the door. "I'm feeling somewhat overwrought this morning. Would you mind seeing yourselves out?"

"Of course, but if you wish me to investigate for you, please let me know."

"That won't be necessary. The police have it in hand."

He opened the door just as Mr. Henderson was about to knock. Beside him stood a gentleman of slim build with thinning blond hair and small lines fanning out from worried blue eyes. Mr. Warrington's mood instantly lifted as he greeted the newcomer with a look of relief.

The visitor clasped Mr. Warrington's shoulders. "Bertie, I came as soon as I received your message. What happened?"

Mr. Warrington stepped aside to reveal Harmony and me. "Thank you for coming, Pierce. Miss Fox, Miss Cotton, may I introduce my friend, Mr. Pierce Drummond. I asked him to stop by at his earliest convenience. I'm in need of good friends around me today."

The two men exchanged grim smiles, and Mr. Drummond stepped forward to shake our hands. Mr. Warrington did not explain that we were private detectives or why we were there. He simply stood beside the open door, waiting for us to leave.

We bade them goodbye and headed down the stairs behind Mr. Henderson. I stopped at the entrance to the drawing room and Harmony did too. When he realized, Mr. Henderson turned back. He closed the door on the staff who'd turned their attention to the bloodstained chair.

I glanced up and was surprised to see him not scowling. He didn't look angry. He looked sad.

I'd made a dreadful mistake. A mistake that ladies and gentlemen often made, but one I'd not expected to make. I'd treated a servant as if he were invisible, as if his reaction to the previous night's events could tell me nothing.

But Mr. Henderson's shoulders were a little slumped this morning, his face etched with lines of exhaustion that hadn't been there yesterday.

He turned and continued down the stairs, his pace brisk.

I hurried to keep up. "Mr. Henderson, may I ask you some questions about last night?"

"No."

"What about Mrs. Warrington's maid? I believe she found the body. May I speak with—?"

He stopped at the base of the staircase and turned so suddenly to face me that I took a stumbling step back, bumping into Harmony. Mr. Henderson leaned down to my level to look me in the eye. Where before he seemed sad, now he was back to being the austere butler.

"Mrs. Warrington is deceased. Show some respect and leave."

"But it might be important."

"Get. Out."

He gripped Harmony's arm and marched her to the front door.

"Unhand me!" Harmony swatted at him, but he did not release her until the door was open. She adjusted her coat and thrust out her chin at him. "Don't touch me again."

"Don't come back here again," the butler growled.

"Something wrong?" the constable said as Harmony and I joined him on the porch.

"Don't let them back in," Mr. Henderson snapped at him. "Mr. Warrington no longer wishes to see them."

I bristled. "That's not true!"

"Miss Fox? Harmony? What the devil?"

The familiar voice took me by surprise. So much so that I couldn't move for several seconds as I stared at Mr. Armitage, approaching from the pavement. "What are you doing here?" I asked.

"Making a nuisance of himself," the constable said. He crossed his arms and settled his feet apart, blocking Mr. Armitage from joining us on the porch.

Mr. Armitage was still taller even though he stood on a lower step. He put up his hands in surrender. "I'm not attempting to get inside. I just want to make sure my friends are all right. Harmony, are you hurt?"

"I'm fine," she said, somewhat cautiously. Her gaze slid to me, brows arched.

"Miss Fox?" he asked.

"We're quite all right, thank you. Are you here to speak to Mr. Warrington?"

"Yes, but this fellow won't let me in." Mr. Armitage glared at the constable. "How did you get in?"

"Mr. Warrington is my client so naturally I was allowed."

The constable grunted. "Don't think he's your client no more." He jerked his head at the closed door. "Seems he threw you out."

"His butler doesn't speak for his employer." I passed Mr. Armitage on the steps and Harmony followed behind. "Why did you want to speak to Mr. Warrington?"

"To offer my services in the investigation," he said.

Harmony and I stopped and rounded on him. "You can't!" I blurted out. "He's *my* client."

The journalists looked up, sensing an intrigue. Mr. Armitage indicated we should keep walking.

"He was your client in the divorce matter," he said. "This is different."

"It is not," Harmony said snippily.

"It's irrelevant anyway," I said. "Mr. Warrington is leaving it in the hands of the police. He won't be hiring either of us."

Mr. Armitage remained silent. Too silent. I grew suspicious.

"The police have arrested a suspect," I went on.

He scoffed. "You believe the story about the vagrant?"

"You know about that?"

"I called my father as soon as I read the article in the newspaper this morning." He glanced behind us to make sure no one was listening. "He doesn't believe the vagrant did it. For one thing, why did he remain so close to the house after killing her and taking her jewels? He should have got further away. He had time."

"That's what I thought."

"That's not all. The killer appears to have accessed the drawing room via the unlocked window. Since the room was on the first floor, he would have had to climb up the plumbing pipes and crawl through, but he has a bad arm. Even with a ladder, he would struggle."

"So they've released the vagrant?"

His face turned grim. "Unfortunately, the detective assigned to the case wants to wrap it up quickly. My father thinks he's getting pressure from higher up. The vagrant may be the scapegoat unless the real killer is found."

"So the investigation is not being conducted in a thorough manner. I imagine that must frustrate Detective Inspector Hobart."

He gave a wry laugh. "My father does like to make sure everything is done properly. Unfortunately he hasn't got the authority to do anything about it. When he raised concerns he was told to keep quiet."

We walked on, heading in the general direction of Mayfair, although no one had suggested a final destination. It was yet another overcast day, but the rain held off and it would have been a pleasant walk if we'd not just come from a murder scene.

"So what do we do now?" I asked.

"Investigate," Mr. Armitage said. "Find out who really killed her then go to Mr. Warrington with the proof before going to the police. Perhaps he'll pay; perhaps he won't. It's not an ideal way to go about conducting business, but I'm prepared to do some work *gratis* while I establish myself." He flashed me a lopsided grin. "Also, I have nothing better to do."

I smiled.

Harmony cleared her throat. "That's all well and good, but what if Mr. Warrington *did* do it? Maybe he wanted to be sure he kept her money. If they divorced, wouldn't she keep it, but in the event of her death, he'd inherit? Seems like a good motive to me."

"If they married after the law changed in 1882, she'd have kept any property and money she brought to the marriage in the event of divorce," Mr. Armitage said.

"They did," I said. "They married in '83, according to the butler. So if Mr. Warrington divorced her, he would have got nothing. She would keep her inheritance. But if he killed her, it all goes to him, as next of kin, unless her will stated otherwise." A chill ran down my spine. Had I just been in the same room as a killer? Thank goodness I'd taken Harmony with me.

I looped my arm through hers and we exchanged worried looks. She clearly thought the same as me.

"It's not him," Mr. Armitage assured us. "My father told me Warrington has an alibi for the time of the murder. He was at his club."

We turned into Kensington Gardens to take a slightly shorter route back to Piccadilly. The Albert Memorial was visible through the bare winter trees, the gold cross glinting in the sliver of weak sunshine managing to poke through the clouds. It was clear now that we were heading to the hotel.

"I think we ought to return to the house," I said. "We need to question the servants."

Harmony agreed. "If the police aren't willing to look further, then it's up to us. Mr. Warrington will pay us once we find the killer." She said it with conviction and I tended to agree with her. He'd been willing to pay my entire fee this morning, even though my investigation was cut short.

"We won't tell him yet, however," I said. "Not until we have proof that someone other than the vagrant did it. What do you think, Mr. Armitage?"

"There is no 'we' in this investigation, Miss Fox."

"Come now, don't be like that. Even though Mr. Warrington is my client, I'll let you have a piece of the pie this time since you have nothing better to do."

"I meant, I'll work this investigation alone."

I gave him a sweet smile. "I know what you meant." I turned and retraced our steps back towards the house. Harmony kept pace beside me.

Mr. Armitage muttered something then fell into step alongside us. "I've created a monster."

"Merely unleashed her."

He grunted. "I'm not sure you were ever leashed, Miss Fox. Not while I've known you, anyway. You strike me as someone who has always been a free spirit who does as she pleases."

"If I could do as I pleased, I wouldn't go to dull dinners with my family and sit through conversations with dull men who only have one thing on their mind."

"Marriage?"

"Finance."

He laughed. "Would you prefer it if they wanted to talk about marriage?"

"Good lord, no. I'll take financial conversations over personal ones any day."

Several paces later, he asked, "How many men are there, anyway?"

"Just the one, and that's more than enough." I shouldn't talk about Edward Caldicott in such a way. It was hardly fair. He'd been friendly to me at dinner, and hadn't been as dull as I'd made out. I suspected after he returned from his holiday that he would be rather more interesting. Travel tended to change a person and expand their viewpoint.

That's if he decided to travel at all. His mother had made

it sound like he was putting it off. I only hoped he wasn't putting it off so he could court me, as she'd implied.

"I think we should avoid the butler." Harmony's voice cut through my thoughts and reminded me of the task at hand. "But I do think we should speak to the other servants, if possible."

"It won't be easy to get them alone," Mr. Armitage said. "Not without the constable seeing us, or the butler."

"We'll wait for them to leave," I said.

Mr. Armitage lengthened his strides. "I have a better idea."

His better idea was to inform the journalists that he'd heard the constable was in possession of some scandalous information about the Warringtons. They swarmed up the front steps and surrounded the poor constable, peppering him with questions.

We took advantage of the commotion to take the stairs to the basement and slip into the house via the service door. Mr. Armitage went ahead to make sure the butler wasn't present, then returned a few minutes later with a small woman wearing a black uniform and white cap. I recognized her as the lady's maid caught listening at the door when I'd spoken to the butler in his office yesterday. I didn't know what Mr. Armitage had said to her but going by the way she batted her lashes at him, I suspected he'd employed his charm.

He introduced her as Miss Jennet. She was young for a lady's maid, only mid-twenties, with brown hair pulled back severely under her cap. She had an angular jaw and high cheekbones, and dainty hands that wrung together in front of her.

"Miss Jennet, this is Miss Fox and Miss Cotton, my associates." To us, Mr. Armitage added, "I told Miss Jennet how we are private detectives employed by Mr. Warrington to find the killer as he doesn't believe the police have the right man. She knows she mustn't talk about it with the others."

She barely even looked at Harmony or me. She blinked up at Mr. Armitage. "I think what you do is thrilling."

Good lord, this was getting us nowhere, and the house-keeper or butler could interrupt at any moment and then we'd get no answers. "Can we go for a walk outside, Miss

Jennet?" I said. "It's just that I feel somewhat claustrophobic in this narrow corridor."

Footsteps echoed on the flagstones in the distance. "Is someone there?" It sounded like the housekeeper.

"Let's have a nice chat in a teashop," I said cheerfully.

The footsteps grew louder.

Harmony opened the door and Mr. Armitage ushered Miss Jennet out. I just managed to close the door before the housekeeper came into view.

We found a teashop on Kensington High Street and sat at the back. It was too early for most customers, so we were able to talk without being overheard.

"I know it's difficult to talk about," Mr. Armitage began, "but can you please tell us what happened last night. Begin with when you found the body."

Miss Jennet rested her hands on the table in front of her. Her busy fingers hadn't stopped twisting together since we'd sat down. "I went into the drawing room at midnight to ask if she was going to bed soon and if she wanted help undressing. Sometimes she does it herself if she gets in late so I can go to bed." She drew in a shuddery breath and released it slowly. "She didn't move so I went over to her chair, and that's when I found her, covered in blood." Her voice trembled and her eyes filled with tears.

Our tea arrived in a pretty blue and white teapot with matching cups. Harmony poured as Mr. Armitage continued with the gentle questioning.

"Where was she in the drawing room?"

"On the wingback chair by the fire."

"Forgive me, I haven't been inside the drawing room. Which way does it face in relation to the window?"

"She had it turned to the fireplace, which she likes to do in winter. The window is a little behind and to the right. That's how the killer got in, isn't it? The vagrant? He climbed through the window and cut her throat from behind then stole her jewelry?" Her voice became increasingly high with each question.

I placed a hand on her arm and she instantly calmed. "What happened then?"

"I called for help. Mr. Henderson arrived first, but he

wasn't any use. He broke down and wept. Then the house-keeper came. She sent the coachman off to Mr. Warrington's club. We telephoned the police while we waited for his return."

"Does anyone else live in the house besides Mr. and Mrs. Warrington, the butler, housekeeper and you? What about the cook?"

She shook her head. "She lives in her own place with her husband. She leaves after she makes the dinner."

"Did anyone touch the body?" Mr. Armitage asked.

"Mr. Henderson fussed over her coat a bit and removed her hat. I don't think he meant anything by it. He was just trying to make her look presentable." She grimaced. "I know how it sounds, but he's very fond of her. He would know she'd like to look her best, no matter what."

I tilted my head to the side. "Why was she wearing a coat and hat inside? Was she going out?"

She nodded. "She planned to, but that all changed after the argument."

"What argument?" Harmony asked.

"Between Mr. and Mrs. Warrington."

"I think we need to know what led up to you discovering the body," I said. "You say Mrs. Warrington was going out for the evening. Where was she going?"

"For a walk."

We all arched our brows at that. A well-to-do lady going out for a walk at night in winter wasn't just odd, it was suspicious. It certainly implied she was up to something she shouldn't be.

"Oh, don't worry," Miss Jennet went on. "She often did it and always stayed in well-lit areas. She also wore men's clothes. Nobody pays men any attention, but a woman would be preyed upon, so Mrs. Warrington would say."

"Was she wearing these men's clothes at the time of the murder?" Harry asked.

Miss Jennet nodded. "Cap and all."

"Was that why Mr. and Mrs. Warrington were arguing? He didn't want her going out?"

She shrugged. "I don't know. I could hear harsh voices but not the words."

"And what time was this?" I asked.

"About nine. It lasted a few minutes and then he stormed out." She sipped her tea, cradling the cup in both hands, her elbows tucked in. Seated next to Mr. Armitage, she appeared very small and fragile, and somewhat nervous. "I don't think I should be telling you this. If Mr. Warrington wanted you to know, he would have told you."

"He isn't aware of what may be important at this point." Mr. Armitage's quick response coupled with his encouraging smile, seemed to ease her a little. "We'll speak to him about it later and get his side of things. We won't tell him who gave us the information."

She looked relieved. "Thank you. I know I can't stay on now that my mistress is gone, but I need a good reference. "

"Tell us what happened next," I said. "Where did Mr. Warrington go after he stormed out of the drawing room?"

"He went to his bedroom. At about nine-thirty, he went out to his club. By then, I assumed Mrs. Warrington had changed her mind and decided not to go for her walk. At ten, she rang the bell and Mr. Henderson answered it. She asked for tea."

"Who delivered the tea to Mrs. Warrington?" I asked.

"Mr. Henderson."

"And what did you both do after that?"

"I was in the servants' dining room doing some mending. Mr. Henderson was doing the same for the master. The housekeeper was doing her accounts and the cook had gone home. As time went on, we thought it strange that Mrs. Warrington hadn't rung for me to get her ready for bed, but we didn't do anything about it." She touched her fingers to her trembling lips. "By midnight, I'd had enough of waiting so went upstairs to ask her if she needed me. That's when I found her." Her face crumpled and she lowered her head.

I reached across the table and clasped her hand. "It's not your fault. Even if you'd gone up earlier, it's unlikely you could have saved her. She would have bled to death very quickly." Too late, I realized that might be more information than her nerves could cope with.

It seemed to comfort her a little, however. It must have been playing on her mind ever since discovering the body that she could have saved her mistress if she'd checked on her earlier.

Mr. Armitage handed her his handkerchief. "I know this is hard, but we need to know how the body looked when you found it. Can you describe it for us?"

She dabbed at the corners of her eyes with the handkerchief. "I'll try. I don't remember much, except that there was a lot of blood. It was on the back of the chair, on the chair arm and all down here." She indicated her throat and chest. "It came from a wound here." She touched the right side of her throat. "She was seated upright, still wearing the cap with her hair pinned up beneath it. I didn't notice until later that her jewels were missing. Her rings and a necklace, all gone."

I didn't have the heart to ask her if she'd noticed any defensive wounds. It was unlikely the maid had studied the body closely enough anyway. She would have been in shock. Without seeing the body ourselves, we couldn't be certain, but the fact that Mrs. Warrington's cap and hair were still in place meant she probably hadn't fought back. If the killer had crept up from behind, she wouldn't have had a chance to fight him off.

"You said earlier that you called for help and Mr. Henderson came," I went on. "And you said he broke down, crying?"

She nodded. "It was a shock for him. He's very fond of her."

"How fond?"

Her lips pursed. "There was nothing going on, if that's what you're implying. He admired her, that's all."

I hoped Mr. Armitage or Harmony would take over the questioning and ask about Mrs. Warrington's lover, but Harmony had been reluctant to ask questions throughout, and Mr. Armitage had gone oddly quiet. He merely sat there, brow furrowed, the teacup half-raised as if he couldn't decide whether to sip or not.

"I'm sorry to have to ask this," I said. "But it's come to our attention that Mrs. Warrington was an adulteress."

Her face colored and she dipped her head, but did not look shocked. "I wouldn't know about that."

"But you think there was another man in her life?"

She lifted a shoulder in a shrug. "I couldn't say."

"She's gone, Miss Jennet. You don't have to protect her now."

"Her reputation isn't gone. And if people find I've been talking out of turn, I'll never be employed as a lady's maid again."

Harmony caught my eye and shook her head in warning. She was right. It wasn't fair of me to pressure Miss Jennet. She needed an impeccable reference in order to get another job. It wasn't easy for lady's maids to find work these days. So many society women visited salons to have their hair done and dressed themselves that the art of the lady's maid was dying.

But I had to glean as much information as I could. I would kick myself if I didn't try as hard as possible. "Yesterday morning, I spoke to Mr. Henderson in his office. I'd been employed by Mr. Warrington to find evidence of his wife's adultery. You were listening in on our conversation and went to warn your mistress."

Miss Jennet stood abruptly. "I think I'd better get back now."

I caught her arm. "I followed her when she left the house shortly after that. She went to a photography studio in Paddington. Do you know why?"

She shook her head. "She didn't confide in me."

"Was she trying to hide all evidence that she was seeing another man? Were there incriminating photographs of them together?"

She jerked her arm away. "I don't know. I've got to go."

"Please, just one more question. Do you know if Mrs. Warrington knew her half-brother was in London?"

She considered this then must have realized it didn't matter now, and it wouldn't be a scandal if word got out. "She met him yesterday afternoon."

That must have been before he checked into the hotel. "Did she tell you anything about the meeting?"

"No."

"How did she seem when she returned home?"

"Angry. I gathered the meeting hadn't gone well. Now if you don't mind—"

"One more thing." Mr. Armitage stood too. He no longer sported the smiles of a charmer, but the creased brow of a detective with something on his mind. "Can you describe the chair?"

Miss Jennet blinked. "The chair?"

"You said it was a wingback. How large was it?"

She used her hands to show how the wings came out at the sides, shielding the upper body and face once of the person was ensconced in it.

"And you say it was facing the fire, the back to the window."

"The fireplace is on the left hand wall as you look from the door, and the window is opposite the door. The chair would mostly have its back to the window, yes."

He thanked her and watched her leave the teashop. He did not resume his seat, but turned to me, a triumphant look on his face.

"Why the questions about the chair?" I asked. "We already know the killer came through the window and stabbed her in the throat from behind."

He rounded the table and stood behind me. I tipped my head back and looked up, but he gently pushed it forward again. His hand touched the right side of my throat. His warm skin caressed mine. My pulse quickened. I wanted to look up again and see his face, but dared not.

"Go on," Harmony snapped.

Mr. Armitage cleared his throat but did not remove his hand. "The chair was large and facing away from the window. The wings would have shielded the sitter's face and body from anyone approaching from behind. Except perhaps an arm and shoulder, and the top of her head."

I gasped. "And she wore a man's coat and cap. If the killer caught only those glimpses, he might not have realized she was a woman."

"He comes up behind the chair and stabs her, here." His thumb stroked the skin at my throat, sending a wave of warmth through my entire body.

I turned my head a little and caught a hint of his cologne. He stood very close. So close that if I tipped my head back, it would bump him. I ought to be shocked at his proximity, but

I was not. I should put some distance between us, but I couldn't move. Didn't want to.

Harmony set her teacup down hard in the saucer. It was a miracle the china didn't crack. "And?"

Mr. Armitage returned to his side of the table and gathered up his hat and gloves. His eyes shone brightly in his flushed face. "And you know what that means."

"The killer thought she was her husband," I said. "Mr. Warrington was the intended victim, not Mrs. Warrington." I stood and pulled on my gloves. "We have to warn him."

CHAPTER 7

*M*r. Warrington was quite shocked when we told him our theory. He had to sit down and he couldn't speak for a long time.

We'd told the constable and butler that we'd learned something of importance about the murder that Mr. Warrington needed to hear. Mr. Henderson refused to let us in, but we were loud enough that Mr. Warrington himself overheard the commotion. He'd been coming down the stairs with his friend, Mr. Drummond, and invited us in. We returned to his office to speak in private.

"Here, Bertie, drink this." Mr. Drummond handed him a tumbler he'd half-filled from the decanter. "You look like you need it."

Mr. Warrington accepted the glass gratefully and sipped.

"Are you sure he was the intended target?" Mr. Drummond asked us.

"No," Mr. Armitage said. "It's only a theory at the moment."

"But it's quite a solid one," I added. "When you realize the intruder couldn't have seen Mrs. Warrington seated in the large wingback chair, it makes sense that he mistook her for a man. And what other man would be seated alone in the drawing room of an evening but Mr. Warrington?"

"Quite," Mr. Warrington murmured.

"Do you have enemies, sir?" Mr. Armitage asked.

"Too many," Mr. Drummond said darkly.

Mr. Warrington looked up at his friend and shook his head. "That's just politics, Pierce, nothing to murder anyone over."

Mr. Drummond threw his hands in the air. "You're a fool if you think that. Politicians have been murdered for much less."

"You've been receiving threatening letters," I said. "Perhaps the person sending them is following through on the threats."

I felt Mr. Armitage's gaze drill into me but I dared not look at him. I hadn't mentioned the letters to him and they weren't public knowledge.

Mr. Warrington, however, already knew that I knew. "It's possible."

Mr. Drummond scoffed. "It's *very* likely. Do you still have the letters?"

Mr. Warrington shook his head. "I gave them to the police when I reported it. The fools. They did nothing about it. The detective in charge said he would look into it and asked me to hand over any future letters I might receive."

"And did you?" I asked.

"I never received any more."

"Who was the investigating detective?" Mr. Armitage asked. "I have contacts at Scotland Yard so I might be able to find out what progress they've made."

Mr. Warrington rubbed his forehead and squeezed his eyes shut. "Hobart, I think his name was. Yes, Hobart."

Mr. Armitage went quite still except for a curt nod.

"Thank you," I said. "We'll follow it up, as well as any other leads. Now, please forgive me for this, but there's the matter of our fee."

Mr. Warrington waved his hand. "I'm not going to hire you. I'll inform the police of your theory. They can look into it. They already have the letters, after all, and may be well on their way to finding who wrote them."

"Or they might not care," I countered. "If they can close the case quickly, they may not look beyond the vagrant."

"Come now, Miss Fox, Scotland Yard are not inept. If evidence points to the vagrant, it must have been him."

"He has a bad arm. He couldn't possibly have climbed the pipe and got through the window."

Mr. Warrington rubbed his jaw, over and over, taking his time before responding. "But if I present the police with this new theory, surely they'll look at the letters again."

Mr. Drummond did not agree. "You can't trust them. You have to hire Miss Fox."

"Armitage and Associates," Mr. Armitage cut in.

"Miss Fox is right. The police won't look elsewhere if they have a perfectly acceptable scapegoat in their cells." When Mr. Warrington still did not agree, Mr. Drummond added, "How about you hire Mr. Armitage and his associates but also tell the police their theory? That way if the police do a poor job, Miss Fox, Miss Cotton and Mr. Armitage will solve the case with their parallel investigation. You have nothing to lose, old man."

"I suppose."

"You need to protect yourself." Mr. Drummond squeezed his friend's shoulder. "You also need justice for poor Isobel. You two might not have been on the best of terms, but she was your wife, and I know you cared for her once."

"I still did, right up until the end." Mr. Warrington's voice softened. "Very well. I'll hire you, but I will also inform the police of your theory."

"That's fair," Mr. Armitage said. "But if we could ask you to keep our name out of it. We don't want the police knowing you've hired private detectives."

Mr. Drummond's lips tilted in a sardonic grin. "They don't like being shown up, you mean."

Mr. Armitage bristled. "There are some excellent policemen at Scotland Yard."

"Of course, of course. Just not the fellow who arrested that poor vagrant."

Mr. Warrington rang for the butler and Mr. Henderson arrived to show us out.

"You should take all the necessary precautions to ensure your safety," Mr. Armitage said.

Mr. Warrington and Mr. Drummond exchanged grim glances. "I'll make sure he does," Mr. Drummond assured us.

The butler led the way down the stairs. Now that I knew

how distraught he was at his mistress's death, I could see the telltale signs of grief in the swelling of his eyes, the sagging of his shoulders. I wasn't sure whether to feel sorry for him, or suspect him of being her lover.

"Is it all right if we ask you some questions?" I asked as we set foot on the first floor landing.

"No."

"But Mr. Warrington is employing us to find the killer. He will want you to cooperate."

"I have nothing to tell you therefore I have nothing to say." He lengthened his strides, leaving us in his wake.

I picked up my skirts and raced after him. "It's about the threatening letters Mr. Warrington received."

"I don't know anything about those. They arrived, and I gave them to Mr. Warrington along with the rest of his mail. Good day." He jerked open the door and told the constable to make sure we left the premises.

Harmony took my arm. "We have all the information we need to get started," she assured me.

I allowed her to steer me past the constable and the waiting journalists, their number thinner than it had been earlier. Mr. Armitage followed behind then drew up alongside me as we turned the corner.

"Why didn't you tell me he was receiving threatening letters?" he asked.

"I forgot." At his disbelieving look, I added, "Truly, I did."

He glanced at Harmony. She simply smiled innocently at him which only made him more suspicious.

"I'm not going to keep anything from you deliberately, Harry. We're working together now. We must promise to share everything we learn. Between all of us, we'll solve this case quickly."

He walked on, a hand in his pocket. When we reached Kensington High Street, he said, "So...we're on first name basis now?"

"Is that all right with you?"

"Yes." He smiled at me.

Harmony scowled at us both. "It's all very well out here, but you shouldn't be so familiar at the hotel. Someone might overhear."

I glared at her and gave a slight shake of my head, but she wasn't looking my way.

Harry, however, noticed, but he didn't look at all surprised. His smile vanished. "We can't have that." The sarcastic tone was subtle but it was there.

"It's for Cleo's sake, not yours," she shot back.

He frowned. "I know your uncle doesn't like me being at the hotel, but have you got into further trouble because of me?"

I waved his concern off with a flick of my wrist. "Let's talk about our next moves as we walk. Where are we going, by the way?"

"I was planning on going to the hotel to use my uncle's telephone to call my father at work. We need to find out what he discovered about the letters sent to Warrington. But now I'm rethinking. The hotel might not be the best place."

"We can go to Scotland Yard directly," Harmony said.

He shook his head. "I don't want anyone there knowing we're taking on this case. Some of my father's colleagues know me. If I'm seen, someone might ask questions and I don't want to put my father in a position where he has to lie for me."

"That's very thoughtful of you," Harmony muttered, somewhat reluctantly. It would seem Harry's kind nature might soften her attitude towards him eventually. "We'll enter the hotel through the staff entrance," she went on. "We'll meet you in Mr. Hobart's office, Cleo. It's unlikely Sir Ronald will see you."

* * *

I DIDN'T GO DIRECTLY to Mr. Hobart's office, however. I was waylaid by Frank, the doorman. He paced back and forth on the pavement, his hands clasped loosely behind him, his chin buried in the high collar of his coat. I thought he was simply trying to keep warm, but the furrowed brow suggested he was worried. Or perhaps simply in a cantankerous mood, which seemed to be Frank's normal mood when dealing with the staff. He was pleasant to guests, but other staff—and me —were not afforded the same civility.

"Miss Fox, a moment of your time, if you have it."

"Is something the matter, Frank?" I asked.

"It's Goliath. He's disappeared."

"Are you certain he's supposed to be on duty? He is acting as night porter too. Perhaps Mr. Hobart gave him the day off."

"I know the roster. And he was here earlier. Half an hour ago, he brought down a guest's luggage and loaded it onto their conveyance. He told me he would return in a few minutes with the luggage of the next departing guest, but he never came back. The second porter's had to do twice the work. I'm telling you, Miss Fox, Goliath is missing."

"I'll speak to Mr. Hobart—"

"No! Blimey, not him. Make discreet inquiries, but don't let Mr. Hobart know he's disappeared. He could lose his job. He deserves it, but then I'd have to get used to someone new. Goliath's better than most."

It was high praise coming from Frank. "Mr. Hobart isn't as cruel as that. Anyway, I'm sure there's a reasonable explanation. I'll check with Peter."

Frank looked relieved. "Thank you, Miss Fox." He hurried to open the door as the second porter emerged, pushing a trolley laden with a trunk, bag and two hat boxes.

Inside, the foyer was relatively quiet. I waited for Peter to finish checking-out the two guests whose luggage had just left ahead of them. He stood awkwardly, his upper body angled forward rather than upright as he asked for the gentleman to sign the register.

When the guests departed, I approached the desk. "Have you hurt your back?"

He frowned. "No. Why?"

Now that I was closer, I could see that he was leaning forward because he stood back from the counter rather than up against it. "Is there something on the floor preventing you from standing nearer the counter?"

His eyes widened. "Er…"

I tried peering over the counter, but was too short to see the floor on the other side. A soft snuffle sounded from direction of Peter's feet.

Peter moved sharply and the snuffle became a grunt. Peter

smiled at me. "Is there something I can do for you, Miss Fox?"

"Goliath is asleep down there, isn't he?"

"No."

I tilted my head to the side. "Peter, it's just me. I won't tell anyone."

He sighed and stepped back from the counter. He studied the floor where I imagined Goliath was sound asleep, invisible to anyone not on that side of the counter. "He's a great, big log of a fellow all stretched out like that. I had no idea he'd take up this much space when he asked me if he could take a nap there."

"I think you'll need to wake him up. Frank has noticed he's missing, and it won't take long for Mr. Hobart to realize either. He's as sharp as a tack."

As I spoke, Mr. Hobart emerged from the senior staff corridor where his office was located. He nodded a greeting to me which I took to mean Harmony and Harry had arrived in his office and were waiting for me. He continued on and was soon engaged in conversation with a guest.

Peter looked down at his feet again and shook his head. "The problem is, he's really tired. He needs to rest."

"Yes, but not here. Peter, you can't protect him forever. He will be discovered sooner or later if this goes on."

"Then what should I do?"

"Find a solution to the problem before Mr. Hobart finds out Goliath's been sleeping while on duty. And wake him up now. Quietly."

Peter's eyes widened again as he stared past me. "He's coming," he whispered.

I turned to see Mr. Hobart approaching. I went to intercept him before he drew too close to the counter, but he spotted another guest and diverted his course. To my surprise, it was Mr. Trickelbank.

What was Mr. Hobart up to? Or was he simply being the polite hotel manager, checking on a guest?

I moved closer to listen in, using one of the large black vases to shield me from view.

"I was very sorry to hear about your sister," Mr. Hobart

began. "On behalf of Sir Ronald and Lady Bainbridge, may I offer heartfelt condolences."

I held my breath, wondering if Mr. Trickelbank would deny he had family in London as he had done at dinner last night.

"Thank you," Mr. Trickelbank muttered. "If you'll excuse me…"

"You're not checking out today, as initially planned?"

"I'll stay for the funeral."

"I do hope you were able to see your sister before her demise."

"I didn't," Mr. Trickelbank bit off.

I knew that to be a lie. According to Miss Jennet, Mrs. Warrington had met her half-brother on the afternoon of her death.

He tried to move past Mr. Hobart, but Mr. Hobart wasn't yet finished with him.

"I apologize for holding you up, sir, but would you mind waiting a few more moments. I'll write a quick note of condolence for you to pass on to Mr. Warrington. He has never been a guest here, of course, but the Mayfair considers him an extension of yourself."

"I won't be seeing him." Mr. Trickelbank pushed past Mr. Hobart and strode out of the front door.

I emerged from behind the vase. "Well done, Mr. Hobart. You were marvelous. Your questions were more effective than any police detective's."

His eyes twinkled. "Don't tell my brother that. He thinks a blunt club gets better results than honey. You should be on your way, Miss Fox. Harry will send out a search party if you don't join him soon."

Harry was indeed waiting impatiently for my arrival in Mr. Hobart's office. He sat perched on the edge of the desk, his arms and ankles crossed, one finger tapping on his sleeve. The pose was both casually sophisticated and authoritative. The tap added to the air of barely-contained masculinity he exuded. He indicated I should sit on the guest chair while he took his uncle's chair behind the desk.

"Where's Harmony?" I asked.

"She was waylaid by the housekeeper. It seems one of the maids called in sick this morning and Harmony is needed."

"Now I feel awful for asking her to join us here. If she hadn't come in, she would have had the entire day to herself. It's not fair she has to work on her day off."

"Mrs. Short strikes me as someone who would have gone to great lengths to find her and bring her in anyway, no matter where Harmony spent the day."

"She is quite the dragon." I indicated the brass telephone. "Shall we call your father now?"

"I just did and left a message for him to call back."

"So now we wait?"

"We wait."

I removed my gloves and placed them on my lap, only to pick them up again to stroke them in an attempt to do something with my hands. The silence stretched thin, and I hoped the distraction of the gloves would help calm me. It did not. I felt compelled to break the silence.

"It's good of you to share this investigation with me, Harry."

He looked up, blinking in a somewhat dazed manner. While I had been searching for something to say to fill the void, his mind had been elsewhere. "Not at all. *You* are sharing it with *me*."

"It was clever of you to conclude that Mr. Warrington was the intended victim."

"Hmmm."

"And thank you for including Harmony in the investigation."

He gave a single nod.

"I think her work here bores her, and she finds investigating a pleasing distraction. I can't blame her for that, can you?"

"Right."

"She's also very intelligent. She'll be an asset to the investigation." When he didn't even answer me or look up from the spot on the desk he was staring at, I added, "Being a fairy princess is always an asset, don't you think?"

He glanced up, frowning. "What?"

"Harry, you're not listening. What's the matter? Is there something about the case that's bothering you?"

"Actually I was thinking about the hotel. The kitchen, to be precise."

"Did you enter via the kitchen?" The hotel's main staff entrance was on the ground floor, above the basement kitchen. A set of stairs inside the entrance from the side street led directly down to the kitchen and the warren of corridors, storerooms and other basement rooms used mainly by the cooks. The *chef de cuisine* loathed anyone being in his domain who shouldn't be there.

"I avoided the kitchen, but overheard heated words coming from one of the storerooms nearby. I recognized the chef's voice and Sir Ronald's."

"They were arguing?"

He nodded.

My heart sank. It would seem they had not resolved their issue. If this went on much longer, my uncle's temper was going to continue to simmer and he would take it out on everyone, particularly his children. I had successfully managed to avoid it, but that was because I wasn't one of his children, and I was better at eluding him than they were.

"I know what it's about," I said. "My uncle plans to move the restaurant out of the dining room and into new premises next door."

He nodded. "Uncle Alfred told me. I think it's an excellent business decision."

"But for some reason, the chef doesn't like the idea. He's resisting, and getting quite huffy about it. I honestly don't understand his objection. He should be pleased he'll be in charge of a larger establishment. He claims it'll be less prestigious, but I disagree. The public restaurants at other luxury hotels are quite influential on the social and culinary scene."

Harry lifted a shoulder in a shrug. "Perhaps he's worried he'll be out of his depth in a large restaurant. In the current restaurant, he is king of the domain, but it only caters to the hotel guests. In a public one, he'll be subject to reviews in newspapers and journals. He'll also have more staff to manage and more supplies to organize. He'll need to renegotiate contracts with suppliers which could affect his relationship with them."

When he put it like that, I almost felt sorry for the belligerent chef. Almost, but not quite. "The chef does all the ordering, doesn't he?"

"Of the food, yes. The sommelier works independently with wine suppliers. Years ago, before I was promoted to assistant manager and before the current chef came to work here, Uncle Alfred negotiated the original contract with all our restaurant suppliers. It includes a twenty percent discount because the hotel orders large quantities, and a promise that we're offered the choicest cuts of meat and the freshest produce."

"So the chef has never had to do the negotiations himself, but moving to a larger establishment will require the contracts to be renegotiated."

Harry nodded. "Perhaps it scares him. Despite his blustery manner, he's not that bad outside of the kitchen."

"Can't he just ask Mr. Hobart to do the renegotiations on his behalf?"

"Perhaps he will. Sir Ronald won't back down, so if the chef wishes to keep his job, he'll have to re-open discussions with the suppliers. Uncle Alfred will help if asked."

I couldn't see the chef swallowing his pride and asking, but I didn't know him like Harry did. Our only communications had consisted of him shouting at me to get out of his kitchen.

The telephone rang and Harry picked up the receiver. He waited for the operator to connect the call then greeted his father on the other end. The discussion was very brief, then he returned the receiver to the cradle of the candlestick shaped device.

"I'm meeting him at my office where it'll be easier to talk." He rose and buttoned up his jacket. "Coming?"

"Of course." I led the way into the corridor and waited while he plucked his hat and coat off the stand by the door.

"I'll meet you on Piccadilly." He headed off along the service corridor towards the back of the hotel.

"You can come through the foyer," I called after him.

"I've done that before, remember? It was a disaster when your uncle caught us."

"Not a disaster."

It hadn't been pleasant, it was true. With Harry leaving the hotel under something of a cloud, Uncle Ronald didn't want him visible to the guests in the foyer. Indeed, he didn't want him gracing the corridors of the hotel at all. It was not only unfair, it was ungracious. My uncle ought to let bygones be bygones. But he hadn't liked it when Harry had stood up to him. It had been a rather tense exchange, all carried out in the full view of the guests.

I ran after Harry, catching up to him at the end of the corridor. "Don't let him dictate to you. You're perfectly within your rights to come and go through the front door."

"It's Sir Ronald's hotel, and my right to be here is dependent on his whim."

"Don't let him bully you. What will he do to you, anyway? Manhandle you out through the front door? Hardly."

"It's not what he'll do to *me* that makes me wish to avoid him." He strode off.

I frowned at his back. Did he mean he was worried about what my uncle would say to me if Harry was caught leaving the hotel through the front door?

Well, if Harry was going to take the staff exit, then I would too. I followed him. At the sound of my footsteps, he glanced over his shoulder, shook his head, and faced forward again. But not before I saw the small smile tugging at his lips.

* * *

DETECTIVE INSPECTOR HOBART was a slightly more intimidating version of his brother. I didn't think he meant to be intimidating, but Mr. Hobart was such a sweet man that almost everyone was gruffer by comparison. Harry allowed his father to take the main chair behind the desk while he and I occupied the two guest chairs. We sipped on coffees made by Luigi as Harry informed his father of our parallel investigation to the one conducted by Scotland Yard, including Harry's theory that Mr. Warrington was the intended victim.

"I don't think it will be parallel," the inspector said with a sad shake of his head. "My superiors are determined to pin the murder on the vagrant. You're right to take on the case, Harry. Hopefully your efforts will bring justice for Mrs. Warrington."

"We're both taking on the case," Harry said. "Cleo is helping me."

"Working alongside you," I countered. "I think that's what you meant to say, isn't it, Harry?"

He smirked.

His father glanced between us. "Is that wise? It could be dangerous. It may have started out as a case of adultery, but it's now a murder investigation. The killer is still out there."

"Thank you for your concern for my safety," I said, and meant it. "But I've been involved in two other murder investigations. I know what I'm getting myself into."

"Harry is capable of investigating alone."

"As am I. But he muscled his way in *after* he'd already given Mr. Warrington to me."

"For the divorce. This is an entirely different case."

"Or it could be linked."

Detective Inspector Hobart's blue eyes bored into me. He was very good at using them to full effect, whether that was to pretend innocence during an inquiry, or making them seem as cold as ice, like now. "How can the cases be linked if Mr. Warrington was the intended victim, not his wife?"

"Perhaps her lover did it out of jealousy."

My theory was so good that it rendered him speechless. Harry took advantage and stepped in to diffuse the tension. "Cleo is an excellent detective and she's working *with* me. That's final. And anyway, I didn't expect you to object. Mother, yes, but not you."

I sighed. His mother must still be angry with me for getting Harry dismissed from his job at the hotel.

The inspector gave me a sheepish look. "My apologies, Miss Fox. It's nothing personal." He cleared his throat. "To the matter at hand. You asked me for information about the person who sent the threatening letters to Mr. Warrington. I can do better than that. I can give you her name."

"Her?" I echoed.

Harry sat forward. "Are you sure you should tell us? You could get in serious trouble if your superiors find out."

"It might be important," the inspector said. "Indeed, if she's guilty of killing Mrs. Warrington because she mistook her for her husband, then it's my duty to do everything in my power to prevent her from killing her intended target. I would never forgive myself if he was her next victim." He put up his hands. "I'm not saying she is your killer, but she must certainly be considered a suspect. Her name is Elizabeth Parker, and she lives at forty-two Arlington Road, Camden Town."

"How do you know she sent the letters?" Harry asked.

The inspector puffed out his chest and tugged on his lapel. "I'm a good detective."

"Were you able to trace the postmark?"

The inspector smiled. "Her husband recognized the handwriting and had already suspected she would threaten the politicians blocking the bill. He works for me. Good sergeant. It's not his fault his wife has a militant streak."

Harry sat back. "Let me guess. You let her off with a warning."

"I did, but not entirely because of my colleague. We didn't want to make a martyr of her. The women's suffrage movement is gaining momentum, and we don't want to add fuel to the fire. Now before you object, Miss Fox, I want to point out that I'm not against women being given equal rights as men. I'm just saying it's best if progress is achieved without violence. Nothing has escalated that far—yet—and I'd like to keep it that way."

"I wasn't going to object, at all." I gathered up the empty cups and rose. "Does Sergeant Parker know you're giving his wife's name to us to investigate?"

"No one knows anything about your investigation at Scotland Yard, and that's how it must remain until you have irrefutable proof. I hope for Parker's sake it wasn't his wife who murdered Mrs. Warrington, but she must be considered a suspect." He rose and indicated the cups. "Give those to Harry to return to the café. This is his office, so it's his responsibility. Besides, I'm a little slower getting down the stairs these days, if you wouldn't mind waiting for me, Miss Fox."

Harry accepted the cups from me and stepped outside.

The moment he was out of earshot, the inspector turned to me. "I have no objection to you working with Harry under normal circumstances, Miss Fox."

"I'll be all right. You don't have to worry about me stumbling into danger like I did in the hotel when the Christmas Eve killer was on the loose. I'll be very careful."

He dismissed my suggestion with a wave of his hand. "I'm not worried. Harry can take care of you as well as himself. I am more concerned that he will insist on taking only half the fee when he needs it all."

"Oh."

"He's a gentleman and seems to think he owes you this investigation since he'd already given you the client."

"He doesn't owe me anything. We have agreed to work together and split the fee. I don't think Harry would take it all even if I insisted."

"Precisely my point and why I suggest you step down."

"No!"

"Miss Fox—"

"No, sir, I am not stepping down. Do you really want Harry knowing you interfered and guilted me into giving up? Because he will realize," I added when he drew breath to object. "He's not a fool. He'll work it out."

The inspector sighed. "Forgive me for being blunt, but you don't need the money, Miss Fox."

And Harry did, he might have said. My heart sank a little. The fact that Harry's father was asking me to give up my half of the fee behind Harry's back meant finances were dire. My own situation could be classified as wanting, rather than desperate. I had an allowance from my uncle that was more than enough to get by, but Harry had nothing except what he earned. I didn't need the money urgently. My plans to move out of the hotel could wait.

I rested a hand on the inspector's arm. "I will do my best to insure he takes the entire fee for himself. I promise."

He patted my shoulder. "Good. Good. Now all you need to do is solve the case. I suspect that won't be a problem with the two of you working together."

The inspector invited me to go down the stairs before him

then followed, his gait sprightly. I smiled to myself and was still smiling when we met Harry on the pavement, his gaze narrowed. Clearly he was suspicious of his father's motives for sending him on ahead.

He did not ask what we'd talked about, however, and we did not offer an explanation. Detective Inspector Hobart bade us goodbye after informing Harry that his mother expected him home for dinner.

"You have two very caring parents," I said as we watched the inspector walk off.

"I know," Harry said warmly.

Tears filled my eyes as thoughts of my own loving family came flooding back to me. Not just my parents, but also my paternal grandparents. Like Harry, I'd been lucky to be accepted into their home with open arms after my mother and father died in an accident, but unlike him, my grandparents were my blood relatives and not strangers to me. It must have been so hard for the thirteen year-old boy whose mother had died only two years earlier, but at least he'd entered a caring home. Unlike when he'd entered the boys' home and then run away to live on the street, as he'd been forced to do in between. I could imagine Mr. and Mrs. Hobart being kind from the moment they took him in.

I shook off my dreary thoughts and kept pace with Harry. I had no right to feel melancholy when I had so much and others so little. Not only that, we had a solid lead in our investigation. Mrs. Parker might have been let off with just a warning by the police, but I doubted she'd give up on her cause so easily.

I identified with the women calling for equal rights, and although I wouldn't write threatening letters or kill a man for the cause, I also wouldn't be diverted from my plans after receiving a warning. If she thought killing Mr. Warrington was the only way to ensure the bill was passed through parliament, she might be prepared to go to great lengths to remove him.

CHAPTER 8

*M*rs. Parker lived in a modest terrace in an uninspiring street in Camden Town. There was very little to recommend it except that it seemed like a quiet place to raise a family. The thin terrace was one of dozens lined up like cigarettes in a tin. They were all built from exactly the same cream brick with two wrought iron balconies attached to the first floor windows that were barely wide enough for two people to stand on. The front doors were all painted either black or dark gray, with the same iron knockers.

Mrs. Parker answered the door herself. She was a tall woman, aged in her late twenties, with clear eyes and a square jaw that firmed when we stated we'd come to ask her questions about the Warringtons. She scowled and went to close the door.

Harry stopped it. "We're investigating the murder of Mrs. Warrington and your name was given to us by Scotland Yard."

Her eyes widened. "I didn't kill her!"

"Then answer our questions honestly so we can eliminate you as a suspect."

"I've already answered the questions of a Scotland Yard detective. I don't have to answer yours too."

"That was in relation to the letters," I said. "The murder changes things."

"Not for me, it doesn't. I didn't do it." She glared point-edly at Harry but he didn't let go of the door. "Why would I kill *Mrs.* Warrington?"

"It appears to be a case of mistaken identity and *he* was the intended target, not her," Harry said. "Where were you last night between the hours of ten and midnight?"

"Here."

"Can anyone vouch for you?"

"My husband, a Scotland Yard sergeant." She crossed her arms and her glare turned smug.

"Anyone else?"

"Isn't that enough?"

"No. In my experience, husbands and wives lie for one another. Even ones who work for Scotland Yard." He gave her a smug look of his own.

Her confidence melted away, slackening her features and rigid stance.

"We know you stopped writing those letters to Mr. Warrington," Harry pressed. "Did you change tactic? Did you go to his house in order to prevent him blocking the bill?"

"No!" She clutched her throat—on the right side, no less. "I've only ever been to the Warringtons' house once, last week. Not last night. Look, I feel sorry for the wife. If she was murdered instead of him, then that's a tragedy. But it wasn't me that did it."

Harry thanked her, but I wasn't finished. "On the night you went to their house, did you notice anything?" I asked.

"Such as?"

"Anything odd, out of place? Did you overhear any conversations or see anyone come or go?"

"I saw a woman and a man sneaking off together. I say sneak because they closed the front door softly, tiptoed down the steps, and hurried off along the street. Also, the woman was dressed in men's clothes and a cap. But it didn't convince me. Women walk like women, if you know what I mean. Changing their clothes doesn't change their walk."

"Can you describe the man?"

"Taller than me, neither fat nor slim. I didn't really see his face."

We thanked her and Harry let the door go. She didn't shut it immediately.

"Is that why Mrs. Warrington was killed instead of her husband?" she asked. "Because she wore men's clothes and the killer thought she was him?"

She was certainly clever. "Good day, Mrs. Parker," I said. "Thank you for your time."

Harry and I walked side by side in silence until we were several houses away.

"The man she described sneaking off with Mrs. Warrington must have been her lover," Harry said. "It's not Warrington. He's not tall."

"I think I know who it is."

He stopped to stare at me. "How can you possibly know from Mrs. Parker's vague description? It could be anyone."

"It wasn't all that vague. Not when you consider that Mrs. Warrington left the house *with* the fellow. She didn't meet him outside, as she would a stranger to the household. Based on that description, it can only be one man."

"The butler."

I nodded. "No other man except her husband would be leaving the house alongside her. Mr. Henderson was also distraught over her death and was protective of her from the start. He didn't like helping me when I was tasked with finding out the identity of her lover."

"How distraught was he? More than a loyal butler should be?"

"I've never had a butler, loyal or otherwise, but not even Miss Jennet the lady's maid was that upset over the death of her mistress. Based on what Mrs. Parker just told us, I think Mr. Henderson and Mrs. Warrington were lovers."

"And he accidentally killed her, thinking she was her husband."

"Precisely."

Harry walked off. "We need to speak to him."

I fell into step alongside him, having to quicken my pace to keep up with his long strides. "I've tried. He won't talk to me and I doubt he'll talk to you, either. Besides, what will we ask? Did you kill your lover thinking she was her husband?"

He eyed me sideways and his pace slowed. "Do you have a better idea?"

"We need to find the photographs or the negatives to prove he was her lover. He can't ignore definitive proof."

"Particularly if we threaten to take the photographs to the police," Harry said with a sly smile.

"The problem is, it's very likely that Mrs. Warrington collected them from the studio yesterday morning, but if there's a chance she only picked up the photographs, and the negatives are still there, we have to try to retrieve them."

"You're suggesting we break in tonight?"

"No! I'm suggesting we go to the studio and one of us distracts the photographer and his assistant. The other will then search the premises for the negatives."

He scoffed. "And what sort of distraction will get them both out of the studio long enough for a search to be conducted? I do hope you're not planning to set the premises on fire."

"Very amusing. Of course not. Not with you inside, anyway. I'll think of something by the time we get there."

Harry pulled out his watch from his jacket pocket. "Not today. It's getting late. Shall we meet at the studio first thing in the morning? Say nine o'clock?"

"Tomorrow morning suits me. That'll give me time to think."

We parted ways, he heading to the railway station to catch a train to his parents' house for dinner. I returned to the hotel, planning to search for Harmony, but changed my mind when I saw Mr. Trickelbank emerging from the smoking room.

I intercepted him without a clue as to how I was going to get him to confide in me. Our gazes connected and I smiled at him. To my surprise, he did not change course. He smiled back. Perhaps his sister's death had changed his attitude. After all, he'd admitted to Mr. Hobart that he had a sister where before he'd denied it. Perhaps he would admit even more to me.

I would be as honest as possible and use Mr. Hobart's tactic of honey rather than a blunt instrument. "Mr. Trickelbank, what a pleasure it is to see you again. I hoped I would bump into you. I do so wish to pass on my condolences on the death of your sister."

"Thank you, Miss Fox." He swallowed hard. "I, uh, should apologize. Last night at dinner you asked if I had family here and I claimed I did not. As you seem to have discovered, I have—had—a sister. Half-sister, to be precise. I can only explain my little lie by admitting that I felt some shame in my own circumstance. Since you know Isobel was my sister, you probably know how we are connected and that my father was not married to my mother."

I put up my hands. "Speak no more about it. I completely understand." This was going rather well. My hopes rose. "Mr. Trickelbank, may I ask you a few questions about her? You see, I am something of a private detective." Harmony's voice popped into my head, telling me to be more confident. "I mean, I *am* a private detective, and have been tasked with finding out who killed Mrs. Warrington."

He rocked back as if he'd been pushed. "The police have arrested someone, I believe. Do you mean to say he didn't do it?"

"The police think he did, but others believe not."

"Who?"

"That information is confidential."

He frowned. "I see. And you think I can help with your investigation?"

"You might be in possession of important information without knowing it." I glanced back towards the foyer where a small group of guests mingled, chatting and laughing. We were at the far end, almost near the entrance to the senior staff corridor. The smoking room and billiard room were positioned side by side, out of the way so that gentlemen could enjoy their cigars and billiards in peace. "We need to find somewhere more private to talk."

"The smoking room is empty. I just came from there." He led the way and I did not hesitate to follow.

I was no stranger to the smoking room, having followed a suspect into it once. Although the presence of women in the gentlemen's domain was frowned upon, we weren't forbidden from entering. Well, *I* was forbidden, by my uncle. He was worried my presence there would signal that I was of loose moral character and, according to him, the reputation of the Bainbridge women was paramount. Since I had no wish to take up smoking, nor to rock the boat that he captained, I hadn't argued the point. I didn't plan on arguing the point now, but that was because I didn't plan to be discovered. I checked the vicinity carefully before entering.

The small room reeked of smoke. It was so strong, I expected it would never come out, no matter how often the walls, floor and furniture were scrubbed. Mr. Trickelbank sat in one of the deep leather armchairs by the fireplace and I sat in the other. He removed a silver cigarette case from his inside jacket pocket and offered me one. I refused, and he put the case away.

"What is it you want to know?" he asked.

"I'm afraid I have to ask you a question that may make you feel uncomfortable. You see, I suspect that Mrs. Warrington had a lover."

He arched his brows and a somewhat sly smile stretched his lips. "I see."

"Do you know who he was?"

"I'm afraid not. I hardly knew Isobel. We didn't grow up as brother and sister. I knew of her existence, of course, and she of mine, but we never met until our father's funeral. Things were tense from the beginning between us. We exchanged letters, sometimes, but that was all. It was some time ago."

"Perhaps she hinted at her life here in London in her letters. Can you think of anything? Did she mention the members of her household in passing, perhaps?" Surely he would notice if she talked about the butler in glowing terms.

He shook his head. "Nothing like that, but I do know theirs was not a happy union so that supports your theory of a lover. It wouldn't surprise me if they both had one."

"How do you know the state of their marriage if you were barely on speaking terms?"

"In the months after our father died, she tried to befriend me and so her letters were more honest, more open. I suppose she thought I'd be more likely to treat her as a sibling if we shared private matters, as normal siblings do." He scoffed. "In one of those letters, she alluded to the marriage being loveless and it would never bear any fruit, by which I assume she meant heirs. She wrote that I shouldn't feel sorry for her because she didn't want any, and nor did he."

"Heirs." What an odd word to use. Most people would say children.

It suddenly clicked into place. The reason that brother and sister were estranged, the tension at the funeral, and the mention of heirs. Aunt Lilian's friends had informed me that Mrs. Warrington was wealthy, having inherited her father's fortune. Being the illegitimate child, Mr. Trickelbank had either inherited only part of it or none at all. It was entirely dependent on what his father left him in his will. If he'd left him nothing, or died intestate, Mr. Trickelbank might be aggrieved indeed to have been overlooked.

And with their father gone, he might take that anger out on the sister who inherited more than her fair share.

"Why are you here in London, Mr. Trickelbank?"

He looked taken aback by the question. "I have business to attend to."

"Not to see your sister?"

"No. I haven't seen her in years."

I blinked innocently back at him. "Oh? But I heard you saw her on the afternoon of her death."

"That's a lie!"

Considering Miss Jennet had no reason to lie, I doubted it. I didn't question him further about their meeting, however, and decided to press on. "Mr. Trickelbank, forgive me for being so crass, but did you inherit anything from your father?"

He shot to his feet. "These questions are outrageous!"

"It's a standard question given the circumstances."

He walked off and I saw my opportunity slipping away.

"You didn't inherit anything, did you? That's why you argued with your sister. That's why you were estranged, because she didn't give you anything and you felt you were entitled to a portion of your father's fortune."

He suddenly turned and stabbed his finger in my direction. His face was mottled with thick veins bulging on his forehead as he bared his teeth at me. I was glad I'd stayed near the fireplace and the fire iron but wished I was a little closer to the door.

"My father intended me to inherit half his fortune. He *told* me so on his deathbed. But someone made sure he never amended his will. Someone made sure *she* got the lot."

"You think she coerced him?"

"Either her, or Warrington, or both of them. Politicians can't be trusted, in my experience, and make no mistake, they might not have loved each other, but they were in that marriage together. They were a team. Her fortune was also his fortune." He strode off, his fists closed at his sides.

I blew out a measured breath in an attempt to calm my jangling nerves. Despite the way our meeting deteriorated, I was glad I'd spoken to him. Not only was I more enlightened as to the nature of the Warringtons' marriage, but I now had another suspect.

Mr. Trickelbank.

While there was no sibling love between Mrs. Warrington and her brother, she had reached out to him after their father's death to try to heal the rift. But she had not offered him some of the fortune she'd inherited. Was that because her husband controlled the couple's finances? Most husbands did, even when the fortune belonged to their wife. And if Mr. Trickelbank believed he never inherited anything because Mr. Warrington prevented his father-in-law from making a new will, then he might be very angry. Angry enough to kill him.

But why now? Mr. Trickelbank's father died years ago. What could have triggered an anger so fierce that he decided to climb through the window and stab the person seated in the drawing room in the throat, thinking it was the man who orchestrated his misfortune?

I pondered this, as I went in search of Harmony, but came up with no answers. After word got out that I was looking for her, Victor, Peter, Goliath and Frank decided to convene an impromptu meeting in the staff parlor. The three front-of-house men had finished their shifts for the day, as had Harmony, but Victor was about to start in the kitchen. All were keen to hear an update on the investigation.

All except Goliath, who yawned between sips of his tea.

He had a few hours off before he was due to resume duties as night porter.

"You ought to take this opportunity to rest," I told him.

He squared his massive shoulders and puffed out his chest. "I don't need rest. I'm fine. Fit as a fiddle and wide awake."

Harmony rolled her eyes and muttered, "Men."

I informed them of what I'd learned that day and we tossed theories around, but could not find any new angles to investigate. We agreed it was imperative to see the photographs of Mrs. Warrington with her lover to confirm if he was, in fact, Mr. Henderson the butler. My new theory about Mr. Trickelbank was harder to prove. Nobody could think of a way forward with that.

"Hopefully Harry will have some suggestions," I said.

"Harry?" Peter asked.

"Mr. Armitage," Harmony said with another roll of her eyes. "He made Miss Fox share the case with him."

"That's not fair," Frank said.

"Mr. Warrington was his client to begin with," I pointed out. "It doesn't matter anyway. Two heads are better than one."

The five of them exchanged glances.

"I mean, the extra head, on top of all of ours." Oh dear, I'd offended them. "Tomorrow morning, Harry and I are going to retrieve the photographs or negatives from the studio, if they're still there."

"And if they aren't?" Peter asked.

"I don't know yet."

"So that's why Mr. Armitage was at the hotel earlier?" Victor asked. "He came to see you?"

I nodded. "Don't tell anyone he was here. It's best if my uncle doesn't find out."

"Are you going to tell us why Sir Ronald dismissed him?"

"It's not my business to discuss. Speaking of the hotel and my uncle, Harry said he overheard him arguing with the chef. How are things in the kitchen?"

"Bad," Victor said. "Chef doesn't talk, he shouts. When he's not shouting, it's almost silent except for the sound of boiling and dicing. It's like a morgue in there. Everyone's afraid to speak."

"And there are lots of dead things," Goliath added with a chuckle. When Victor glared at him, Goliath swallowed heavily. "You know, fish, beef, pork...all dead...and you described it as being like a morgue..."

I rose. "You really must be tired if you're making such dreadful jokes. Go home and get some sleep."

"It wasn't that bad," Goliath muttered as he stood.

Victor checked the clock then drained his tea. With a hand resting on the hilt of the largest knife in his belt, he gave a nod of farewell and left.

"Come along, Miss Fox," Harmony said. "We'd best get started."

I frowned. "Started on what?"

"Getting you dressed and looking your best for dinner."

"That won't be necessary. It's just an informal affair with the family in the dining room."

She frowned back. "No, it's not. Lady Bainbridge told me you're dining with friends tonight and I should help you to look your best."

"Which friends? And where?"

"The Caldicotts, and here at the hotel."

I groaned.

"You don't like the Caldicotts?" Peter asked.

"I do like them, but everyone is trying to pair me with Edward, the youngest son, and I have no wish to marry him."

"Or anyone," Harmony, Peter and Goliath chimed in as one.

I narrowed my gaze. "Quite."

Peter grinned, Goliath yawned, and Harmony shooed me out of the parlor with a flap of her hands. We parted ways and I headed to the foyer where I joined Flossy waiting at the lift door. I decided to ride it up with her instead of taking the stairs.

"Apparently we have dinner with the Caldicotts tonight," I said. "Why was I not informed?"

"You would have been if you were here today. Where have you been anyway? And don't say the museum. You can't possibly have gone again. Nobody likes museums *that* much."

"The British Museum's collection is vast, and there are other museums in the city too." It was neither a confirmation nor a denial, but I hoped that would suffice.

Flossy seemed keen to move on to other topics anyway. "So what are you wearing tonight? Something not quite so bleak, I hope." She inspected my simple black outfit with a critical eye and a downturn of her mouth.

"Harmony will help me find something suitable. Something in gray, I think."

She sighed. "Gray will have to do, I suppose."

The door slid open and a couple dressed in evening wear emerged. They nodded at us and we nodded back before taking their place inside the lift. We greeted John the operator and rode the lift in silence until we reached the fourth floor.

"Is tonight's dinner for my benefit or yours?" I asked Flossy in the corridor. "And when I say benefit, I use the term loosely."

She giggled. "You do say the wickedest things sometimes, Cleo. I suspect it's for both of us to spend time with the brothers, although my mother isn't sure if the eldest is right for me."

"Would you like the youngest? I'll gladly direct him towards you."

I wasn't sure if Edward would be satisfied with someone like Flossy, however. While she was very pretty and could be a lot of fun and had a good heart, she was not all that clever, and I suspected Edward would prefer someone he could have a decent conversation with.

But men had chosen their wives based on having less in common, so a match wasn't out of the realms of possibility.

"He won't be any better in Mother's eyes," she said on a sigh. "She wants me to marry someone rich and from a distinguished family, preferably with a title."

"Would she like him to farm flying pigs too?"

"Don't be ridiculous. She doesn't want me to marry a farmer."

I thought she was serious until she winked. We both laughed.

We stopped at the door to her suite, but she didn't unlock it. "Mother simply wants me to marry the best man I can."

"Shouldn't you decide who the best man is?"

"Now you're just being difficult on purpose, Cleo. You know how these things are." She sighed. "The only problem is, if she insists that no one is good enough for me, I might never marry. I had my debut last year and I'm still unwed. More than half of the girls from my year are either married, engaged or on the verge of an announcement. Only the dregs from the bottom of the barrel are left."

"That's a little unkind."

She gasped and covered her mouth. "Oh, I didn't mean you, Cleo! You're marvelous and if you had debuted when you were supposed to, you'd be married too, by now."

We'd been through this. She knew I had no interest in marriage, so I felt no qualms about the glare I gave her.

She completely ignored it and rattled on as if nothing were amiss. "Speaking of your debut—"

"I must get ready," I cut in. "Harmony will be waiting. I'll send her to you when I'm done." I strode off as quickly as I could without looking back.

"Tell her not to hurry. I'm having a bath first."

Harmony was reclining on the sofa in the sitting room when I arrived, her shoes off and her feet tucked up beside her, the newspaper on her lap, about to slip off. Her eyes were closed.

The poor thing was tired. It was supposed to be her day off and she'd had to work all afternoon here after spending the morning investigating with me.

I let her sleep on and did my own hair after dressing in an off-the-shoulder dove-gray dress with black lace trim on the sleeves and a twisted pattern in black beads down the front. I decided not to add any color to my lips and cheeks as I didn't want to appear as though I were trying to be attractive to Edward Caldicott.

I delayed as long as possible before waking Harmony. "I am sorry," I said as she sat bolt upright. "But Flossy is expecting you, and I didn't want you to get into trouble for not showing up."

She slipped on her shoes and stood. "Why didn't you

wake me as soon as you got in?" She adjusted her skirt and apron. "Did you get yourself ready?"

"Yes. I keep telling you I'm capable."

She wrinkled her nose at my hair. "Let me fix it."

"There's no time. Flossy is expecting you."

"But it could look better. It's a little flat."

"I quite like it like this. You'd better go. Then make sure you go straight home and get some rest. Between you and Goliath, it's like a nursery around here."

"Goliath?"

"A story for another time." I gave her a little shove. "Off you go."

I added some jewelry then decided to go to Flossy's room for company while she got ready. That proved to be a mistake when Flossy took one look at my hair and asked Harmony why she'd done such a poor job.

"It's so lifeless." Flossy clicked her tongue as she pulled my hair free of the comb holding it in place at the back. "Do it again when you've finished with mine."

"It isn't Harmony's fault," I snapped. "I did it myself."

"Why?"

"Er...Harmony had to mend this dress. I didn't know I'd torn the hem last time I wore it. She didn't have time to do my hair as well as the mending." Thankfully the explanation met with Flossy's approval, but she insisted Harmony re-do my hair.

At eight o'clock, Flossy and I ventured downstairs and joined her parents and brother in the dining room. It was good to see Aunt Lilian up and about after needing the day to recover from her headaches yesterday. She smiled at me, but her color was somewhat wan and her eyes hollow. She was not yet fully herself.

My uncle also seemed to be in a morose mood which didn't bode well for the evening. He sat sullenly, surveying the room as it filled with his guests. He smiled at some, nodded at others, and greeted a few by name. But he lacked genuine warmth.

Aunt Lilian grew quiet. Her fingers fidgeted with the edge of the napkin, plucking at the seam. She constantly glanced at the door, perhaps hoping her friends would arrive soon and put an end to this awkwardness.

It could not go on. There was only one thing that would lift my uncle's mood, but it also had the potential to sink it further if the discussion veered towards the recalcitrant chef. I would simply need to avoid mentioning him altogether.

"How are the plans coming along for the new restaurant, Uncle?"

"They're still in the preliminary stages." He signaled to the sommelier and indicated he'd like our wine glasses filled.

"But the Caldicotts haven't arrived yet," Aunt Lilian said under her breath.

"We can start without them."

"When will we be able to view them?" I asked quickly. "The plans, that is."

He blinked in surprise. "You want to see them?"

"Yes, very much."

He gave Floyd a pointed look. "Then I'd be delighted to show them to you. Come past my office when I'm there, and you can look over what the architect has already sent."

Floyd crossed his arms and sank into the chair. "I was going to ask to see them," he muttered.

"Eventually," Flossy added.

Floyd shot her a withering glare.

Oh dear. I'd put my foot into something I wished I hadn't.

Thank goodness the Caldicotts arrived. Once pleasantries were over, the party divided according to topics of interest. The two sons, seated beside Flossy and me, were keen to talk about business with the other men, so they constantly talked past us. Their mother eventually noticed during the soup course and tried to steer the conversation to something more agreeable to all. Unfortunately, she put me in the firing line.

"Have you made a decision about your debut, Miss Fox?" she asked in a loud voice.

I choked as my mouthful of soup went down. "I'm not doing my debut. I'm too old."

A round of polite rebuffs followed in which my age took center stage. It was all rather embarrassing, and I wanted to sink into the floor and disappear.

To my surprise, it was Edward who came to my rescue.

"Leave Miss Fox alone, Mother. She doesn't want to do her debut and that should be the end of it."

Considering it was not up to his mother whether I did my debut or not, Aunt Lilian felt his rebuke more than Lady Caldicott. She fell silent and concentrated on her soup. Lady Caldicott scowled at Edward.

The older men returned to their discussion about the hotel's plans for expansion while Floyd and the elder Caldicott brother discussed the motor car business. Edward leaned a little closer to me.

"I'm sorry for that," he said quietly. "My mother has a habit of sticking her nose into things that do not concern her."

"Thank you for diverting her attention, but I can fight my own battles."

He smirked. "I don't doubt it."

"What's this I hear about you not going on your Grand Tour?"

His smirk turned to a genuine smile. "Have you been talking about me?"

"Your mother made a point of telling me."

His smile slipped. I think I'd disappointed him by admitting that I hadn't been the one to initiate that conversation. "It's true that I've delayed my departure."

"Whatever for?"

"A matter here has caught my attention." A slight blush rose to his cheeks and he could hardly meet my gaze.

I focused on my soup, finishing it amid awkward silence. If I was the matter he was referring to, I ought to tell him that we had no future together. But what if I were wrong and he meant something else? It would be positively humiliating to tell him I had no wish to pursue a relationship with him when he was referring to an investment opportunity.

"Don't put off traveling, Edward," I said. "Not for anything." I paused, waiting for him to lift his gaze to meet mine. When he did, I added, "Or anyone."

The waiters came and collected our soup bowls. Edward hardly seemed to notice as his was taken away. His fingers absently stroked the fish knife before stilling. He turned to me, and I was left in no doubt of his meaning. His gaze had turned earnest, hopeful.

I steeled myself for what was to come.

"It's early days," he said softly, "but I think the matter will be worth delaying my travel plans for. Perhaps even delaying them indefinitely." He shifted in the chair, angling himself ever so slightly to me. "At the very least, I should stay in London and throw my hat into the ring." His knee touched mine.

I jerked away. "It won't be worth the delay."

He swallowed hard. "I see," he said heavily.

I regretted my bluntness, but it was a situation that required it. It wouldn't be fair to allow him to hope.

"Flossy," I said, perhaps a little too brightly. "Did you know Edward is going traveling soon. Isn't that exciting?"

"Oh yes," she gushed. She looked relieved to be included in a conversation. The poor thing had been stuck between Floyd and the other Caldicott brother, talking over her head. "Are you going to Paris?"

"I plan to spend a week there," Edward said.

"And America?"

"I'll be staying in Europe."

The three of us enjoyed a pleasant conversation about European countries with no awkwardness whatsoever. When the evening came to a conclusion at midnight, Edward made a point of thanking me for my honesty.

"Very few ladies would be as frank as you, Miss Fox. You are quite remarkable in that regard."

"Frankness is not necessarily an admirable quality. Sometimes life is easier when one is not so blunt."

"But an easy life is a dull life, is it not?"

I smiled. The more I got to know him, the more I liked him. "If I don't see you before you leave, I wish you safe and happy travels."

He took my hand and bowed over it. "I'd like to tell you all about it when I get back."

"I look forward to that."

From the smile he gave me, I suspected I'd inadvertently given him back some hope. From the way his mother kissed my cheek in parting, I was certain she held out a great deal of hope.

I sighed. One day, perhaps in the not-too-distant future, I

would be too old to be considered a suitable prospect and I could be free of matrimonial-minded mothers, and aunts. Until then, I would need to be on my guard.

It wouldn't be easy. Being a member of the Bainbridge household was like being a warrior on a battlefield. I would have to remember to keep my head down and my shield up.

* * *

MY BREAKFAST WAS INTERRUPTED the following morning by a brisk knock on the door. To my surprise it was Mr. Hobart. I did not invite him in, since there were two cups and two plates on the table in the sitting room. I didn't want to get Harmony into trouble. Fortunately he didn't ask to come in.

He looked troubled. "Harry is downstairs in my office and wishes to speak with you urgently."

"Is he all right?"

"He received a message early this morning. Mr. Warrington has been stabbed."

CHAPTER 9

*M*r. Warrington's left hand was heavily bandaged when he received us in the drawing room of his Kensington house. It was the first time I'd had access to the scene of the murder, and I found myself more interested in the room itself than Mr. Warrington.

Apparently Mrs. Warrington had a penchant for dead birds, stuffed and presented to look as though they'd just flown into the Warringtons' drawing room. There was a sparrow-hawk perched on a branch in the corner, an eagle-owl lamp base, and a pair of glossy white gannets on rocks in a glass cabinet. There were also ostrich and peacock feathers shooting out of vases, and a fan made out of green parrot feathers positioned on the table beside one of the wingback chairs. Both chairs now bracketed the fireplace, whereas according to Miss Jennet, the one in which the victim sat had been turned to face the fire. The wings were so large that it was quite obvious to me that the seated Mrs. Warrington's face would not have been visible to anyone coming through the window.

A chill crept over me as I forced myself to focus on what Mr. Warrington was saying.

"I was walking home from my club last night and she stepped out of the shadows and attacked me."

"She?" Harry echoed. "Are you certain it was a woman?"

"Quite certain. It's why I was able to fend her off, but not before she cut my hand. Fortunately, the doctor says the wound isn't deep, but my movement may be affected. We won't know until it heals. Damned inconvenient, not to mention painful." He gently rested his hand on the chair arm, wincing slightly.

"Why were you walking home from your club when you knew your life might be in danger?" I asked.

Mr. Warrington shook his head and shrugged. "It was foolish. I have no explanation except that my mind has been elsewhere ever since Isobel—" He cleared his throat. "I often walk home from my club of an evening, no matter the weather. I enjoy the peace and quiet of the city at night. It helps me think, and I have a lot to think about these days. Last night, I simply followed my usual routine out of habit."

"Do the police know?" Harry asked, indicating the bandaged hand.

Mr. Warrington nodded. "They're at the scene of the crime now, looking for evidence. I doubt they'll find anything. She ran off when I struck out, taking the knife with her." He clicked his tongue. "They're treating it as a random attack, unrelated to the letters or the murder. A third fellow has been assigned, this one from the local constabulary, not Scotland Yard, even though I gave them the names of the two detectives I've dealt with there already. That makes three different investigations—one for the letters, another for Isobel's murder, and now this. It seems inefficient to me."

"Is there anything else you can tell us about your attacker?" Harry asked.

"I'm afraid not. I didn't get a look at her face. She wore a hood and it was dark."

Considering we had only one female suspect, our next step was clear. Our plan to go to the photographic studio would have to wait.

We thanked Mr. Warrington and made to leave.

"One moment." He collected a large envelope from the table beside his chair and handed it to Harry. "Before I went out last night, I was feeling nostalgic. I spent some time alone in Isobel's bedroom. I suppose I wanted to feel closer to her again, to remember how things used to be between us in the beginning and not how it was at the end. We were fond of one another, once. Not in love, but we were friends. Anyway, I found these in the drawer of her dressing table."

Harry opened the envelope and peered inside. He immediately closed it again and glanced at me with wide eyes.

Mr. Warrington shifted in his chair. "Yes, they are quite inappropriate. I suggest you don't show them to Miss Fox. A young lady should not be subjected to the images contained in those photographs."

Now I was intrigued even more.

"I'm loaning them to you in the hope you can identify the fellow, Armitage. He is clearly my wife's lover and perhaps he can help you with your investigation. It crossed my mind that he might be the one who wanted me dead. Perhaps he's even colluding with the woman who did this." He lifted his bandaged hand. "Please see that they don't fall into the wrong hands—or anyone's hands, for that matter. For obvious reasons, it would be damaging to my reputation if they did."

"Did you find the negatives too?" I asked.

Mr. Warrington shook his head. "I wasn't looking for them, however. I'll conduct a more thorough search this morning. If I can't find them, does that mean the studio still has them, do you think?"

"Most likely. Or it could be that Mrs. Warrington destroyed them. If she did that, I'm not sure why she kept these."

"Keepsakes?" He shrugged.

"There are no negatives at the studio," Harry said.

I frowned.

"How do you know?" Mr. Warrington asked.

"I checked."

I glared at Harry, but he ignored me.

He got up to leave, but I hadn't finished. Mr. Warrington should be made aware of something. It was his reputation that could be ruined, after all, if copies were made from the negatives.

"There's something you should know," I began. "The studio where those were taken has a reputation for making copies from the negatives of their more risqué images and reproducing them on cards. Those cards are sold to collectors."

Mr. Warrington paled. His Adams apple bobbed furiously. "What do you mean by collectors, Miss Fox?"

"Sailors, dock workers..."

His eyes closed and he buried his face in his good hand.

"If it's any consolation, they're not the sort of men who would recognize Mrs. Warrington." It was hardly a consolation at all, really. It was highly likely that collectors of that sort of material existed beyond the docks. It wasn't out of the realms of possibility that the cards could be obtained by men within the Warringtons' circle. Mr. Warrington may not have loved his wife, or even liked her much at the end, but he would be utterly humiliated if his friends saw her naked image.

He dismissed us with a wave of his hand, without looking up or speaking. We saw ourselves out, Mr. Henderson being nowhere in sight.

I held out my hand as we walked off. "May I see the photographs?"

Harry tucked the envelope under his arm. "No."

"I'm hardly going to faint at the sight of them. I am not delicate."

"Even so, these photographs are very...very..." His cheeks pinked.

"Inappropriate, yes I know." I beckoned with my fingers. "Hand them over, please."

He shook his head vehemently. "I couldn't live with myself if I was to blame for ruining your innocence."

I barked a laugh. "I am hardly innocent." Too late, I realized how that sounded. It was my turn to blush, and I did it much more fiercely than he. "I didn't mean to imply... That is to say..." Damnation. I couldn't possibly tell him what I meant. The truth was, I *was* innocent. I'd only been kissed once. I hadn't been overly enamored with the man, but I'd wanted to see what all the fuss was about. The kiss had been a disappointment, all dry lips and a great deal of awkwardness.

Telling Harry that would be beyond humiliating, however. I gave up asking to see the photographs.

We walked on in painful silence, heading in the direction of the omnibus route that traveled to Camden Town. Even though we didn't discuss it, we both had the same idea—to ask Mrs. Parker where she was last night.

I was conscious of Harry looking directly ahead, his gaze not diverting from the pavement. My face remained hot until we sat down on the bus. Finally, as the vehicle jerked forward, my brain emerged from the fog of embarrassment it had descended into.

I remembered something. "You told Mr. Warrington you'd checked the studio for the negatives and hadn't found them." I lowered my voice to a whisper. "Did you break in last night?"

"Yes, and I don't regret not telling you. You would have insisted on coming, I would have insisted you didn't, and we would have argued. I don't wish to argue with you."

"We're arguing now." I huffed out a frustrated breath. "First the photographs and now the break-in. You must stop excluding me from the investigation."

"I'm not excluding you. It's for your own protection. I didn't want you getting caught."

"And I don't want *you* getting caught! If I'd accompanied you, I could have kept a look out and whistled if someone came near. I have experience with break-ins, you know. If you'd been caught..." I shook my head. "It would have been dreadful."

He blinked at me. "You were worried about me," he said flatly.

"Yes, of course. You have more to lose than me. You have a criminal record already, for one thing, and your father's reputation is at stake. If I were arrested, my uncle would make sure it was swept under the carpet. All I'd endure would be his lecture. If you were arrested, you could have been sent to jail and your father forced to leave his job."

"I wasn't caught."

"Not this time. Next time, tell me when you're going. If you insist I don't accompany you, you can take Victor. He's rather good at getting into locked rooms."

We turned the corner sharply and I slid across the seat into his side. I quickly shifted back to my end, but not before my face heated once more.

"So you didn't find the negatives," I said to distract myself.

"No, but I only looked under W for Warrington and H for Henderson. There were a lot of negatives and two constables kept pacing past the shop. I was worried they'd see my lamp's light."

"So if they used a false name, they could have been filed elsewhere."

He tapped the envelope. "Considering the nature of the photographs, it's likely they did. Either that, or they bought the negatives and destroyed them."

I eyed the envelope on his lap. "It doesn't matter to us anyway. We can hopefully identify the lover from those."

"*I'll* take a closer look after we interview Mrs. Parker again."

It was an argument I wouldn't win. Not in an omnibus anyway, and perhaps not at all. I tried not to let it bother me, but it galled to be left out of part of the investigation. So much so that I gave Harry the silent treatment for the rest of the journey to Camden Town.

Neither of us spoke until we turned the corner onto Arlington Road. Up ahead, Mrs. Parker stood in her doorway, addressing a giant of a man on her doorstep.

I caught Harry's arm and we stopped. "Wait. Something's going on."

"Indeed. You're talking to me again."

I ignored the jibe. "She's looking this way!"

We pretended to be friends greeting one another on the street, all the while I watched Mrs. Parker out of the corner of my eye. She handed the man some papers which he flipped through before pocketing.

"Money," Harry said with certainty. "She's paying him."

The giant pocketed the bills then headed towards us.

"He's coming this way," I hissed. "We have to leave."

"Stay calm. Don't let him see your face." He held the envelope between us, pretending to discuss it.

I bent my head as if reading the writing on the front of the envelope where in fact I was watching the man lope towards us, his strides purposeful. He was huge, as big as Goliath, but with shoulders that strained the seams of his coat. His features were just as broad. His brow protruded like a Neanderthal ledge over sunken eyes, and his prominent nose dripped. He sniffed then swiped at his nose with the back of his hand. He did not wear gloves, probably because he couldn't find any that fit those large paws.

I held my breath but he passed without noticing us. Once he turned the corner, I released my breath and glanced towards Mrs. Parker's house. She had retreated inside.

"The local thug?" I asked Harry. "Do you think they even have one around here? It's rather a quiet area."

"Wherever he's from, I'm certain she was paying him to perform a duty for her. Something either outside of the law, or barely in it."

"It wouldn't be for attacking Mr. Warrington last night. He said his attacker was a woman. He couldn't possibly have mistaken that caveman for a female."

"Or fought him off. But what about the night before? Perhaps she paid him to kill Mr. Warrington in his home."

"Then I hope she only gave him half for killing the wrong person."

He chuckled. "Your sense of humor is a little dark at times."

"*You* laughed."

I headed off and he fell into step beside me. I knocked on Mrs. Parker's door and smiled at her when she opened it. Before she'd even drawn breath, Harry put his hand up to ensure she didn't slam the door in our faces.

"What do you want now?" she growled.

"First of all, we want to know who that man was," Harry said.

She rocked back on her heels, her gaze wary. "A friend."

"Why did you pay your friend?"

"He loaned me money so I was paying him back."

"Does your husband know about the loan?"

"It's my money and my business. I can do what I want." She thrust her chin out at me. "I hope he treats you with more respect than he's treating me."

"Mrs. Parker," I went on, "where were you last night?"

She frowned. "Why?"

"Just answer the question, please."

Her tongue darted out and she licked her bottom lip. She was delaying answering. "I called on a friend. She can vouch for me. Do you want her name and address?"

She must be very confident in her alibi if she was offering up the details unasked. That meant she was either telling the truth or she knew the friend would lie for her. Either way, we weren't going to learn anything there.

Harry stepped away and Mrs. Parker did indeed slam the door. We headed back along Arlington Street. Instead of continuing on to the omnibus, however, Harry spotted two constables strolling along the pavement outside the row of shops.

"I've got an idea," he said, rushing off.

I waited in case the omnibus arrived so I could detain it while he spoke to the constables. He returned just as driver pulled on the reins. We climbed in and paid the conductor for our journey.

"Well?" I asked as we sat. "You seem satisfied. What did you find out?"

"That caveman's name is Ricketts. Bob Ricketts. They know him well. He's a local low-life who terrorizes the shop-keepers, demanding money to leave them alone. If they refuse, he destroys their stock."

I pulled a face. "That doesn't sound like the sort of friend the wife of a Scotland Yard sergeant would have."

"But it sounds exactly like the sort of person you would hire if you wanted to kill someone."

* * *

WE RETURNED to Harry's Soho office to discuss the evidence. I told him to go up ahead while I bought two coffees from Luigi. When I entered the office of Armitage and Associates, Harry was drawing up a list of suspects.

"Have you had a proper look at the photographs yet?" I asked as I handed him a cup.

He glanced at the drawer of his desk. "I have."

"And?"

He picked up the pen and dipped it into the ink pot. "Mrs. Warrington's face is clear; the lover's is not."

"Is he turned away from the camera?"

"His head is cut off at the neck."

"What about distinguishing features? Was he tall, for example?"

He wrote something on his notepad. "It was hard to tell."

"Why? Wasn't he standing next to her? Mrs. Warrington was average in height—"

"He wasn't standing." He picked up his cup and gulped a mouthful of coffee before turning his attention to the notepad once more.

He was avoiding looking at me. Those photographs must be inappropriate indeed.

I set my cup down and waited.

A moment later, Luigi burst into the office without knocking. "Harry! Harry, come quick! The café's on fire!"

"Bloody hell." Harry sprang up and raced out of the office behind Luigi.

I didn't have much time. I opened the top drawer and spilled the contents of the large envelope onto the desk. There were three photographs in all, and each one made me blush fiercer than the last. Mrs. Warrington's face was only clear in one of the images, and her lover's face couldn't be seen in any. Indeed, he only appeared in two. One of the photographs showed Mrs. Warrington standing in front of a tropical beach scene alone, her face obscured by a large hat. In the second, she stood beside a man, but the photographer had cut off their heads. In the third, Mrs. Warrington was lying down on the sand covered floor, facing the camera. The man lay behind her, his arm around her and his hand cupping her breast. Positioned behind her like that, his face wasn't visible.

The subjects were completely naked in all the photographs. If one of Mr. Warrington's political rivals got hold of them, it would be disastrous for his career.

I felt they contained a certain beauty, however. Mrs. Warrington looked amused, with a spark of mischief in her eyes as she stared at the camera. To think, these photographs could exist forever, a reminder of the spirited woman who'd agreed to be photographed naked. One day, when she was long forgotten and her murder was a distant memory, I hoped these photographs would be considered beautiful, not disgusting.

"That was a low act." Harry strode into the office and snatched up the photographs.

"I thought it rather clever. You fell for it easily enough."

"Luigi is a convincing actor. When I saw the flames, I thought the building would go up."

I gasped. "He truly set fire to the café?"

"Just an old rag which he placed in a copper pot." He beckoned me to get out of his chair. "You should be ashamed of yourself using your feminine wiles to get him to do your bidding."

"Unfortunately it doesn't work on all men. Pass me my bag, please. I left it beside your chair."

He reached down to retrieve it. I took the opportunity to snatch the photographs back.

He tried to grab them off me, but I danced out of his reach. He growled in frustration as he got to his feet. But he did not try to take them again. I held them to my chest and no gentleman would dare touch a woman there.

He stood with his arms folded and gave me his sternest glare. I found it very hard to keep a straight face. "You're not playing fair, Cleo."

"I am not playing at all, Harry. Anyway, it's too late. I've seen almost everything there is to see."

"Almost?"

"There's something on the man's hand. I need to take a closer look. If I place these on the desk, do you promise not to stop me looking at them?" I smiled sweetly. "Otherwise I'll take them back to the hotel and Harmony can view them with me."

He groaned.

"And Flossy too."

"You *are* playing a game, and it's one you're very good at. Very well. You win. Put them down."

I returned the photographs to the desk and spread them out. "You see far more of Mrs. Warrington's body than you do of his in this one where they're lying down."

"So?"

"So *you* shouldn't look. What about your innocence?"

He rolled his eyes. "You think you're amusing, but you're not."

"I beg to differ. I'm having a lot of fun." I bent closer to the photographs, and Harry leaned in too. Every little part of me was aware of him, from the hairs on my arms to the blood throbbing in my veins. Being so close to him as we studied such risqué images was a sensation like no other. Although it was discomforting, I didn't feel embarrassed. Indeed, I felt emboldened. Almost emboldened enough to—

"There's definitely a mark on his hand." His voice cut through my thoughts like a sharp blade. "Perhaps a wound or birthmark." He opened a drawer and retrieved a magnifying glass. He peered at the photograph of the couple lying down. "I think it's a mole." He gave the glass to me and I inspected the image. "Does Henderson have a mark on his hand?"

"I haven't noticed." I handed back the glass. "We need to find out."

"We'll go back to Kensington now." He checked his watch. "After lunch. Hungry?"

"Lunch is an excellent idea. I think you should lock those away somewhere safe while you're not here."

He retrieved a set of keys from his pocket and opened a small wall safe behind the print of the Tower Bridge building plans. He placed the envelope containing the photographs inside and relocked it.

I retrieved my coat from the stand by the door and handed him his.

We didn't go far. According to Harry, Luigi charged a mere threepence for the most delicious bowl of *pesto alla genovese* pasta. He was right; I'd never tasted anything quite like it, and devoured it all.

With full stomachs, we returned to Kensington but stopped two houses away from the Warringtons'. Mr. Warrington stood on the doorstep with his friend, Mr. Drummond. They were having a heated discussion, but I couldn't hear what it was about.

I was considering whether to edge closer when Mr. Drummond stormed off down the steps and strode away in the opposite direction to Harry and me.

Mr. Warrington watched him for a few moments then, with a shake his head, returned inside and closed the door.

"You speak to Mr. Henderson," I said to Harry. "I'll follow Drummond."

"I should be the one to follow him."

"You're too tall and conspicuous. Besides, a man won't expect a woman to follow him."

"That logic is flawed."

I waved him off and walked away, quickening my pace to catch up to Mr. Drummond. I soon realized he was taking the same route as Mrs. Warrington the day I followed her to the photographic studio. Mr. Drummond didn't travel quite as far, however. He entered Paddington Station instead of passing it by. I almost lost him in the crowd, but then spotted him entering the call office where the public could pay to make telephone calls.

A few moments later, he re-emerged. He did not leave the station, but purchased a newspaper and joined the throng of passengers waiting for the next train on platform one. He stood under the sign for the cloak room and opened the newspaper.

Ten minutes later, he was approached by the photographer's assistant, Jeffrey Deacon, clutching a large package in both hands. I couldn't hear their exchange, but the youth looked nervous as he spoke to Mr. Drummond. Mr. Drummond answered with a nod then accepted the package and passed over something smaller.

Jeffrey inspected it before Mr. Drummond snapped at him. I didn't need to hear the words to know what he said. I could read his lips. He'd told the youth to "Put it away." Jeffrey quickly tucked what I suspected were folded bank notes into his pocket. He touched the brim of his hat but didn't receive the same courtesy from Mr. Drummond in return. Instead, Mr. Drummond pointed his finger at Jeffrey, and spoke sternly to him.

Jeffrey went a little pale. He nodded quickly then, ducking his head, hurried away.

Mr. Drummond studied the package in his hands. Wrapped in brown paper and tied with string, it was too thick to be photographs. The only other explanation I could think of was that it contained plate glass negatives encased in padding.

But why was Mr. Drummond buying them? Why didn't Mr. Warrington collect them himself? Or why not ask Harry to do it on his behalf? At least tell us he knew the negatives were there, instead of pretending not to know. And how had Mr. Drummond or Mr. Warrington known what name to ask for? They must have been under an assumed name or Harry would have found them last night. Did Mr. Warrington know the name of his wife's lover, after all, and it wasn't Mr. Henderson?

I gasped as a thought struck me. If *Mr. Drummond* was her lover it would explain how he'd known what name the negatives were filed under. How diabolical to have a liaison with his friend's wife. Perhaps that was what they'd argued about on the doorstep. Mr. Warrington must have discovered evidence of their relationship while going through his wife's things and confronted Mr. Drummond about it.

There was only one way to know for certain, but it was not only risky, it was morally dubious. I really shouldn't do it.

On the other hand, this was a murder investigation. Sometimes, the end justified the means. Or so I told my conscience.

When Mr. Drummond walked off, I knew I had to act now or miss the opportunity altogether.

I followed him outside and ducked into the first shop I passed where I asked for some brown wrapping paper and string. I thought I'd lost Mr. Drummond when I re-emerged from the shop but spotted him some distance ahead.

I raced after him, weaving my way around pedestrians, but stopped when I spotted a broken crate in a dead-end lane. It must have been discarded by a shopkeeper. I broke it further with a firm kick, and picked up the piece that splintered off. It would do nicely. I checked around the corner to make sure I hadn't lost Mr. Drummond, and wrapped the piece of wood in the brown paper, tying it with the string.

I left the lane and hurried to catch up to Mr. Drummond. But what I needed to do next was the hardest part of my plan, and I feared I didn't have the skills to do it properly.

Fortunately, being so close to the shops and a major railway station meant pickpockets were easy to come by. I spotted a dirty-faced boy dressed in rags wandering idly up to a cart full of fruit positioned at the front of a grocer's. I intercepted him before the shopkeeper did.

"I'll give you sixpence if you bump into that man and make him drop the parcel tucked under his arm," I said quickly, pointing out Mr. Drummond. "Then while he's recovering his balance, swap his parcel for this one. I'll pay you half now, half later. Meet me in that lane."

I deposited the coins into his outstretched palm and handed him the parcel, then retreated back to the lane.

I waited for what seemed an inordinate amount of time. Worried the lad had been caught, I gave up. Just as I rounded the corner, he barreled into me, almost knocking me off my feet.

He handed over the parcel and thrust out his palm. I gave him the other half of his payment. He grinned a gap-toothed smile and went on his way.

I ought to return to Harry's office and look at these with him, but the temptation was too great and I was not known for my patience. I unwrapped the paper, being careful not to drop the contents of the parcel.

Positioned between slim pieces of card and fabric for protection, were two glass plate negatives, not three. They did not show Mrs. Warrington with her lover.

They were of a naked Mr. Drummond. And he was with another man.

CHAPTER 10

The identity of the man standing behind Mr. Drummond wasn't clear in the negatives. His face was partially obscured and the inverse light and dark of the negative made it more difficult. But it wasn't a great leap to assume it was Mr. Warrington. The two men were clearly as close as two friends could be. Mr. Drummond had been at his friend's side the day after Mrs. Warrington's murder. He had also gone directly from Mr. Warrington's house to collect the negatives. It was likely their argument on the doorstep had been about collecting them. Perhaps Mr. Warrington hadn't wanted to make a song and dance about it, but Mr. Drummond was keen to get them back.

It would have been a benefit to discuss what this discovery meant for our investigation, but I wasn't even sure where Harry would be. It was almost time for the hotel staff to have their afternoon break. Perhaps I could make it back to the Mayfair in time and meet them in the parlor.

I stared down at the negatives. I felt no shame in viewing them. It was difficult to determine individual parts of Mr. Drummond's body anyway. Harry wouldn't see it that way, however. I couldn't help smiling at that.

If Mr. Drummond could see me now, smiling over the negatives of his naked image, he'd probably never be able to face me again. Mr. Warrington would probably dismiss me from the investigation.

So many things became clearer now that I knew about Mr. Warrington's inclination for men. It explained why his marriage was one of convenience, and why his wife had taken a lover. It also raised questions. If Mrs. Warrington knew her husband preferred men and agreed to let him live his life as he wished if she could take lovers, why did he want to divorce her? Wouldn't it protect his reputation if they stayed together?

And why would Mrs. Warrington's lover grow jealous of her husband and kill him? If Mr. Henderson was her lover then he must know she could never marry him, a butler. It was best for him, and her, if the Warringtons stayed married. A man in Mr. Henderson's situation couldn't afford jealousy.

Unless her lover *wasn't* Mr. Henderson, but another fellow. Someone who didn't know about Mr. Warrington's preference for men. Someone who flew into a jealous rage and killed Mr. Warrington—or thought he had.

Or perhaps jealousy had nothing to do with it, and the lover wanted to get his hands on Mrs. Warrington's fortune by marrying her. He would need to remove the obstacle in his way—her husband. If he wasn't aware Mr. Warrington was about to sue for divorce, he might have taken matters into his own hands.

And if he *was* aware of the divorce, then he might have wanted to save his lover's reputation. Divorce proceedings would ruin her reputation, making it difficult for them to remarry after the dust settled if he was someone important.

The more I thought about it, the less likely it seemed that the butler was the lover. And the more I realized I needed to learn the man's name.

Since I was already in Paddington, my next course of action was an easy decision to make.

I wrapped the paper around the negatives and tied it up with string. With the parcel tucked under my arm, I headed towards the studio of D.B. Sharp. Jeffrey looked like he wanted to scurry into a hole when he saw me enter. The poor lad was having a trying day after being confronted by an angry Mr. Drummond at the station, and now having me show up.

"I wish to speak to Mr. Sharp," I demanded.

"He's busy with customers." The youth's voice cracked. He cleared his throat. "He won't be long."

"Unless he comes out here to talk to me now, I will go in there. I don't think his customers will like that, do you?"

Jeffrey swallowed heavily. "Wait here."

He rounded the desk then disappeared into the adjoining room. A few moments later, he emerged behind Mr. Sharp. The photographer glowered at me.

"What do you want?" he snapped.

"I want to know the name of Mrs. Warrington's lover."

"I don't know who that is."

"You do. She came here on the day she was murdered to collect her photographs. You would have seen her likeness in the newspapers after her death. Now, unless you tell me the name of the man in the photographs with her, I will have to tell the police that she called here mere hours before she died."

Mr. Sharp attempted to straighten, but his spine remained bent. "I had nothing to do with her death, so your threat doesn't concern me."

"No? Then perhaps it will concern you if I tell the police about your little operation."

"It's not illegal to photograph couples in any manner they choose. Nobody is forcing them to do it."

"But it is illegal to make copies of their images without their knowledge and on-sell them. If word got out, you would be ruined. No one would trust you with their photographic needs ever again."

Jeffrey emitted a hiss of breath and sat heavily on the desk chair, as if he were a balloon I'd just burst.

Mr. Sharp's tongue darted out and licked his lips. "Well. You can threaten all you like, but I don't know the man's name. That's the truth. But I can describe him."

It would have to do. I nodded.

"He was tall with reddish-blond hair and thick sideburns. That's all I remember."

"I remember his name!" Jeffrey blurted out. "She called him Xavier."

Mr. Sharp pursed his lips and glared at his assistant.

"His surname?" I asked.

Jeffrey shrugged. "That's what she called him. Xavier. She ordered the photographs under the name Smith, if that helps."

That was likely a false name, but a given name of Xavier was unusual enough to be real. It was a promising start.

Mr. Sharp opened the door. "Good day, Miss."

"One more thing." I turned to Jeffrey. If I wanted answers, I was more likely to get them from him. "The negatives you just delivered to the man at Paddington Station—do you know who is in the photographs with him?"

Jeffrey smiled.

"We don't," Mr. Sharp growled. "Good *day*, Miss."

I left. It didn't matter anyway. Jeffrey's smile had been enough for me to know they'd known it was Mr. Warrington in those photographs. As a politician, his name and face would be in the newspapers from time to time.

I started to pass all of this information along to Harry when I found him at his office, but didn't get very far. He sat in stunned silence after I told him who Mr. Drummond had met at Paddington station and what I'd done afterwards. He leaned forward, clasping his hands together on the desk then opened his mouth to speak. I expected a lecture. What I got was a long exhalation and a shake of his head. He settled back into the chair with another shake of his head.

"I can't believe it," he muttered. "Not only did you pay a boy to thieve for you, which could have been very dangerous for him."

"He looked nimble, and I paid him well."

"But then you studied the negatives and saw—" He indicated the glass plate negatives which lay side by side on the paper wrapping. "Couldn't you have waited for me?"

"Why?"

He threw his hands in the air. "For decorum!"

"You're being a prude, Harry. Just accept that I have seen things now that have broadened my horizons and we'll speak of it no more. Unless we have to, that is."

He dragged his hand through his hair. "Your uncle would gut me like a fish if he found out."

"Now you're just being melodramatic. My uncle is smart enough to know that you couldn't stop me. It's hardly your fault I'm too nosy for my own good." I went to pick up the negatives to wrap them up again, but he snatched them away.

"I'll do it."

I rolled my eyes. "Aside from learning that Mr. Warrington is most likely the second man in those negatives, which means he prefers men, I also learned something else today when I confronted the photographer."

"You did *what*?"

"Mr. Sharp was somewhat reluctant to speak to me, but he gave up some information when I mentioned that I would inform the police about his extra source of income."

Harry groaned again. "You should have collected me so we could do it together. It could have been dangerous."

"He's an old man and his assistant is barely more than a child. In fact, Jeffrey was more helpful than Mr. Sharp. He told me Mrs. Warrington called her lover Xavier. He has red-gold hair and sideburns. That doesn't fit Mr. Henderson at all."

"Unless the description is a false one. Highly likely considering you were threatening him. He had to give you enough to get rid of you without compromising his customer."

I hadn't thought of that. "Did you see Mr. Henderson's hand? Did it have a mark on it?"

"He wasn't there."

"I don't think he's her lover anyway. I think it's someone with more to gain with Mr. Warrington out of the picture." I explained my theory that the lover, Xavier, would want to make a widow of Mrs. Warrington so he could marry her and gain her wealth for himself, as well as avoid the scandal of her divorce. "If he wanted to marry Mrs. Warrington and required her reputation to be intact, he must have some standing in the community."

Harry rubbed his jaw. "That narrows down our suspects."

His sarcasm was warranted. We were further away from the truth than ever. Indeed, by excluding Mr. Henderson, we'd struck our main suspect off the list. We had to start all over again to find Mrs. Warrington's lover.

Harry reached into his inside jacket pocket. "I almost

forgot. Warrington gave me this letter. He received it late yesterday in the mail."

Two things immediately struck me about the handwritten note. It was unsigned and it was written on what was probably personalized stationery but with the identifying information at the top torn off. I read it and had to re-read it again to make sure I hadn't misunderstood. The letter demanded a thousand pounds be left at the foot of the Albert Memorial in Kensington Gardens at midnight tonight. It was an extraordinary amount of money. If Mr. Warrington didn't pay, the anonymous author threatened to go to the press with information that could ruin him. It did not specify what that information was.

"It's different to the other threatening letters he received," I said. "The sender isn't demanding he let the bill go through parliament. He or she wants money."

"So it's unlikely that it's from Mrs. Parker," Harry finished.

"Mr. Warrington must be worried."

"Actually he's not, because he thinks he knows who wrote it. He recognized the handwriting from letters his wife received and kept. Warrington showed them to me and I agree they're written by the same hand."

"Whose?"

"Her brother, Trickelbank. Not only that, he wrote this on hotel stationery." It certainly appeared to be the same thickness as the Mayfair's paper, but without the identifying hotel's emblem of an M inside a circle, it was impossible to tell. "Warrington wants me to deal with it on his behalf."

"How?"

"He didn't offer a suggestion, but insisted he won't be paying a penny to the blackmailer."

"He wants you to threaten Mr. Trickelbank, doesn't he? But what if he doesn't go away quietly? What if he insists on going to the newspapers with what he knows about their marriage? Does Mr. Warrington expect you to beat the brother into submission?"

He picked up the letter. "I'll *speak* to Trickelbank. Once he knows that Warrington knows he sent this, he'll back down."

"I hope you're right."

"Are you worried about me?"

"Don't be ridiculous. You're younger, taller and broader than Mr. Trickelbank."

He smiled smugly. "Thank you."

"It wasn't meant as a compliment." Perhaps I should have just admitted that I was worried. After all, we didn't know a thing about Mr. Trickelbank. He could be a murderer.

"I'll come with you," I said.

He rose. "No."

"We're partners."

"We are not partners." He collected our coats from the stand and handed me mine. "We're working together on the murder, not this."

"It's most likely the same investigation."

He shook his head. "I don't think so."

"Harry—"

"*Cleo*, you are not speaking to Trickelbank and that's final. It doesn't require two of us. Besides, he knows you and will lodge a complaint about you to your uncle. He isn't aware of my connection to the hotel."

He had a point. My uncle already had enough reasons to lecture me. I didn't need another. "Very well. I'll walk with you to the hotel and then we'll enter separately."

He held the office door open for me. "I'll go through the staff entrance."

"No. You have official business to conduct at the hotel on behalf of Mr. Warrington. You have a right to use the front entrance."

He gave no response as he locked the office door behind him and I suspected he was just avoiding an argument. However, he did do as I suggested and entered the hotel through the front. I waited outside, speaking to Frank to pass the time, then followed a few minutes later.

Harry stood at the check-in counter, talking to Peter. Upon seeing me, Peter jerked his head, beckoning me.

"Harmony is looking for you," he said. "She's in the parlor. Goliath and Victor are there too."

"They'll want an update on the investigation. I'll go now."

Harry frowned. "They *all* want an update?"

"Of course. They help sometimes so need to be kept informed about developments. Peter too, and Frank."

"It doesn't take us away from our duties here," Peter said quickly.

"Even so, don't tell your uncle," I told Harry.

He put up his hands. "The hotel business has nothing to do with me anymore." He leaned a hip against the counter and folded his arms, regarding me with an air of amusement. "You should be the one with 'associates' on your door, not me."

"Or you could just add my name to *your* door. We are partners, after all."

He bent to my level. It was rather disconcerting being eye to eye with him without a desk separating us, and I struggled to hold my nerve and not blink or look away. "We are *not* partners and my business name won't be changing. I bought a thousand cards that all say Armitage and Associates, not Armitage and Fox." He straightened. "After this case, we will return to the way things were."

"Oh Harry," I said, instilling as much mock sympathy into my tone as possible. "You are naïve if you think anything will be the same after this." I strode off without waiting to see his reaction.

I opened the door to the staff parlor and almost bumped into Harmony about to leave.

"I thought you were never going to return," she grumbled as she resumed her seat between Victor and Goliath.

The three of them were alone in the staff parlor, and Goliath was sound asleep stretched out across eight chairs pushed together to accommodate his length. His feet still extended over the end. With him sleeping, it meant Victor and Harmony had been virtually on their own in here. Considering Victor liked teasing Harmony, and Harmony didn't take it all that well, I wondered what they'd been talking about. Or if they'd been talking at all.

I was convinced the teasing and prickly banter meant they liked one another, but I didn't think they'd reached the kissing stage of their relationship. It was much too soon and there was a great deal more flirting to be had.

Neither of their faces gave anything away, but they did

avoid looking at one another. I wasn't sure what that meant, however. They could have been arguing or kissing—either was possible with those two.

Goliath yawned and stretched, but did not sit up. "Did I miss anything?"

"Miss Fox is about to update us on the investigation," Harmony told him.

I poured myself a cup of tea and sat with a sigh, savoring the first sip before I reported everything Harry and I had learned so far. It sounded significant when laid out like that, but unfortunately it all resulted in very little.

Harmony pouted. "So that's it?"

"Did you expect more?"

She lifted a shoulder.

"What is it, Harmony?" I asked.

"Nothing."

I appealed to Victor, hoping he would be able to decipher her.

"She's disappointed you don't need her help," he told me.

"Oh, I see. I am sorry, Harmony, but Mr. Armitage and I have it in hand. Events are moving rather quickly and coming back here to fetch you would have delayed things."

"Is there nothing we can do?" she asked.

"Actually there is, but I just need Victor."

Her gaze narrowed. "Why just him?"

"I think the task is better suited to his talents."

"It involves cooking?"

"It involves speaking to a dubious character with a tendency for violence. And while I do think you are quite capable of many things, I don't think you can get answers from thugs."

"Don't be so sure," Victor said with a bland look on his face. "That tongue of hers is a sharp instrument designed for cutting a fellow down to size."

Her jaw dropped as she swung around to face him. "Are you saying I'm cruel?"

"You have a certain way with words."

"I am *not* cruel. I've merely learned to stand up for myself. One has to when one doesn't look like everybody else." She sniffed. "If you don't like the way I speak to you, why are you always in here when I am?"

He shrugged. "I didn't say I don't like it. Your sharp tongue doesn't bother me in the least. I like a strong woman with opinions. Makes life more interesting."

Goliath chuckled, earning himself a glare from Harmony.

"To the matter at hand," I said in an attempt to rein in the conversation before it ended in an argument. "Victor, there is a man connected to one of our suspects who may be persuaded to tell us what he knows about her."

I told him about Bob Ricketts, the local thug of Camden Town, who we'd seen accepting money from Mrs. Parker. I asked him to see what he could learn from the fellow.

Victor nodded without hesitation, but Harmony was affronted on his behalf. "You can't ask him to do that! It could be dangerous."

"I'll be fine," Victor assured her. "But thanks for worrying about me." He winked at her then stood and swaggered out of the parlor.

Harmony clicked her tongue. "That's not why I'm worried," she assured Goliath and me. "It's the hotel I'm worried about. The kitchen, to be specific. We can't afford to lose any cooks loyal to the hotel, and if Victor does something illegal and is caught, he'll lose his position here, even if the police let him go."

"What do you mean by cooks loyal to the hotel? Are some leaving?"

"Not yet, but they will. Chef says he'll walk out if the new restaurant goes ahead and take those loyal to him with him. Victor said the kitchen is divided into two—those who'll follow the chef and those who want to stay at the Mayfair."

Goliath scratched his head, messing up his hair. "They're mad if they leave good employment for a chef who may not be able to get them work where he goes."

"I'm sure it won't come to that," I said. "The chef is trying to throw his weight around. When he realizes my uncle won't stand for it, he'll back down. My uncle won't give up his plans for expansion."

Goliath stood and picked up his porter's hat from the table. "Don't be so sure. French chefs of his quality aren't easy to find in London. He can walk into a dozen other restaurants and demand his own terms. Plenty would be happy to bend over backwards for him."

"My uncle is a stubborn man."

"But he'd do anything for the hotel," Harmony pointed out. "Even if it means swallowing his pride and giving the chef what he wants. Goliath's right. You can't operate a restaurant in a luxury hotel without a quality chef overseeing it."

With the hotel's troubles on my mind, I returned to the foyer and absently headed in the direction of the front desk where Peter was still working, even though it was past time for him to leave for the day. His gaze darted between Harry and Mr. Trickelbank, having a heated discussion. Or, rather, Harry was standing there while Mr. Trickelbank spat at him in loud whispers. Other guests were beginning to stare and poor Peter attempted to politely and quietly get Mr. Trickelbank's attention.

I hurried over. "Is something the matter?"

Mr. Trickelbank took one look at me, and curled his top lip in a sneer. "This is none of your affair, Miss Fox. I wish to make a complaint to the manager about this fellow." He flicked a finger at Harry. "But this idiot servant won't fetch him." He thrust his chin at Peter.

Peter's mouth snapped shut and his lips pursed. As a front-of-house clerk, he was used to dealing with frustrated guests when something went wrong, but this was a little different to the usual complaint. The subject of the complaint had been his superior a little over a month ago. Poor Peter wasn't quite sure what to do.

"He is neither an idiot nor a servant," Harry said, his jaw hardly moving. "Furthermore, Peter has told you that Mr. Hobart is not present. Kindly refrain from your tirade and simply answer my questions then we can both be on our way."

Mr. Trickelbank's fists closed at his sides. "I am not answering your bloody questions!"

A couple approaching the desk quickly diverted their course away from us, the gentleman's hand at the lady's lower back. With a flare of her nostrils, she glared over her shoulder at Mr. Trickelbank.

"Please keep your voice down, sir," I said.

"If you won't fetch the manager, then get Sir Ronald Bainbridge. This fellow ought to be thrown out, and if you are not prepared to do it, I'll see what Sir Ronald thinks."

The last thing we wanted was my uncle down here. Harry was treading a precarious line. I tried to catch his attention, but he wouldn't look at me. He simply gazed back at Mr. Trickelbank with a composure that inflamed Mr. Trickelbank even more. In my experience, men who couldn't control their tempers loathed men in complete control of theirs.

Peter cleared his throat to get our attention. "I believe Sir Ronald is also busy, sir. Would you like me to see if Mr. Floyd Bainbridge is in the hotel?"

Mr. Trickelbank scoffed.

"Perhaps I can help," I said. "As a representative of the Bainbridge family—"

"Anyone would be better than you," Mr. Trickelbank snarled. "Even that brainless cousin of yours."

"I can assure you, if you refer to either of Sir Ronald's children as brainless to his face, he won't be inclined to help you."

"And I am inclined to stay elsewhere in future. This hotel has too many nosy people."

"Perhaps you should," I said sweetly. "Perhaps you'd like to complete your stay *this* time at another hotel, seeing as the Mayfair is not to your liking."

The muscles in his face twitched with indignation at not being begged to stay. No doubt he'd expected me to apologize and do anything to keep him here. But the Mayfair didn't need an angry guest spraying his venomous accusations around the place. It was better to lose one customer who could never be pleased rather than risk more being infected by his vitriol.

"If it wasn't for the funeral tomorrow, I would," he said, his temper somewhat cooler. "But it's late in the day now, and I'll be leaving as soon as the funeral is over. I won't be spending a moment longer here than I have to."

"I think that's best." I smiled for the benefit of the other guests nearby.

Mr. Trickelbank strode off towards the lift. I wanted to talk to Peter to see if he was all right, but a guest commanded his attention. I moved away from the front desk with Harry.

"Nicely done," he said. "It's a pity your uncle and mine didn't witness that."

"Why?"

One corner of his mouth lifted. "No reason."

"What did you say that got him so incensed?"

"I simply asked him if he sent the blackmail letter to Warrington."

"Then what did you expect? He had to make a scene to avoid answering. Couldn't you have been subtler?"

He gave me an arched look. "I can be subtle, but in this instance I thought direct was the only way."

"I suppose you're right." I sighed. "Poor Peter. That was a terribly cruel thing for Mr. Trickelbank to say."

"You should talk to him. Lifting the spirits of the staff after a bruising encounter with a guest is an important skill." He tugged on the brim of his hat in farewell and walked off.

"Skill for what?" I called after him.

He turned and, walking backwards towards the door, gave me a smile and a shrug, then faced forward again. There was a spring in his step as the doorman opened the door for him. Harry didn't leave, however. He stopped to have a conversation with him.

I turned to Peter and watched as he completed his end-of-day tasks. He didn't look quite so harried now as he closed the reservations book and placed it in a drawer behind the counter, but he wasn't his usual happy self either. Harry was right. Peter needed cheering up.

"Sorry, Miss Fox," he said as he locked a metal box and placed it on a shelf under the counter. "I didn't have the authority to do anything."

"You do, Peter. In Mr. Hobart's absence, you are the most senior member of the front-of-house staff. Mr. Armitage is not a guest here, so you have every right to ask him to leave if he is upsetting someone."

"But then he wouldn't get the answers he needed to solve the case."

"I don't think Mr. Trickelbank was going to offer him answers."

He disappeared into the storeroom behind him and reappeared carrying his coat and hat. "If Mr. Armitage was in the wrong, why didn't you throw him out?" he asked.

"Because it was too late by the time I got there, and Mr. Trickelbank was rude to you when you had done nothing to deserve it. His rudeness was uncalled for, and I wasn't going to allow it to stain the Mayfair's reputation. Perhaps my uncle would have seen it differently, and wouldn't have liked how I spoke to a guest, but in his absence, I had to do what I thought was right. And I don't think behavior like that is acceptable from anyone, guest or not."

"I wish I had your bravery."

"Bravery comes with authority. If you remember you are the senior front-of-house staff member in Mr. Hobart's absence, then you *will* feel brave. Trust me on that."

I was taken aback somewhat to realize that I had felt enough like a member of the Bainbridge family, and therefore a part of the hotel, to speak to Mr. Trickelbank in that manner. It probably helped that I knew him to be the villain who'd tried to blackmail Mr. Warrington.

Peter rounded the counter and joined me. "When Mr. Armitage worked here, either he or Mr. Hobart were almost always in the foyer or within earshot. They both had a sense for when an issue was about to escalate and would intervene before it did. I don't know how they do that."

"Experience and a natural affinity for reading people. You have that affinity too, Peter. You're very good with the guests. They think you're wonderful."

He blushed. "That's very kind of you to say, Miss Fox."

"You also have experience. And if you remembered that you have the authority to make the sort of decision that I just made, you'd be an excellent assistant manager."

His jaw dropped and he stared at me.

I smiled. "Now, has Mr. Hobart truly left for the day? It seems a little early. Goliath hasn't started his night porter duties yet."

"He's in a meeting with Sir Ronald, Mrs. Short and Mr. Chapman." He glanced at the clock on the wall behind the front desk. "He assured me he'd be back by now. It's my mother's birthday and we have a surprise for her. We're having an early dinner then we're taking her to a show at the Hippodrome."

"How wonderful! Then you must go or you'll be late. I'll stay here until either Mr. Hobart returns or Goliath's shift starts."

He chewed his lower lip.

"Go, Peter. I can take care of things here for a few minutes."

He left, bypassing Harry who was still in conversation with the doorman. It was mostly quiet in the foyer, being the time of day after guests had returned from their outings and before they came down to dine or go to the theater or opera. I found it rather peaceful, and it gave me time to think.

Indeed, an idea struck me and I stopped in the middle of the foyer under the central chandelier and smiled to myself. Mr. Trickelbank's tirade hadn't been entirely pointless.

I needed to speak to Mr. Hobart, and was glad to see him emerge from the lift as it arrived on the ground floor. He did not emerge alone, however. He was followed by Mr. Chapman, Mrs. Short and Uncle Ronald. Not a single one of them smiled. But my uncle's fury was palpable, even from a distance.

Harry spotted them too. He excused himself, but instead of leaving the hotel, he headed towards me, directly into the path of my wrathful uncle.

$\mathcal{M}$y first instinct was to pretend I needed to be somewhere else, but my uncle bore down on us so quickly that he cut off all escape routes. My second instinct was to protect Harry. I would receive nothing more than a lecture, but Uncle Ronald might be angry enough to remind Harry of his thieving past, and thereby inform everyone within earshot. So far, the reason for Harry's dismissal from the hotel had been kept quiet, and I wanted to keep it that way for his sake.

I stepped in front of Harry, but Harry immediately moved out of my shadow and intercepted my uncle.

"If this is about Trickelbank, then the fault is entirely mine," he said. "He's trying to blackmail my client, and I wanted to gain a confession from him. He became irate and Cleo stepped in to calm the situation. She did everything she could, but he was having none of it. She had no choice but to ask him to leave."

At the mention of my first name, something flashed in Uncle Ronald's eyes and his lips thinned. I suspected he was too angry to hear the rest of Harry's words. "Get out of my hotel," he snarled.

"Not until you assure me you won't blame her. Trickel-bank is—"

"I said get out. Don't come back here and don't speak to

my niece again. I know what you're trying to do, and she's far too good for the likes of you."

Something exploded inside me. It took a great deal for me to anger, but in that moment, I was so furious I couldn't form words. I could barely manage to think over the pounding of the blood in my veins.

Beside me, Harry stiffened. Perhaps he was too angry to speak too, because he remained silent, although the tension emanating from him thickened the air.

Guests pretended not to notice us as they passed. Mrs. Short had not remained to hear the confrontation, but Mr. Chapman hovered at a nearby vase as he pretended to re-arrange the flowers. He would be relishing seeing me get into trouble.

Beside me, Harry's intake of breath was loud in the silence. Mr. Hobart shook his head at his nephew and whatever Harry had been going to say was left unspoken.

If he was forced into surrender, then it was up to me to go into battle. "You don't have a say in who I keep as friends, Uncle." My voice shook and didn't sound like my own.

He bared his teeth. "I do have a say if you want to stay here, under *my* roof, receiving an allowance from *me*."

My heart jumped into my throat and my skin suddenly felt cold, clammy. To say that in front of others was cruel. "Guests are watching. If you wish to continue this conversation further, I suggest we do it elsewhere."

"My office. Now." He did not move, however, but glared at Harry. "And you must go."

"I'm not leaving until I have your assurance that you won't blame Cleo for what happened with Trickelbank."

My uncle took a step towards him.

I quickly moved between them. "Harry, please, I can handle this."

I didn't expect to reach him through the icy wall of his fury but he blinked at me and some of the ice melted. "If you're sure."

"I'm sure."

He gave a single nod and walked off.

I walked off too, heading in the opposite direction, my skirts snapping at my heels. I bunched them into my fists so I wouldn't trip over the hem as I raced up the stairs. It wasn't so much anger that fueled me now, but humiliation. Uncle Ronald had firmly reminded me of my place, and he'd made sure others knew too.

If he'd known how contrary I could truly be, he would never have tried to dictate to me. I was more determined than ever that I should keep the friends I'd made.

His office door was unlocked and I entered. I paced in front of the desk, too agitated to sit or to be still. When he finally arrived, he did not close the door. He didn't even enter.

"I don't think there's any more to say to one another," he said. He was calmer now, that initial anger having dissolved with the exertion of climbing four flights of stairs.

"I agree, there is very little to say. You've made your position clear. I'll pack my things and leave in the morning."

He scoffed. "Don't act the hysterical female, Cleo. You're better than that. No one wants you to leave, least of all me."

"You have made it impossible for me to stay. If the choice is to keep my friends or to be at the mercy of your whims then it's an easy decision. I'll leave in the morning. Kindly stop your allowance payments from tomorrow. I don't want to owe you anything."

"You don't *owe* me; I am your uncle."

I could think of so many things to say to that, but all of them were hurtful and somehow, despite the fog of anger returning again, I knew I'd regret saying them in the morning. I merely shook my head and approached the door to leave.

But he blocked the exit. "I am not asking you to stop having friends, merely choose them more wisely. That boy is—"

"He is not a *boy*. He is my friend and I will continue to see him when I feel like it."

"Friend? Ha! Don't be so naïve, Cleo. He wants one thing from you—to use you to shackle himself to this family and gain all the benefits that come with our name for himself."

"Do you honestly think so little of me that you believe I don't know when a man is trying to seduce me for his own gain?"

His features softened and the look he gave me was one of sympathy. I was taken aback by it. "You forget how well I know him, Cleo. He was a lad when he came here. He grew up in this hotel. The fact is, I know him better than you. He has a silver tongue and a way with women. To say anything more would be beneath both of us."

"I am not like other women, and Harry and I are merely friends."

"If you think he'll be satisfied with that, you're more naïve than I thought."

I threw my hands in the air. "Why wouldn't he be satisfied with that? Why would he want to marry me if he is after a woman with a fortune? As you just informed everyone within earshot, I am poor. Everything I have was given to me out of charity." Tears burned my eyes and clogged my throat. I hated that I was close to breaking down. He would see my tears as weakness, and not the angry tears they were.

"Not charity," he said gently.

I scoffed. "Obligation, then."

"Nor that."

"Move aside, please."

He did but caught my elbow as I passed him. "I spoke out of turn earlier. Don't move out of the hotel, Cleo. Your aunt will never forgive me. Your cousins, too. Please stay."

I pulled free and stormed off along the corridor. Tears streamed down my cheeks, blurring my vision, and I fumbled with the key as I unlocked the door to my suite. Once inside, I strode into the bedroom and threw myself on the bed. The pillow muffled my shout of frustration.

Later, after a warm bath and a large glass of sherry, I felt somewhat calmer. My head cleared and I was able to think without emotions getting in the way.

My uncle had not apologized. Nor had he given in and agreed to allow me to be friends with Harry. What he had done was beg me to stay.

I would stay, but not because of him. I would stay for my aunt and my cousins, and for me. Where would I go, anyway?

* * *

THE FOLLOWING MORNING, after stewing over the confrontation with my uncle for much of the night, I opened the door to an excited Harmony holding my breakfast tray.

"I have news," she said, moving past me into the sitting room.

I padded after her in my slippers, yawning.

She placed the tray on the table and frowned at me. "Don't you want to know what it is?"

"Of course. What happened?"

Her frown deepened. "Are you all right?"

It would seem she hadn't heard about the confrontation. "I'm fine. I couldn't sleep. The case kept me awake. Tell me your news."

"It's Mr. Trickelbank."

I groaned. "What has he said now?"

"Nothing. He left."

"Left for the funeral already?" I glanced at the clock on the mantel, suddenly worried it was later than I thought. But it was only eight.

"No, he left the hotel. He ran off in the middle of the night, taking his luggage with him."

"Without paying for his stay?"

She nodded as she poured coffee into the cups. "Goliath saw him and tried to stop him, but Mr. Trickelbank jumped into a waiting cab and fled. He must have organized it beforehand with the driver."

"How extraordinary," I said as I sat.

"Sir Ronald is furious. He says he's going to call the police on him, so Goliath told me. Mr. Trickelbank won't be hard to find. Even if he gave a false address when he checked in, Mr. Warrington will know where he lives."

"Unless Mr. Trickelbank has gone into hiding, which he may well do if he's guilty of murder."

Her mouth formed an O. "Do you think he killed his sister?"

I accepted the cup from her and put it to my lips. "He's high on our suspect list. If he felt wronged for not getting his inheritance, then he might have done it. Perhaps not deliberately, but accidentally, out of anger."

She nodded. "People often do things they regret in the heat of the moment."

"And things they say," I added wryly.

She narrowed her gaze at me. "Are you sure you're all right, Cleo?" she asked, slipping into the familiarity of my given name now that we were alone.

I smiled. "Perfectly. Now, I have a funeral to attend today. Help me choose something to wear."

* * *

I CHECKED the notices in the newspaper for the time and place of Mrs. Warrington's funeral, then went in search of Mr. Hobart. I met him as he was about to leave his office behind Mrs. Short and Mr. Chapman. The housekeeper and steward returned to their own offices, while Mr. Hobart invited me inside.

"I hoped to see you this morning," he said as he closed the door behind us. "Harry was worried about you. He thought you might move out of the hotel, and he would be devastated if you had done so because of him."

I hadn't thought of that. It wasn't fair that Harry should feel guilty if I moved out, but I knew he would. If the positions were reversed, I would too. "I'm not leaving. Not today, anyway. About that encounter...I'm sorry you had to witness it."

He signaled for me to sit. "You don't have to apologize. It was a difficult situation and you handled it well. I'm sure Sir Ronald will come to see it that way. His anger is quick to ignite, but just as quick to extinguish."

"Indeed. But he was unfair to Harry."

He sighed. "He has certainly made up his mind about him and won't change it."

"Is Harry all right?"

"Harry is Harry."

I wasn't sure what that meant and was about to ask when he added, "He's fine. His temper should have cooled by now, although as I said, he was worried about you."

"He shouldn't be."

"He was...taken by surprise."

I frowned. "In what way?"

"I'll let him explain." He clasped his hands on the desk and leaned forward. "That is, if you are going to see him again."

"Of course."

"Is that wise?"

"Wisdom has nothing to do with it. It's about what is right and wrong, and seeing my friend is right. At least, it is to me."

The smile he gave me was both sympathetic and pleased. "Harry might see it differently."

"I hope this doesn't affect your relationship with my uncle."

"We have a professional working relationship. That won't need to change. This is a family matter, between you and him. Speaking of work, I suppose it's out of the question for you to step into the role of assistant manager now, considering the way things are."

I blinked rapidly. "Me? Assistant manager? What makes you think it was a consideration?"

"Harry told me how well you handled Trickelbank yesterday, and how you stood up for Peter and the hotel. He thought you'd make an excellent assistant manager. But your uncle wouldn't stand for it. Before last night, I thought he might consider it, but now I don't think it's worth bringing up. For the sake of peace, you understand."

Despite everything, I couldn't help chuckling. "I don't want to be assistant manager."

"Harry thinks you'd be excellent. And so do I. It's a shame your uncle won't allow a family member to take a more active role."

"A *female* family member." I shook my head. "Thank you for your confidence in me, but I'm not interested. Anyway, there is another candidate you should consider."

"Is this about Peter again?"

"Don't dismiss him yet, Mr. Hobart. I think he'd be very good."

"I'll think about it." He checked his pocket watch and rose. "I must go. I have a meeting."

We approached the door together, only for it to open from

the other side. My uncle entered. "There you are, Cleo. I've been looking for you." He was cheerful today, but it sounded forced, as if he were trying too hard. He turned to Mr. Hobart and Mr. Hobart offered us the use of his office for privacy.

My uncle waited for him to leave before turning to me. "I wanted to apologize. I should have taken your side and not his."

I felt as though we were reading a different book. "Pardon?"

"Trickelbank. He fled overnight without paying. I should have trusted your instincts yesterday and not accepted his version of events." He placed his hands at his back and stood to attention like a soldier on parade. "I shouldn't have taken the word of a guest over that of family, and I want you to know I'm sorry."

I opened my mouth to remind him that our disagreement wasn't about Mr. Trickelbank, but about my friendships, and Harry in particular. But perhaps it was wise not to. Perhaps his apology was all-encompassing, but he couldn't bring himself to say it.

Part of me didn't want to let him off the hook so easily. But that was being petulant, not smart. In truth, my uncle probably wasn't capable of offering a full apology. His pride wouldn't let him.

And I had more sense than to allow this to come between me and the only family I had. While it didn't change my ultimate goal to save up enough to move out of the hotel, I could bide my time until I was ready and not cut off my nose to spite my face.

"Thank you for saying so," I said.

He cleared his throat. "There's no need for your aunt or cousins to know about our little disagreement. I've asked Hobart not to mention it to anyone."

"If that's what you want."

"About you leaving… I hope I made it clear that I don't want you to go. You're family and Bainbridges must stand together."

I opened the door. "I'm a Fox. But I will stay. Now, if you'll excuse me, I have a funeral to go to."

* * *

CHRIST CHURCH in Kensington was full by the time I arrived. I sat near the back with the Warringtons' servants and watched the mourners, looking for any gentlemen who matched the description of Xavier. There were a number of people crammed into the small church and being seated near the back made it difficult to see their faces until it was time to leave. Even then, I couldn't see any gentlemen who looked distraught. Except for Mr. Henderson the butler. As her coffin was carried out, he burst into tears.

Mr. Warrington followed close behind the coffin, looking somber but not upset. Behind him came Mr. Drummond, then the other mourners followed. Mr. Trickelbank was notable by his absence.

I made sure to be one of the last to leave and checked the faces of each of the men as they passed me up the aisle. While all were grave, only one appeared to be on the verge of breaking down. He also happened to have reddish-blond hair and thick sideburns, and he wasn't wearing gloves. The small brown birthmark on the back of his hand was the confirmation I needed.

"Xavier," I said quietly as he passed.

He looked up and blinked watery eyes at me. Realizing he didn't know me, and thinking he'd misheard, he continued on the slow procession behind the coffin.

I joined the line of mourners at the end. Harry stepped in beside me. I'd noticed him earlier, seated in the pew in front of me and on the other side, and wasn't surprised to see him in the church. He seemed surprised to see me, however.

"What are you doing here?" he whispered.

"Investigating. I think I've found the lover." I nodded at the man a few paces ahead, dressed in a dark gray coat and black hat.

"You shouldn't have come. Not after your uncle's threats. If he makes you leave the hotel because of me…"

"Don't worry, he asked me to stay this morning. Come on, we have to speak to Xavier."

We emerged from the church into weak sunshine and

scanned the faces of the mourners for the gentleman. I couldn't see him. "He's gone."

"There he is." From his higher vantage point, Harry could see more clearly.

I followed him down the stone steps and hurried in his wake as he caught up to the man named Xavier. I suddenly wished I'd thought more about what to do next. I'd been so intent on simply finding him that I didn't know what to say. Introduce ourselves and tell him we were investigating Mrs. Warrington's murder? Or make something up?

Harry had no such difficulty making a decision. When Xavier stopped upon being hailed, Harry immediately slipped into a smooth, friendly tone designed to win our quarry over. He introduced us and said we were attempting to solve the murder of Mrs. Warrington.

"We don't believe a vagrant with a bad arm could have climbed through the first floor window," he finished.

The man named Xavier looked past Harry to me. I smiled sympathetically. I liked to think it was the icing on the cake that won him over although it was likely more to do with his desire to find the killer. Still, he was wary.

"Who is paying you?"

"No one has paid us," Harry said. While it wasn't a lie, it wasn't the entire truth either. Mr. Warrington hadn't paid us *yet*. Whether it was right to let Xavier think we were amateur detectives investigating in our spare time was debatable. "Let me begin by saying we're deeply sorry for your loss. We know Mrs. Warrington was important to you."

Xavier swallowed heavily and his gaze became unfocused. "Thank you."

"Are you up to answering questions?" Harry asked.

"I suppose, but I don't see how I can help you." He was softly spoken, but that could have been his grief making it difficult for him to speak. "I didn't know there was any doubt about the vagrant. Why haven't the police come to ask me questions?"

"Because they're not looking elsewhere."

"They also don't know of your existence," I added.

"Then how do you?"

I wasn't willing to admit that I'd seen the photographs of he and Mrs. Warrington so I didn't answer at all.

"When was the last time you saw Isobel Warrington?" Harry asked.

"The day before she died. We were supposed to meet up on the night of her death, but..." He swallowed. "She never arrived."

"What time should your meeting have taken place?" I asked.

"Ten."

"And how far away do you live?"

"A fifteen minute walk."

I exchanged glances with Harry. If Mrs. Warrington only lived fifteen minutes away from her lover, she should have left by nine forty-five. But she was still in the house at ten when she ordered tea. Had she changed her mind? Had the argument with her husband earlier given her reason to change it?

"How long were you two together?" Harry asked.

"Almost six years."

"Did her husband know?"

"He knew *of* me, but not my name or anything to identify me. According to Isobel, he didn't want to know. It was probably best that way, for everyone."

"Did you know he wanted to divorce her?" I asked.

His mouth dropped open. "My god. No, I didn't. She didn't tell me."

"She only found out on the morning of her death. If you didn't see her that day, or had no communication from her—"

"I did. I received a brief message from her in the late afternoon, asking if she could see me that night."

"What did it say?"

He shrugged. "Just that she needed to speak to me and she was worried. It must have been because she learned he wanted to divorce her. At the time, I thought it was about her half-brother. She was going to meet him that afternoon and hadn't been looking forward to it."

"There was nothing in the note about how the meeting went?"

He shook his head. "I can't believe Warrington wanted to divorce her," he said quietly. "They had an agreement."

"What sort of agreement?" Harry asked.

Xavier glanced towards the small crowd lingering near the church door. "Their marriage has never been consummated because he...isn't interested."

"We know Mr. Drummond is more than just a friend," I added. "Is that what you're referring to?"

He inclined his head in a nod. "That's why I never felt any guilt over being with Isobel. Why couldn't we be together when it was all right by her husband? No one was harmed by our arrangement. Indeed, everyone was happy. Or so I thought. Now you're telling me he wanted a divorce. I don't understand. Why now, after all this time? Why attract attention to himself and risk exposing his proclivities?"

It was a very good question.

"You must have been jealous of Warrington," Harry said.

"A little, in the beginning. I would have liked to marry Isobel in those days, but I came to accept the way things were. As I said, the arrangement suited everyone and that includes me. I quite like the bachelor's life, you see." His thumb absently stroked the birthmark on his other hand and his mouth drooped at the corners. "She was so full of life and spirit. I can't believe she's gone. I can't believe someone would want to kill her."

Neither Harry nor I informed him that we suspected Mr. Warrington was the intended target. If Xavier knew we suspected Isobel's death had been an accident, he might be less inclined to help because it would make him the prime suspect.

I glanced towards Mr. Warrington as he climbed into the carriage to transport him to the cemetery. Mr. Drummond followed, but not before he lifted his gaze and met mine. It wasn't clear from this distance if he knew that the man we spoke to was Mrs. Warrington's lover. The carriage drove off with the curtains wide open, which I thought was a little dangerous considering someone wanted Mr. Warrington dead. Perhaps he assumed no one would attack in broad daylight. I hoped he was right.

"Have you considered the possibility that the killer didn't come through the window?" Xavier suddenly asked.

"We're considering all possibilities," Harry said. "Is there something you'd like to tell us?"

"I...I don't know if it's relevant."

"Tell us anyway and we'll decide," I said.

Xavier's thumb continued its stroking as he took his time answering. "I went to the house once, last year. I had to give Isobel an urgent message so delivered it myself. I spoke to the butler, and he must have realized who I was. He was rude to me. Quite nasty, in fact. He warned me off, telling me he'd make my life difficult if I didn't stop my harassment of his mistress. That was the word he used—harassment. There was no reasoning with him. It was obvious to me that he was jealous of our relationship, and that he was in love with her."

"Are you suggesting he killed the woman he loved so no one else could have her?" Harry asked. "It seems a little extreme."

Xavier shrugged. "One reads about these things happening in the newspapers. Or perhaps it was an accident and the butler didn't mean to kill her."

It was so close to the truth that I wondered if he'd reached the same conclusion as us, that *Mr.* Warrington was the intended target.

Harry thanked Xavier and asked for an address where we could find him if we had further questions. The smile he gave us upon departing was a sad one.

"What do you think?" I asked as we walked off in the other direction.

"I think he's devastated over the loss of his lover," Harry said. "But that doesn't mean he didn't kill her, accidentally mistaking her for Warrington."

"True. I found it interesting that he tried to implicate Mr. Henderson."

"Very interesting indeed. But of all our suspects, the butler knew it was Mrs. Warrington in that chair, not her husband. Our theory that he was the intended victim doesn't hold water if Henderson is guilty."

We walked on in silence. The late morning sunshine tried valiantly to stay out, but the clouds soon closed in and smothered it. The air chilled and a brisk wind picked up. Harry suggested we attempt to speak to the butler to get his version of the confrontation between he and Xavier a year ago. I agreed and we changed our course, heading towards the townhouse. The servants had not followed the carriages going to the cemetery but had headed off on foot in the direction of the Kensington residence.

"You have a theory?" Harry asked.

I looked up at him. "Why do you think that?"

"Your brows draw together when you're lost in thought and a small dent appears between them."

I pressed a finger to my forehead to iron out the dent. "Do we agree that the timing of the murder has something to do with the divorce?"

"I think so, yes. It's too much of a coincidence for Mrs. Warrington to learn about the divorce on the day someone tries to kill her husband, only to accidentally murder her instead."

"So the murderer is someone who believes being a widow is better for her than being a divorcee. They are trying to save her reputation, which would be ruined after a divorce."

"There are only two people who love her enough to commit murder for her. Xavier and Henderson."

"Xavier is pointing the finger at Henderson," Harry said, "and Henderson knew his master was out. So it *must* be Xavier."

I agreed. "We'll see what we can learn from Mr. Henderson about that confrontation."

* * *

OUR VISIT to the Warrington house was a waste of time. Mr. Henderson slammed the door in our faces and refused to reopen it, despite our continued knocking. Our questions would have to wait for a time when Mr. Warrington was home and could order his butler to speak to us.

We caught an omnibus back to Harry's office so we could discuss the investigation further without being overheard. He was quiet on the journey, but I got the distinct feeling he wanted to speak.

"Is something the matter?" I asked, as we walked from the omnibus stop to his office.

He lifted a shoulder in a shrug and shook his head.

I ought to leave it there, but my interest was piqued and I couldn't. "Is it something to do with the case or the confrontation I had with my uncle?"

He waved to Luigi through the window of the café and removed the key to the door from his pocket. He inserted the key into the lock and frowned.

The door wasn't locked.

He put up a hand to order me to stay back then entered. He crept up the stairs and paused on the landing. I followed, taking pains to be as quiet as possible, and withdrew the small knife I kept in my bag. Harry wasn't armed. His gun was inside the office.

I pressed the knife into the palm of his hand and received a scowl in return. He jerked his head, ordering me back down the stairs. I complied, but only for three steps.

He gently turned the office door-handle then, drawing a deep breath, shoved it open.

He stopped in the doorway and swore loudly.

I pushed past him and stopped too. A gasp caught in my throat.

We had a visitor. An unwilling one going by the way he was tied to the chair with a cloth covering his mouth.

CHAPTER 12

"Sorry for bringing him here, but I didn't know what to do with him, once I caught him." Victor lounged in the brown leather armchair, dressed in street clothes, not his cook's uniform.

There was no look of triumph in his eyes, no sign of satisfaction that he'd managed to tie Bob Ricketts up and bring him here for questioning, all on his own. He looked like he'd just come in from the market and dumped his purchases on the chair at the desk in the hope someone else would unpack them.

He stretched out his legs and crossed his arms over his chest. "He wouldn't speak to me, but maybe you'll have better luck, Armitage."

"How did you manage to get him in here without being seen?" I asked.

"I can't give away all my secrets. I'm already teaching you how to pick locks."

Harry's gaze slid from Victor to me.

I approached Ricketts and tugged the cloth covering his mouth down to his chin. He snarled and went to bite my hand, but I jerked it back just in time.

Harry stepped forward. "Try that again and you'll leave here looking even uglier than when you came in."

Ricketts spat on the floor near Harry's feet.

"We just have some questions to ask you," I said. "Answer them truthfully and we'll let you go."

"And if I don't?" he snarled in a Cockney accent. "You going to keep me 'ere forever?"

"I'll tell the local bobbies where I found you," Victor said from the armchair. "I reckon they'd be interested in your lair."

Ricketts' top lip curled in a sneer. "Dog. If I ever find you—"

"You won't." Victor's cockiness remained, despite the fierce glare Ricketts fired back at him.

Ricketts might not be able to find Victor, but he could come here and find Harry. If we didn't want him to retaliate, we had to be smarter in our strategy.

I started to untie the rope binding his hands together behind the chair but Harry stayed my arm.

"I'll do it. Go and stand near Victor."

I relinquished my position and Harry continued untying the rope. The moment he was free, Ricketts leapt up and swung a fist at Harry. If it had connected, Harry could have lost a tooth, but he was ready for it and darted out of the way. Ricketts might be built like a bear, but Harry was quicker and smarter. The punch had thrown Ricketts off balance, and Harry swooped in and wrapped his arm around Ricketts' throat. Given their positions and the awkward angle of Ricketts' bent body, his attempts to free himself were in vain.

"You don't seem to understand," Harry said in a calm voice. "This is a business transaction that benefits both you and us. I will pay you for answers and we will not tell the police where to find you. *But* you must answer honestly and you must leave peacefully. Understood?"

Veins bulged across Ricketts' face, the shade of which ran the spectrum from pink to red to purple. Harry could choke him to death if he didn't release him soon.

Ricketts managed to whisper an agreement and Harry let him go. Ricketts doubled over, his hands on his knees, coughing and spluttering.

Beside me, Victor had got to his feet the moment Ricketts was free. He remained standing, his hand resting at his hip beneath his coat where his knife belt was strapped.

Harry moved the chair with his foot. "Take a seat."

Ricketts sat, but no one else did.

Harry removed a gold sovereign from his pocket and placed it on the desk. "You'll get more if I believe your answers."

Ricketts pretended to ignore the money, but by not looking at it, it was obvious he desperately wanted it.

"Why did Mrs. Parker pay you yesterday?"

Whatever question Ricketts had expected, it wasn't that. "What makes you think she paid me?"

"We saw you."

The big man's brow plunged as he tried to recall seeing us. But he was clearly as unobservant as he was subtle and couldn't remember passing us on the street. "She asked me to do some business for her."

"What sort of business?"

He looked pointedly at the coin.

Harry placed another on top of the first.

"Will you keep my name out of it?" Ricketts asked.

Harry nodded.

Ricketts considered this then said, "She paid me to rough up a bloke for her. I don't know who. She didn't give me his name, just told me where to find him."

"Did she ask you to kill him?" Harry asked.

"No!" Ricketts rubbed his paw over the back of his neck. "She just told me to scare him into not attending parliament on the day some new law was going to be discussed. So I followed him into a lane near his Mayfair house and we had words."

I frowned. "Mayfair?"

"That's what I said. Mayfair, in a lane, last night."

"Last night?"

"Are you deaf or just stupid? I did the job on that politician last night, in Mayfair, just like she wanted. Roughed him up real good, too. It even made the papers." He grinned, revealing a mouth like a chessboard with broken or missing teeth.

This man sickened me. He might not be our murderer, but he was revolting nevertheless.

"What about Tuesday night?" Harry asked. "Did you work for Mrs. Parker that night too?"

"I didn't work for no one on Tuesday night. I was at The Three Sails down by the docks. Why? What's Tuesday night got to do with anything? The job she paid me for was last night, Thursday." We must have given him blank looks, because he felt the need to clarify. "I always get payment in advance. The job you saw her pay me for yesterday was to be done last night, not Tuesday and not Wednesday."

Harry sat on the edge of the desk, his hands pressing on the surface on either side of him. He looked as deflated as I felt. Mrs. Parker hadn't hired Ricketts to kill Mr. Warrington in the drawing room on Tuesday or the lane on Wednesday. She could be struck off our suspect list.

Unless she did it herself. Perhaps murder was a job Mrs. Parker felt required her personal attention since Ricketts clearly couldn't be trusted to keep his mouth shut. And Mr. Warrington claimed a *woman* attacked him in the lane. If Mrs. Parker was his attacker, it stood to reason she was also the one who tried to murder him on Tuesday night, but unfortunately mistook Mrs. Warrington for him.

Harry jerked his head at the door. "Get out."

"I want more."

Harry placed another coin with the other two, but this time it was a mere sixpence.

Ricketts screwed up his face. "That all?"

"That's what your information is worth to us."

Victor opened the door and stood by it. Ricketts made a point of towering over him as he passed, making sure Victor noticed the difference in their sizes. Victor merely watched him with mild amusement.

Ricketts tugged on his forelock. He had no hat or cap. Perhaps he lost it in the scuffle with Victor. "Pleasure doing business with you. If you ever need a businessman like me, let me know. I can be useful."

Victor closed the door on him. "He's slow and tires easily," he said. "He might fit through a window, but I don't reckon he could climb up pipes to the first floor."

Harry and I both agreed. Bob Ricketts hadn't killed Mrs. Warrington, but Mrs. Parker was still a suspect.

How to find evidence against her? Or against anyone, for that matter?

Our investigation was once again at a standstill.

Victor left, and I opened my bag to retrieve a pencil and notebook to make notes on our suspects. I hoped something would jump out at me when I saw their details in writing, something I hadn't realized earlier.

"Do you pay them?" Harry asked.

It took me a moment to realize he was talking about Victor, Harmony and the others. "Not as much as I'd like, although I don't think they do it for the money. Anyway, I've only had the one murder case where I've been paid. Mr. Warrington has only paid me for the investigation into his wife's lover, and that wasn't much."

He sat in the chair behind the desk and passed the small knife I'd given him back to me. He hadn't needed it. "What's Victor's background?"

"I'm not entirely sure. Thief? Swindler?" I rummaged in the bottom of my bag for the pencil, but couldn't find it.

"You should be more careful about who you trust."

"You're a thief, and I trust you."

He flinched and I felt sick at how casually I'd tossed out the barb. "I'm sorry, that was awful of me. I didn't mean it."

"You didn't mean to say you trust me?"

I tilted my head to the side and regarded him. It was difficult to determine if he was poking fun at me or not. His eyes were flat and his handsome features set, but I swear his lips twitched at one point. "Of course I trust you. What I meant to say was that I trust Victor, too. He's been helpful in my investigations."

"The question is, why? If you're not paying him, what is he getting from it?"

"Something interesting to do?"

"You think dragging hardened thugs around London is interesting?"

"It's certainly more challenging than working in the hotel kitchen, even when a feud is brewing between the two factions of cooks. Anyway, perhaps he's simply doing it to please Harmony. There's something going on between those two, I'm sure of it." I continued rummaging in the bottom of my bag and finally found the pencil.

I pulled it out, managing to grab hold of a loose piece of paper too. I couldn't remember putting it there and unfolded it. It was the list of places Mrs. Warrington had visited in the days before her death, given to me by Mr. Henderson on his employer's orders.

I skimmed the list of names and addresses. They were mostly shops and the private homes of women who must be her friends. Except one. A doctor in Earl's Court.

"Mrs. Warrington had a medical appointment last Monday, the day before she was murdered." I handed Harry the list. "Shall we see what it was about?"

"We have no other leads at this point." He stood and handed the list back. "Do you want to go now?"

"I have nothing better to do this afternoon."

"What about your uncle? Won't he be checking up on your movements today?"

I sighed. "Probably."

"Then go back to the hotel," he said gently. "I'll visit the doctor alone."

The very notion of not following the investigation to the end was disagreeable and I told him so.

"Then what will you tell your uncle when he asks where you've been all day?" he asked.

"I'll say I went to the museum."

He opened the door for me. "And how long will that excuse last?"

"For as long as I need it to."

He caught my arm as I passed. "Cleo..." He released me and dragged his hand through his hair before putting on his hat. "You can't afford to antagonize him further. I had no idea about your situation—"

"My situation is none of your concern." I regretted my snippy tone when he flinched. I wasn't sure why I was angry at him. None of this was his fault. My face heated and I turned away. "Let me handle my uncle's moods. I've done a fine job so far and there's no reason to think I can't continue."

"A fine job? He berated you in front of the staff and guests." He locked the office door and followed me down the stairs to the ground floor. "Bainbridge must have been furious to make a scene in the foyer. It's not like him."

"He doesn't like being defied, and I defied him. It inflamed his temper further." I went to open the door, but he reached past me and put a hand to it, keeping it closed.

He stood close, his arm touching mine, his head dipped so he was more level with me although he still towered above me. I was never more aware of his height and his broad shoulders, or how handsome he was.

"Don't antagonize him, Cleo," he murmured. "The consequences aren't worth it."

I drew in a deep breath, drawing the pleasing scent of him into my lungs. "Let me be the judge of that."

He released the door and I opened it. He fell into step alongside me as we headed in the direction of the omnibus to Earl's Court. My awareness of him remained constant for the entire journey.

* * *

It wasn't easy to extract an answer from the doctor. He refused to tell us what ailed Mrs. Warrington, even after we explained we'd been hired by her husband to find her killer.

"I will speak to Mr. Warrington if he comes here in person," Dr. Fitzpatrick told us. "But I cannot speak to you. I have an ethical responsibility to my patient, deceased or not."

He sat across from us on the other side of the desk, his hands clasped over his protruding stomach. For a doctor, he wasn't the healthiest looking man, with florid cheeks and nose, and yellow teeth. He didn't seem unsympathetic to our plight. Indeed, he told us he'd been very upset when he read about Mrs. Warrington's murder in the newspapers. He'd only seen her the day before.

This hint of a sympathetic nature might work in our favor, if we played our cards right.

"You will have to speak to the police if they question you," Harry said. Frustration was making him desperate. Did he think his father would come here on our behalf? I wasn't so certain Detective Inspector Hobart would be willing to step into an investigation that wasn't assigned to him.

173

"If they come, I will." Dr. Fitzpatrick checked his watch but refrained from asking us to leave.

We had mere minutes to convince him. I sat forward and leveled my gaze with his. "The police won't come," I said. "The thing is, they believe they've caught their killer and are in the process of closing the investigation. We believe they have the wrong man, as does Mr. Warrington. Please, sir, help us give poor Mrs. Warrington justice. She didn't deserve to die so horribly. Her killer should be held accountable for taking her life."

His small wince was slight, but encouraging. I was getting through to him.

"Doesn't your ethical responsibility towards your patient include catching her killer?"

He shifted in the chair, making it creak under his weight, and shifted back again. He gave a single nod. "You're right, Miss Fox. The killer should be held accountable...for taking *two* lives."

I sucked in a breath. "She was with child?"

He nodded. "I informed her that day."

"How did she seem when you told her?"

"Not as thrilled as a woman usually is upon hearing that news. I assumed she was worried about the birth, as many women are, so I told her if she wished to return the next day with her husband, I would talk to them both, to reassure her, you see. She told me she would make an appointment in due course." He cleared his throat. "She left here looking somewhat dazed."

We thanked the doctor and exited the clinic. As soon as we set foot on the pavement, we turned to one another. I imagined my eyes were as bright with excitement as Harry's.

"It must be Xavier's child," I said, at the same time that Harry said, "The father isn't Warrington."

"The question is, who knew about it?" I asked. "If it were me, I'd tell the father first."

"It falls into place now. She told Xavier and he decides he's no longer content with their current arrangement. He wants to claim their child as his own, and to do that, he must marry Isobel. He can't wait for the divorce—it would take too long and it would also ruin her reputation, damaging their future together as well as that of the child."

"So he plans to murder Warrington, but kills Isobel instead after thinking she is her husband," I finished. "Dear lord, it's a tragedy of Shakespearean proportions. The poor man."

"That poor man is a murderer, Cleo."

"Perhaps. It's only a theory at this point. I've made the mistake in the past thinking I know the culprit only to find out that I don't."

He grunted in wry amusement. "So I recall. Very well, we won't assume anything. Not until we have proof. But I'm putting him at the top of our suspect list."

"As am I."

* * *

XAVIER HAD GIVEN his address as a flat in one of the handsome red-brick mansion blocks in Earl's Court Square, popular with well-heeled bachelors, according to Harry. It was furnished with old, thick-legged chairs and tables that were more suited to a smoking room than sitting room. There was a small cluster of framed photographs on top of a cabinet. One of them was of Mrs. Warrington standing next to a seated Xavier, her hand on his shoulder in a touching gesture of unity.

Xavier welcomed us without reservation and his manner was courteous. He told us he worked for a financial company in the city, but had taken the entire day off to mourn Mrs. Warrington. He looked as miserable as he had this morning at church.

Harry and I had decided to speak to Xavier as if he were helping us, and not a suspect. We agreed that we'd get more answers that way. If he knew we suspected him, he might close up and tell us nothing.

"We have just come from the practice of Dr. Fitzpatrick," I said gently.

Xavier's eyes remained a little unfocused, as if he were only half listening. If the name meant anything to him, he was a very good actor.

"He told us that Isobel was expecting," I finished.

Slowly, as if my words sank into him like drips of water, he lifted his gaze to mine. His face paled, his lips parted but it took several heartbeats for him to speak. "My god. Are...are you sure?"

I nodded. "Do you think it was yours?"

"Y-yes. Of course. She was faithful to me and I to her."

"You didn't know?" Harry asked.

"No."

"She found out on Monday and died on Tuesday night. Why wouldn't she have told you as soon as she knew?"

Xavier sat back and rubbed his fisted hands along his thighs, up and down, up and down. "I don't know." He continued to rub, his gaze focused on the floor.

Harry and I exchanged glances, neither of us quite sure what to say next.

Xavier suddenly stopped rubbing and looked up. "She would have told Warrington."

"Before informing you?" Harry asked.

He nodded eagerly. "She would have tried convincing him to raise the child as his own. She would have seen it as the best way, not just for her but for the baby. After all, Warrington has a solid reputation and I am merely a clerk." The more he warmed to his theory, the more animated he became, his eyes growing wider and wilder. I worried he might be going mad. "Perhaps that's why he wanted a divorce now, after all these years of a mutually beneficial arrangement. Because he didn't want to raise another man's baby."

Harry merely nodded, and I did too. Neither of us wanted to agitate Xavier any more than he was. If he were going mad, we didn't want to say something to push him over the edge.

"I know what you're thinking," Xavier went on. "You think if I discovered another man was going to raise my child, I would get angry and kill her. But I didn't do it. I swear to you, I didn't. I loved her, and I would welcome our child, even if she insisted another man was acknowledged as the father."

"We believe you," I said to placate him. "But it begs the question, who did kill her?"

"My money is still on the butler, out of jealousy. He seems like the type to go to such an extreme."

We thanked him and left. It was growing late and we were both hungry, having forgotten to stop for lunch. It also looked like it would rain. Harry suggested we discuss the new evidence at a teashop and we found a quaint one with pretty pink and green floral curtains and matching tablecloths. Inside there were a few gentlemen accompanying their wives or mothers, so Harry didn't feel too out of place. It was also perfectly acceptable for an unwed woman and man to be seen together in such a respectable establishment.

We ordered tea and sandwiches, and as soon as the waitress was out of earshot, we both leaned forward a little. Harry allowed me to speak first.

"Do you think Xavier was telling the truth and knew nothing about the baby?"

"It's hard to say," he said. "He was acting oddly, but that could be because it was the first he'd learned of the pregnancy. Or it could be because he knows we suspect him."

"Let's assume he was telling the truth and hadn't known. And let's assume he's right and Isobel did tell her husband. It explains the divorce proceedings *if* she confided her suspicions about her condition before the doctor confirmed it. Warrington wanted to hire you several days before the murder took place, after all."

"I'm not sure. If I were him, I might want a child, even if it weren't my own."

I shook my head. "Mr. Trickelbank once told me that the Warringtons didn't want children. Heirs, he called them. To me that means *Mr.* Warrington never wanted a child. Perhaps Isobel did but had resigned herself to never having any. But then she finds herself with child and decides she does want it, and she wants her husband to claim it as his. He refuses and decides to divorce her."

"She only learns about the divorce on the morning of her death, when her maid overhears you talking to Henderson about it," he noted.

"The first opportunity she has to talk to Mr. Warrington about the divorce is that night," I went on. "That's the argument the servants overheard at nine. If faced with ruination from a divorce, and uncertain if her lover would marry her afterwards, she would fight back to save herself. That's what I'd do."

"And how would you fight back?"

"I would use the best weapon in my arsenal—damning information. Warrington has a very big secret that if the world discovered, he would be more than ruined. He could find himself in prison, like Oscar Wilde. He would lose his reputation, his friends and be demoted by his party if not ousted altogether. He would be publicly shamed. It would be utterly devastating."

He nodded along as I spoke, warming to my theory. "So that night, when they argued, she threatened to expose him if he continued with divorce proceedings."

We paused and sat back as our tea was delivered in a silver teapot and dainty china cups were placed in front of us. I picked up a cucumber sandwich as the waitress poured our tea.

She flashed a small smile at Harry as she filled his cup. "I hope everything is to your liking, sir."

He hadn't been watching her, but now looked up and returned her smile. "Thank you."

"I'll be over there if you need anything else." She sauntered off, hips swaying. Unfortunately for her, it was a wasted effort as Harry was more interested in the food.

I pressed my lips together to suppress my smile.

"What's so amusing?" he asked.

I didn't think he could be so oblivious to the waitress's flirtations, but perhaps he was so used to it, he no longer bothered to flirt back unless he was genuinely interested.

My uncle's words echoed in my head—*he has a silver tongue and a way with women.* He could have been referring to something as innocent as flirting. Or he could have meant something more.

I shook my head to dismiss the thought. It was none of my business.

"The problem is," I said, "that all of this leads me to question everything we've assumed so far. If Mr. Warrington told her he wanted nothing to do with the baby, and she threatened to tell the world his secret, then the next logical step is for him to stop her."

"By killing her," Harry said quietly. "You're right. It throws into doubt everything we've assumed so far. It means he wasn't the intended victim that night. *She* was."

"And the killer was her own husband," I finished. "Except he can't be. He was elsewhere at the time."

CHAPTER 13

*H*arry and I nibbled on sandwiches as we thought through the implications of our theory. It was a lot of information take in, and there was much to consider. But I kept coming back to one conclusion—that Mr. Warrington wanted to ensure his wife never told anyone his secret, and the best way to silence her forever was to murder her.

"He did it," I said. "He must have. It feels right to me. But how? He has an alibi. He was at his club when it happened."

"We should check," Harry said. "So far we only have his word for it. I'll go there after leaving here and ask the manager." He tapped his finger on the side of the teacup, his brow furrowed. "If Warrington did it, he must have faked the stabbing in the lane."

I nodded. "When we told him we assumed *he* was the intended victim, he realized our theory benefited him. To make it seem like we were on the right track, he stabbed himself in the hand then claimed it was a woman who attacked him. He knew a woman sent him the threatening letters, but he didn't know her name. Is that right?"

"So my father said." He removed his hat and ruffled his hair. "We helped him, Cleo. We helped him get away with it."

"Inadvertently. We can't blame ourselves. But we can fix it. Finish your tea and we'll go to the club."

"You're not coming. It's getting late and you need to

return to the hotel. Your uncle will be cross if you get in after dark."

I shot him a withering glare over the rim of my teacup. "I told you, don't worry about my uncle."

"Don't antagonize him, Cleo. I know him better than you, and I know how he likes everyone to do as *he* pleases."

I huffed a humorless laugh. "My uncle said the same thing, that he knows you better than I do. You two think alike, in some ways."

He scowled. "Even Floyd is careful not to be caught doing something his father won't like. If Floyd knows he can't get away with it, you can't expect to either." He ate the last sandwich then drained his cup. "I'll call you from my parents' house if I learn anything at the club."

I gathered my gloves and bag and stood. "I'm glad you're dining there most nights. Only until your business gets on its feet, of course." Which would take longer now if Mr. Warrington was guilty of murder. A guilty man is hardly going to pay us our fee.

"It turns out that my stomach is bigger than my pride. And my mother is a very determined woman."

"So I noticed."

We parted ways at the front of the teashop. Almost half an hour later, Frank opened the front door of the hotel for me.

"Has anyone asked after me today?" I said.

"Only Miss Bainbridge. She wanted you to join her for afternoon tea. I told her I didn't know where you'd gone."

I thanked him and strode through to the foyer. Peter stood alone at the front desk, his body leaning forward at an awkward angle once more. "Is Goliath asleep down there again?" I whispered.

His lips flattened and he nodded. "Hopefully this is the last time. I suggested someone to Mr. Hobart as a new porter. He's agreed to let him have a trial this week. He'll work with Goliath during the day and one of the daytime porters will move to night duty so Goliath won't need to do it anymore."

"Who did you find?"

"My brother."

"William? He's a little young, isn't he?" Peter's twelve year-old brother had helped me watch the house of a suspect once, pretending to operate his shoe-shine stand as he kept an eye on the premises. He was something of a scallywag.

"One of my other brothers, George. He's seventeen."

"How many brothers have you got?"

"Four, and two sisters."

"Tell your mother I take my hat off to her."

He grinned. "We're a handful. Or we were. Most of us are older now. William is the youngest."

He stiffened as someone approached behind me. I tensed as I turned to greet them, and was relieved to see it was Mr. Hobart, not my uncle. So relieved, in fact, that I gave him a wide smile and enthusiastic greeting.

Unfortunately he immediately suspected something was amiss. "Is everything all right, Miss Fox?"

"Everything is fine, Mr. Hobart. I've been out for a walk." I winced. Why had I offered an explanation when he didn't ask for one?

"How pleasant. Was Harry with you?"

My face heated.

He leaned closer and lowered his voice. "You don't need to be anxious around me. It doesn't concern me if you want to see my nephew."

I blew out a breath, relieved that he thought my nervousness was because I was worried about being caught with Harry, not about Goliath sleeping on the floor behind the counter.

A soft snore emanated from the direction of the sleeping giant. Mr. Hobart frowned at Peter. "What was that?"

Peter made a great show of clearing his throat and snuffling. "I'm afraid I might be coming down with something, sir."

Mr. Hobart's frown deepened and he took a step closer to the counter. He stood on his toes and tried to peer over, but he was too short to see the floor where Goliath slept. Peter made a snorting sound again.

Mr. Hobart took a step back from the counter. "Don't give your cold to the guests. Miss Fox, I have news which might please you. It's about Mr. Trickelbank."

"Oh? Has he been found?"

"It seems he arrived home just in time to collect my

telegram. He sent a response back promising to organize payment first thing tomorrow morning when his bank opens."

"That is good news. I'm sure my uncle is relieved."

"Very." He rocked back on his heels, a smug smile on his face. Clearly there was more to it.

"How did you manage it?" I asked.

"I told Trickelbank it would be a shame if the newspapers heard he was somehow involved in his sister's murder."

I gasped. "Mr. Hobart, that's diabolical!"

"I thought it rather clever. It certainly got the intended result." He looked around. "Keep this to yourself. I'd rather nobody knew I resorted to blackmail."

"I will. And in my book, there's nothing wrong with blackmailing a blackmailer."

Goliath emitted another soft snore. Peter covered it again by clearing his throat, but sooner or later, Mr. Hobart would realize. I took him by the elbow and steered him away.

"How is my uncle's mood today?" I asked.

"Better. I believe he plans for the family to all dine together tonight."

"Alone?"

"As far as I am aware. You can check with Mr. Chapman if you like."

"I'm sure I'll find out sooner or later."

I bade him goodnight and took the stairs to my suite. After a calming bath, I sifted through my clothes for something to wear for dinner and settled on the black dress I usually wore for such occasions. Despite receiving a comfortable allowance from my uncle I was loathe to spend it on clothes. For one thing, I hoped not to have to wear mourning again for some time, and for another, I preferred to save it for when I needed it.

Flossy stopped by my suite at six to inform me of our dinner plans. She did not immediately leave, however, and I could see she wanted to say something. I steeled myself for her questions.

"Where were you today, Cleo? And don't tell me you were at the museum or library. No one believes that anymore."

"I don't see why not. People go to libraries and museums

all the time. But in this case, you're right. I've been lying because I didn't think you'd approve of what I am actually doing."

She arched her brows. "Which is?"

"Investigating a murder."

She pressed a hand to her chest and released a breath. "Is that all! I am so relieved."

"You're relieved I'm investigating a murder?"

"That's more acceptable than meeting unsuitable men."

I refrained from pointing out that murderers were highly unsuitable. And I certainly wouldn't mention the encounter with Bob Ricketts in Harry's office. She might faint if she learned I'd questioned a known bruiser.

"What qualities make a man unsuitable?" I asked.

She flapped her hand in the air. "Someone low."

"You mean low born," I said flatly.

She smoothed her hand over her dark burgundy velvet skirt and avoided my gaze. "I overheard Father telling Mother that you'd been spending time with someone unsuitable." She blinked her lovely blue eyes at me. "Who is he?"

I almost blurted out Harry's name. I wanted to tell her. I hated lying to her. But I didn't want to put her in a position that if he asked who I was with today, she had to lie.

"I spoke with a number of men today, some of them were certainly unsuitable." At her shocked gasp, I chuckled. "They were all suspects and witnesses. Rest assured, Flossy, I am not flirting with them, or any man." At least that wasn't a lie. "You know I have no intention to marry. I also have no intention of being romantically involved with anyone. I've told Uncle Ronald as much but he doesn't seem to understand. He thinks I can't judge when a man is trying to trap me."

She sighed. "He has become suspicious of any man who speaks to me, too. I have to be careful not to talk to any particular boy for too long or my parents start planning my wedding."

I reached forward and clasped her hand in my own. She had it much worse than me. At least, as a mere niece, I wasn't in the direct firing line.

She patted my hand. "Don't anger him, Cleo. If you must

meet with an unsuitable man, please try to be discreet. Make sure Father doesn't find out."

I tilted my head to the side. "*You* have no objection to me meeting up with a man?"

"Does it matter if I do object?"

"Your opinion matters to me, but it won't change anything. I will see whomever I wish to see."

"I thought so. But thank you, Cleo. That's sweet of you to say that my opinion matters." She huffed out a breath. "It doesn't always, in this family."

"Don't worry about me, Flossy. I am a good judge of character and I won't put myself in a compromising position."

"I know. You aren't stupid."

"Thank you."

"And you are quite worldly," she went on. "I mean, you know all sorts of things that I don't."

"I'm older than you." And less cosseted, I could have said.

"Sometimes I see you coming and going from the hotel and I feel so frustrated that I can't do that too."

"If you could come and go as you pleased, where would you go?"

She blinked back at me as she thought about it. "The shops, I suppose."

It was so absurd, since she went to the shops all the time anyway—chaperoned, of course—that I burst out laughing. She started laughing too, and we both collapsed into giggles until a brisk knock on the door broke us apart.

It was Harmony with the excuse of helping me get ready for dinner. I knew she wanted to know about the case, but neither of us mentioned it in company. She bobbed a curtsy to Flossy who, thankfully, wanted to have a bath before dinner.

"Come and do my hair when you're finished with Cleo's," she said before leaving.

"Yes, Miss Bainbridge."

I closed the door on my cousin. As soon as I set foot in the sitting room, Harmony threw her questions at me.

"Well? What happened at the funeral? Did you see the lover? And why is Victor whistling like he hasn't got a care in the world? All the other cooks are tip toeing around the kitchen and he's making a fool of himself."

"Why is he making a fool of himself? Isn't he a very good whistler?"

She merely shrugged.

I headed into the bedroom and sat at the dressing table. "He's probably proud of himself for bringing Bob Ricketts to Mr. Armitage's office, all by himself."

Harmony stood behind me, staring wide-eyed at my reflection in the mirror.

I smiled as I withdrew the pins and combs from my hair. "I don't know how he did it, but he managed to bring in a man twice his size, tie him up and gag him. We learned enough from Ricketts to rule him out as a suspect in the murder. Later, Mr. Armitage and I came to the conclusion that Mrs. Parker should also be ruled out. Listen to this, Harmony. You'll never believe it, but we think we've been wrong all along."

Harmony brushed out my hair and listened to my account of the day, from our conversation with Xavier, to discovering that Mrs. Warrington was with child, and our latest conclusion that she was the intended victim after all.

"The problem is, our main suspect is now her husband, but he has an alibi for the time of the murder." I scooped up a handful of pins and held them out to her. "Harry is checking with the club's manager to ensure that Mr. Warrington was indeed there that night. He should be on his way to his parents' house now. He'll call and tell me what he learned once he gets there."

Her gaze narrowed when I used Harry's first name. "If it's not him, then who else is still on your suspect list? The half-brother? He seems like a no-good character to me, sneaking off in the middle of the night without paying."

"He will pay tomorrow, according to Mr. Hobart."

She placed a hair pin between her lips and poked a second one into my hair. "How'd he manage that?" she asked around the pin.

"I told him I wouldn't tell anyone." I winked at her in the mirror's reflection. "Let me just say that Mr. Hobart shouldn't be underestimated."

She thrust more pins into the arrangement then stood back

to admire her handiwork. "Pass me the black enamel and silver combs, the ones shaped like petals."

I retrieved them from the box of combs and handed them to her, one at a time.

"I don't think Trickelbank should be struck off the list entirely," she said as she tucked the combs into my hair at the back.

"You're probably right. Do you know he also lied to us about seeing his sister on the day she died? Apparently they met in the afternoon. It must have been soon after he arrived in London but before he checked in here."

She clasped the sides of my face and made me look into the mirror to admire her handiwork. "That's not why I think you shouldn't take him off the list just yet, though it doesn't help his case. I think we need to find out if he inherited anything from her death. If he did then he should still be a suspect, in my book."

She was absolutely right. While we hadn't dismissed Mr. Trickelbank, we hadn't investigated him properly, either, because we didn't think his sister was the intended victim. That was an oversight. In fact, the more I thought about it, the more I came to the conclusion that he had a very solid motive for murdering his sister—an inheritance. By all accounts, she'd tried to connect with her brother years ago, only for her friendship to be rejected. If she'd felt guilty for inheriting everything from their father, she might have written her brother into her will to make amends. Perhaps she even told him that at their meeting on the afternoon of her death.

Or perhaps they'd argued and she'd threatened to take him *out* of the will. Trickelbank would be desperate to stop her before she had a chance to communicate her wishes to her lawyer.

Mr. Trickelbank also had the means and opportunity. He'd dined with us on the evening of her murder, but he'd left by eleven. He seemed fit enough to climb up to a first floor window, kill Mrs. Warrington, then climb down again.

I needed to find out the contents of Mrs. Warrington's will. And I knew who might know.

"You're brilliant, Harmony," I said, smiling at her reflection.

She lightly patted my hair. "It does look nice considering how simple it is."

"I mean your theory about Trickelbank and an inheritance. I'm going to call Detective Inspector Hobart at his home and see if he knows." I checked the watch I'd placed on the bedside table. "I'll wait a little longer to give Mr. Armitage time to arrive. That way I can speak to him about the club, too."

Harmony surprised me by smiling. "You look nice tonight, Cleo."

"Oh. Thank you, that's very sweet of you to say." I checked my reflection in the mirror, but I looked the same as I always did. The dress wasn't a special one and Harmony hadn't gone out of her way to create an elaborate arrangement.

"If Mr. Armitage makes you happy and is willing to share cases with you, then I approve."

I swung around to face her. "I'm not in a good mood because of him. It's because we're approaching a conclusion to this investigation. I can feel it. And I have no reason not to be happy, of course. That always helps one look their best."

"If you say so. Do you want to apply some color to your cheeks and lips?"

"Not tonight. It's just the family."

"Make sure your uncle doesn't dampen your good mood. I hear there's nothing pleasing him lately."

She left to assist Flossy to dress for dinner. I waited another thirty minutes then took the lift down to the foyer. A number of guests gathered in small groups, waiting for friends, or chatting before they went in to dinner or out to the theater. Phillip, the other night porter who now shared the role with Goliath, greeted me and asked if he could be of assistance.

"I need to use a telephone," I said. "May I use the one on the front desk?"

"Of course, Miss Fox. Just make sure you put everything back the way it was. Peter hates for anything to be out of place when he gets in."

I didn't want my uncle to see me if he happened to pass, so I picked up the telephone and bobbed down out of sight behind the counter, stretching the cord as far as it could go. I plucked the receiver off the cradle and asked the operator to put me through to the Hobarts'. I'd remembered their number by heart, as well as a few other common numbers in London. Although I'd never used a telephone before moving into the hotel, I was beginning to wonder how the world ever functioned without the service. The device was a marvel.

When Detective Inspector Hobart's gruff voice came through the earpiece, I realized too late that I'd probably disturbed their family dinner. His wife would have another reason to dislike me when she found out I was on the other end. At this rate, I might never win her over.

"It's Cleopatra Fox," I said down the line. "Something has occurred to me. Something that relates to our investigation. You might be able to answer it for me."

"You aren't calling to speak to Harry?"

"Yes, that too. But I also wanted to ask you about Mrs. Warrington's will. Do you know if she had one, and who benefited from her death?"

"It's not my investigation, so I don't know. I can find out for you."

"Would you? That would be marvelous, thank you."

"Harry's here and wants to talk."

There was some noise at their end and some muffled voices then Harry came on the line. "My father just told me you asked about the will. He then scolded me for not being curious about the beneficiaries from the beginning, considering Mrs. Warrington is a wealthy woman."

"It's an amateur's mistake," I agreed. "What did you discover from the club's manager?"

"Warrington can't be our man. The manager checked his book and said Warrington arrived at nine-forty and signed out at midnight. He arrived in his own conveyance so the coachman can confirm the time. Warrington was also seen throughout the evening by the manager himself as he passed through the main gaming room."

"So it's not him. Damnation. I was convinced."

"As was I, but I was thinking about it on the way home, and have another theory. What if Warrington asked *Drummond* to kill her? Or what if he wasn't asked, but Drummond took the task upon himself because he could see how it would benefit his lover to have his wife out of the way?"

I shifted my weight on my haunches as my legs began to ache. "It's a possibility. If Drummond loves Warrington, he might do anything for him. They could have worked together or he could have acted on his own. What do you propose we do about it?"

"Cleo?" My uncle's voice sounded very close. "Cleo, are you there?"

My heart leapt into my throat. He was on the other side of the counter. If he came around to this side, he'd see me crouching, clutching the telephone. He'd know I was avoiding him.

"Cleo!" he snapped.

CHAPTER 14

J returned the telephone earpiece to its cradle, not even daring to whisper a hasty goodbye to Harry first. I remained in a crouched position, as close to the counter as possible, and tried to think of an excuse if I were discovered. I could claim to be searching for spare stationery, but the telephone would give me away.

"Cleo?" Uncle Ronald's voice came from the end of the counter. He was about to look behind it. When he did, he'd see me.

I closed my eyes.

"I think I just saw Miss Fox heading towards the dining room," Phillip said. "Sorry, sir. I didn't realize she'd gone."

"Thank you, Phillip."

The sound of retreating footsteps was music to my ears. I blew out a breath.

"It's safe to come out now," Phillip said. "He's gone."

I stood and returned the telephone to its position on the counter. "Thank you, Phillip. It's not that I'm hiding from my uncle, you understand. It's just that I needed some privacy."

Phillip clasped his hands at his back and rocked on his heels. "It's none of my business who you're telephoning, Miss Fox." He leaned forward and lowered his voice. "Don't worry, I'm always discreet."

"Always?"

"Mr. Bainbridge has made it clear to me that I mustn't talk

about the family's comings and goings, even to other members of the family."

If Floyd had told him that, then Floyd had more to hide than me. I knew my cousin went out a lot in the evenings, and not always with his father's approval, but perhaps it was more often than I realized.

I thanked Phillip and headed to the dining room where I found my uncle seated at the family table. He was speaking to a guest, thankfully, or I would have walked out again. The last person I wanted to be alone with was my uncle.

Unfortunately, the guest walked off as I sat. Uncle Ronald sat beside me.

"Phillip says you're looking for me," I said before he could speak. "He apologizes for sending you in here, but he thought he saw me. I was in the senior staff corridor, hoping to see Mrs. Short, but she wasn't there."

"Is there a problem with your maid?"

"No! Not at all. My maid is excellent."

"Then what—?"

"Oh look. Here's Flossy and Aunt Lilian. And Floyd is just behind them too. How marvelous."

We greeted them and resumed our seats. The ever-present waiters wasted no time asking us for our orders. Once we were alone again, my uncle fixed a glare on me. It would seem I wasn't going to be let off the hook so easily.

"I was looking for you earlier, Cleo, because I wanted to ask you where you've been all day." The hard line of his jaw was a sign of his determination to get an answer.

I doubted claiming I was at the museum would suffice. Like Flossy, he didn't believe a woman would spend day after day wandering around museums and libraries. One of these days I wanted to prove them both wrong, but not today.

I was at an utter loss to explain my whereabouts, however. Tell the truth and I'd be in trouble twice over—for spending the day with Harry *and* for conducting a murder investigation. But no believable lies presented themselves either. My mind had gone utterly blank.

"Well?" he barked.

"Cleo was shopping with me," Flossy said quickly. "We

got measured at the dressmaker's and looked for gloves and hats, but I didn't find anything I liked."

"You shopped all day?" he asked.

"We stopped at a teashop on Bond Street in the afternoon and lost track of time."

"What did you buy?"

"Nothing, in the end. But it was an enjoyable day out, nevertheless."

"Did you go with them, Lilian?"

"I had a headache," my aunt said without looking up from the table.

Uncle Ronald's frown deepened. "The girls need a chaperone."

"Cleo is my chaperone," Flossy said. "She doesn't need one at her age."

"Doesn't she?" he bit off. "I beg to differ."

My uncle needed to be distracted from this line of questioning before he gave a directive I wouldn't like. The best way to distract him was to get him talking about something that would make him forget about me. Once I realized that, the rest was easy.

"Can you show me the architect's plans for the restaurant after dinner, Uncle?"

If he thought the sudden change of topic jarring, he gave no indication. He eagerly agreed then dove into a discussion about the restaurant with enthusiasm. His entire demeanor changed and he was happy to answer our questions. Everyone joined in, even my aunt and Flossy. I doubted they were as interested as they made out, but it was as if they'd decided to rally around me by presenting a united force. Uncle Ronald seemed entirely oblivious to it.

The rest of the evening went smoothly enough, but no one felt like lingering at the dinner table once we'd finished our three courses. As promised, I went with my uncle to his office to look over the plans. Floyd came too, and I shot him a grateful smile when he said he was interested. The last thing I wanted was to be alone with Uncle Ronald. At least Floyd could help deflect him from making any rash decisions, like demanding I be chaperoned whenever I left the hotel.

After a suitable amount of time looking over the plans, I

yawned and announced I was ready to retire. Floyd walked me out, but we only got as far as his suite. His friend Jonathon leaned against the wall near the door, his legs crossed at the ankles. He straightened upon seeing us.

"Good evening, Miss Fox." He removed his hat and bowed. His blond hair flopped over his forehead and he flipped it back with a toss of his head as he straightened. I wondered if he knew how boyish the movement made him look. He probably wouldn't like hearing that. Most young men didn't like to be told they seemed younger than they are.

"Don't I get a greeting too?" Floyd asked.

Jonathon bowed to his friend, flourishing his hat in an elaborate sweep. When he straightened, he leaned conspiratorially towards me. "Your cousin is the jealous type."

Floyd rolled his eyes. "Pay him no heed, Cleo. Jonathon is a scoundrel."

"I am not! Well, not anymore. I've changed my ways."

Floyd snorted.

Jonathon winced. "I *plan* to change my ways. All I need is the love of a good woman to help me."

"You'll always be a scoundrel, my friend."

Jonathon winced again, but this time there was no theatrics or grand statements accompanying it. I suspected he was genuinely hurt by Floyd's comment.

I had seen Jonathon regularly at the hotel in recent weeks. He was Floyd's closest friend. When they weren't playing cards in Floyd's suite, they were attending parties or their club. They moved in illustrious circles, so Flossy told me. Illustrious and fast.

I'd thought him too forward when I first met him, but I quite liked him now that he'd stopped trying to impress me. His good looks were only enhanced by the small scar on his cheek. It gave him a ruggedness, which I sometimes wondered if he knew. He certainly knew he was handsome. Like most handsome men, Jonathon was confident in his appeal to women, and that gave him a general air of confidence in every aspect of life. Harry was the same.

"Are you two going out tonight?" I asked, careful to keep my voice low.

"We are," Floyd said. He offered no more information and

I didn't inquire further. It was best if I didn't know; I wouldn't have to lie if asked.

Jonathon cleared his throat. "I thought we should stay at the hotel for a while. We could play cards, just the three of us, and Flossy too, of course."

Floyd's eyes narrowed ever so slightly as he regarded his friend. Then his gaze slid to me.

"Actually I'm very tired," I said. "Another time, perhaps."

Jonathon's face fell for a moment before he bowed again. "Another time. Goodnight, Miss Fox."

Although I wanted to walk quickly back to my suite, I maintained a steady pace. When I reached my door, I glanced back. They were both gone.

* * *

I LEFT the hotel early the following morning to avoid my relatives. I headed to Harry's office. Although we hadn't agreed to meet there, it was the most logical place.

I called in at the café first and ordered two cups of coffee to take up. Luigi was quite busy serving coffees to five customers, all of them Italians who seemed to know one another. The two regular customers were there, stuck to their stools. Did they go home at night or sleep where they sat?

Luigi informed me that Harry already had a coffee so he gave me only one cup. I took it up the stairs to the office, not bothering to knock.

Harry sat in the chair, the fingers of both hands holding the coffee cup. He didn't appear to be doing anything, just thinking. I sat on the chair opposite.

"Good morning," I began. "Have you had any more thoughts about Drummond?"

He sat forward and set the cup down, his movements careful, deliberate. He looked up through his lashes at me with the same measured effort. "What happened last night?"

"The telephone line went dead." I didn't want to tell him about my uncle looking for me to interrogate me. Harry might feel the need to end our friendship to make life easier for me at the hotel. I didn't want to end it.

The arched look he gave me was filled with skepticism. "I

heard your name being said in the distance. It sounded like Sir Ronald."

"You must have been mistaken."

"Cleo—"

"Can we discuss the investigation? The more I think about Mr. Drummond, the more I'm certain he must be the killer. He either colluded with Mr. Warrington or took matters into his own hands. Either way, love makes people do things they usually wouldn't, particularly when backed into a corner."

Harry heaved a sigh. "And Warrington was backed into a corner. He couldn't go ahead with the divorce or his wife would tell the newspapers about his proclivities."

"And he didn't want to raise another man's child as his own," I finished. "So the question is, how do we prove it?"

"Speak to him."

"Speak to them both," I said.

A knock sounded on the door and Harry invited the newcomer inside. To our utter surprise, it was Mr. Drummond himself. He removed his hat and nodded at each of us as his hands worried the hat brim.

Harry invited him to sit. As he did, Harry indicated that I should join him on the other side of the desk. Perhaps he did it as a safety measure, to keep me out of reach of a potential murderer. I did it because of the symbolism. On the visitor's side of the desk, it looked as though I were a guest too. Standing on the same side of the desk as Harry, it signaled that I was as much involved in the investigation as he was.

Harry gave up his chair for me. Instead of dragging around one of the guest chairs, he stood at my side.

"How can we help you?" he asked.

Mr. Drummond continued to fidget with his hat, now in his lap. "I came to find out how far away you are from catching the killer."

"I'll be making a report to Mr. Warrington when the time comes," Harry said.

Mr. Drummond licked his lips and drew in a deep breath. "The thing is, I'm worried about him. While the killer is still out there, he's in danger." If he was lying, it was very convincing.

"Has something happened?" I asked.

"Someone followed us last night. We were on our way out and it was dark. We changed our minds and decided to stay in instead. But we can't go on like this."

"Did you see the person?" Harry asked.

"No."

"Then why do you think you were followed?"

"Oh, I thought you were asking if I saw them personally. I didn't, but Warrington did. He thinks it was a woman. In fact, he's sure of it."

I wanted to exchange glances with Harry but kept my gaze forward. Harry remained silent, and I was sure he was thinking the same as me. To get answers, one had to ask the right questions. It was time to ask Mr. Drummond for the truth.

"Are you sure Mr. Warrington saw a woman following you?" I asked. "Or did he make that up, just like he made up the stabbing in the lane?"

Mr. Drummond's mouth dropped open. "What the devil? That's a serious accusation, Miss Fox." He appealed to Harry, but received no support from that quarter.

Harry opened the wall safe behind the Tower Bridge sketch and removed the glass plate negatives I'd stolen from Mr. Drummond. "We believe you might like these back."

Mr. Drummond grasped at them and hugged them to his chest. He lowered his gaze to the desk and swallowed hard.

"Let us tell you what we know," Harry said. "We know that you and Warrington are lovers."

Mr. Drummond looked up, his face crimson. "It…it's not him in these negatives! It's someone else."

"We know it's both of you."

"But you can only see my face, not his."

I tilted my head to the side. "Mr. Drummond, you are at his house all the time. We've seen you together. We can see that you are in love."

He adjusted his hold on the negatives. "Please, please, don't tell anyone. If people knew, it would ruin him. Ruin us both. But he has more to lose than me, with his career."

"We will only tell the police if it becomes necessary," I said, my voice gentle. I felt sorry for him, even though I knew I shouldn't. He was probably a murderer.

"You would do anything for him," Harry pressed.

Mr. Drummond cleared his throat. "I've lied for him, it's true. Our entire lives are a lie. That's why I couldn't leave these in the hands of that snake as he asked me to do. I had to retrieve them."

"The negatives?"

He nodded. "We argued about it. When he told me he'd learned that the photographer sells copies of these sorts of images to purveyors of pornographic material, I knew I had to get them back. Warrington wanted me to leave well enough alone, telling me there was no point and that it would cost a fortune. I told him I had to get them back. I *had* to. It's fine for him. His face isn't visible. Mine is. One look at these and the entire world will know. I might not be a member of parliament, but I have a family. It would destroy my parents and siblings, and I'd probably lose my position as permanent secretary. Anyway, I can't bear to think of others looking at them." He managed to lift his gaze to meet mine, but I got the feeling he was forcing himself to be brave and face me. "What do these negatives have to do with your accusation?"

"It proves that you love him and will go to great lengths to please him, even if that means doing something that goes against your better judgement." I nodded at the negatives. "Posing for those, for one thing, and going along with the story about the stabbing in the lane."

"Bertie *was* stabbed. I've seen the injury myself."

"It's easy enough to stab your own hand," Harry pointed out. "The wound is superficial."

Mr. Drummond's face drained of color as our accusation sank in. "My god," he murmured. "You think he faked his injury to make it seem as though he was the intended target that night, not Isobel."

Neither Harry nor I spoke. We both watched as Mr. Drummond worked through the implications, following the thread of the theory until eventually arriving at the end. "No!" His voice was a low snarl and the color returned to his face as his anger rose. "You have it all wrong. Bertie didn't kill her. He can't have. He was at the club."

"Were you at the club that night?" Harry asked.

"No. I was at home."

We fell silent. Once again, Mr. Drummond took a few moments to reach the conclusion we had. When he did, he leapt to his feet. "You think I did it! You think I killed her because I love him? Are you mad?"

After retrieving the negatives from the safe, Harry hadn't rejoined me behind the desk. He now moved to block the door.

"Get out of my way!" Mr. Drummond shouted.

"Please calm down," I said, also standing.

"Calm down? You are accusing me of murder! I think that gives me every reason to shout. I am innocent, Miss Fox! Your accusation is absurd. Why would I want to kill Isobel?"

"For him."

"Why would he want to kill her? She was a convenience, not a hindrance. A politician who loves men needs a wife, Miss Fox."

"Then why was he was going to divorce her?"

His mouth snapped shut.

"We actually know the answer to that," I went on. "He was going to divorce her because she was with child. She must have confided her suspicions before the doctor confirmed it the day before she died."

Mr. Drummond didn't look surprised by the news. "I didn't know."

"I think you're lying. Mr. Warrington told you that she wanted him to bring up the child as his own, but he didn't want that. Did he?"

Mr. Drummond had gone quite still. Not even his gaze moved to meet mine.

"They argued just before she died," I went on. "Earlier that day, she learned that he wanted to divorce her. She was going to be a ruined woman with a baby, unsure if her lover would rescue her and marry her. She tried to convince her husband to stay married, but he refused."

"If he was going to divorce her, why kill her?"

"Because she was going to tell the world about his proclivities if he insisted on a divorce. You said yourself, it would be disastrous for him. Once she threatened him with public exposure, there was only one sure way to save him. You had to silence her."

"Not me," he whispered. "It wasn't me."

"It must be you. It can't be him because he was at the club. You're the only who loves him enough to do it and you don't have an alibi. You just told us you were home alone."

The hands clutching the photographic negatives trembled. "I swear to you, I didn't do it. I wasn't even at the house that night."

"You climbed up the pipe and through the window," Harry said.

"No! No, that's impossible. I overheard the butler tell Bertie he's sure he locked the window."

Harry and I exchanged glances. "Why weren't we told this?" Harry asked.

"I assumed you'd already spoken to Henderson about it and dismissed it, thinking the butler got confused. The night must have been chaotic and he simply misremembered."

It was likely, of course. Henderson might have made a mistake. Or he might not. Either way, he had told Mr. Warrington, and Mr. Warrington had not informed us.

"May I go now?" Mr. Drummond cautiously approached Harry, as if Harry were a vicious dog guarding the door. "After all, you have no evidence. You can't detain a man without proof."

Harry's chest heaved with his intake of breath. He stepped aside and watched as Mr. Drummond departed. His footsteps could be heard pounding down the stairs, culminating in the slamming of the front door.

"What do you think?" I asked.

"I think we need to speak to the butler and find out whether the window was closed or not."

"And if it was? If the only way the killer could have entered the house is through the front door? What then?"

He shook his head. "I have no idea."

* * *

ONCE AGAIN MR. HENDERSON refused to speak to us, but Harry was not going to let that stop him.

"We have authority from your employer," he said. "He wants you to answer our questions."

Mr. Henderson lifted his chin. His nostrils flared. "He's not here." He went to shut the door.

Harry put his shoulder to it and forced Mr. Henderson back. He barreled through to the entrance hall and I followed. He was proving rather useful to have along when questioning witnesses.

"Can we go somewhere to talk?" I asked.

"No," Mr. Henderson said. "Get out or I'll call the police."

"No, you won't," Harry said mildly. "Because if you do, we'll be forced to tell them how you were in love with Mrs. Warrington and jealous of her lover. That jealousy led you to kill her."

The butler gasped and took a step back, towards the stairs. Harry stepped forward, perhaps worried he would run off. He couldn't go anywhere but up, however.

"I...I...you're mistaken." The butler's breathing came hard and fast and I grew worried he was going to have an episode in the entrance hall.

"Is there somewhere we can go and sit?" I asked.

Again, Mr. Henderson shook his head, but I wasn't sure if it was in answer to my request, or a denial of Harry's accusation. "I would never harm her. I've known her for years, ever since she came here as a young bride."

"And you fell in love with her then." Harry arched his brows.

Mr. Henderson swallowed heavily.

"Were you two lovers?"

"No! Good lord, what do you take me for?" Mr. Henderson scrubbed a hand across his mouth. "Please, you have to believe me when I say I would never harm her. You're right. I did love her." His eyes suddenly filled with tears. "I miss her terribly. It's not the same here without her. It never will be." He clutched the newel post and lowered his head. His breathing became shallow.

Harry went to ask another question, but I put my hand out to stop him. Perhaps a gentler approach was in order. He relinquished the interrogation to me.

"You have avoided speaking to us from the beginning," I said. "You have refused to talk, and slammed the door in our faces. Mr. Henderson, do you see how that looks?"

He gave a small nod. "It makes me look guilty. But I didn't kill her. I swear to you. I didn't want to speak to you because I knew what angle you were pursuing, and I owed it to her to save her reputation."

"She's gone, Mr. Henderson. You can't save her now."

"I *can*. I *must*. Her reputation is all that's left. She was a good woman with a good heart and spirited nature. She doesn't deserve to be remembered as a harlot. And I know—I *know*—if anyone found out about her relationship with that fellow, her name would be blackened in the newspapers." He looked up. He was crying now, his tears flowing down his cheeks. He dashed them away with the back of his hand and reached for a handkerchief from his pocket.

"Whatever you tell us will remain private," I assured him. "We won't sell any information to the journalists."

He spluttered a humorless laugh. "Is that so? *You* will protect her reputation? *You*, a lackey for her husband employed to find evidence of her adultery? Forgive me, Miss Fox, but I don't believe you."

I drew in a breath. This was going to require as much delicacy as I could muster. "I was initially employed to do that, it's true. But after her murder, everything changed. Now I want to find her killer. Don't you want that too, Mr. Henderson? Doesn't Mrs. Warrington deserve justice?"

He dabbed at his eyes with the handkerchief.

"At this point, the police don't care," I reminded him. "Mr. Armitage and I are the best chance she has of receiving justice. If you want that for her, then you must answer our questions honestly."

He choked back more tears and nodded into his handkerchief. "She needs to rest in peace. Go on then. What do you want to know?"

"It's come to our attention that the drawing room window was locked at the time of her death."

"It was. I check all the locks when it gets dark. It's part of my evening routine. I do it every night, and I did it that night. But the police insisted it was unlocked when they arrived."

"Was there anyone else in the house that night other than you, Miss Jennett, the housekeeper, and Mr. and Mrs. Warrington?"

He shook his head. "The coachman was in the coach house, and the cook had gone home."

"Could someone have come into the house through the front door without you noticing?"

"Yes, if they had a key. If they were quiet, I wouldn't have heard it opening from the servants' hall."

"Who has a key besides Mr. and Mrs. Warrington?"

"Mr. Drummond."

Harry and I exchanged glances.

"He rarely uses it, but I know he has one. I caught him once, coming out of Mr. Warrington's chambers when Mr. Warrington was not at home. I asked the other servants and no one had let him in. I realized that's where the spare key had gone. Mr. Warrington had asked me to have one made some weeks before."

"Take us through the events of Tuesday evening again, the night of the murder."

He was calmer now, the tears having abated. His hands shook a little, and he was pale, his eyes hollow. He no longer resembled the formidable man I'd first encountered. "Mrs. Warrington was dressed in men's clothes to go out for the night. She needed to speak to her husband so I directed her to the drawing room where I knew he was reading. She closed the door behind her, but I heard them arguing. I couldn't make out the words, however. That was about nine. Several minutes later, he came out. I'd waited nearby, in case she needed me, and I saw him emerge. He went immediately to his rooms."

"And Mrs. Warrington remained in the drawing room?" Harry asked.

He nodded.

"Then what happened?"

"About nine-twenty, Mr. Warrington asked me to have the coach sent around. He was going to his club. Ten minutes later, he left. I returned to the servants' hall, where Miss Jennett and I both did some mending. The housekeeper was doing her accounts. We were surprised Mrs. Warrington had decided not to go out, but we assumed the argument had upset her and she changed her mind. Then at ten, the bell for the drawing room rang. I answered it and Mrs. Warrington asked me to bring her tea."

"Tell us how the room looked," Harry said. "Picture the window in your mind." He paused to allow Mr. Henderson time to think. "Was it open?"

He shook his head. "It was closed. I would have noticed a draft if it were open. But I didn't check if it was locked. I assumed it was. I *know* it was."

"And the rest of the room?" I asked. "How did it look?"

"As it often did on cold nights, with one of the wingback chairs angled to the fire."

"And how did Mrs. Warrington seem? Was she upset?"

"I don't know. I didn't see her face and—"

"You didn't see her?" Harry echoed.

"No. I told you, her chair was facing the fire. At that angle, the seated person isn't visible to anyone entering the room. Or from the window, for that matter."

My mind whirred as the new information clicked into place. It was all starting to make sense now, although I was well aware of some very large holes opening up too. "What did Mrs. Warrington say to you at that point?"

"She said 'tea.'"

"Just one word?" When he nodded, I asked, "Is she usually so short with you?"

"No. I thought it odd. She's always kind, but I assumed she was still upset over the argument with her husband and had no wish for a lengthy exchange."

"So you made the tea and brought it up," Harry prompted. I could tell from the pitch of his voice that he was on the same path as me. "Where did you place it?"

"On a table near the door."

"Why there? Isn't that far away from where she was seated?"

"Yes, but that's where she directed me to leave it. She pointed at the table."

"Pointed? She didn't speak?"

"No."

"What did her hand look like?"

Mr. Henderson frowned. "Like any hand wearing a glove."

"And what happened then?" I asked.

"That was about ten past ten. I returned downstairs where I continued with my work. At midnight, Miss Jennett decided to see if Mrs. Warrington needed anything. She wanted to retire for the evening herself. That's when she screamed and…" He pressed his trembling lips together and closed his eyes. After a moment, he drew in a shuddery breath and continued. "Mr. Warrington was sent for, and then we telephoned the police."

"The coachman will confirm this?" Harry asked.

"Of course. You can ask him now. He came home after driving Mr. Warrington to his office this morning."

He took us through to the back of the house where we exited through the rear door and crossed the courtyard to the stables and coach house in the mews. The coachman confirmed that he took Mr. Warrington to his club, arriving at approximately nine-forty-five, and fetched him around midnight after the murder had taken place.

"So we potentially have a new time of death," Harry said as we walked out of the mews. His strides were long and I had to quicken my pace to keep up. I doubted he was aware of how fast he walked. "If the butler didn't see her face and didn't hear her voice except for that one word, tea, then she might have already been dead by ten. And the killer pretended to be her so that the butler would think she was still alive when he delivered the tea at ten past ten."

I clutched my throat and nodded. "It must have been Warrington. He must have killed her when they argued then left to go to his club, only to come back and re-enter the house."

"Probably through the window which he unlocked before he left the drawing room earlier. He seems fit enough to climb up the pipe."

"He rang for tea then sat in the chair, perhaps moving her body aside and squeezing in beside her." I shivered at the gruesome image. "He ordered tea and, with gloves on, pointed to the table when Henderson brought it in ten minutes later. Then he left through the window, returned to the club, and waited for the alarm to be raised."

"There's only one problem," Harry said heavily.

"He was at the club during that time," I finished. "The coachman took him and he remained there, according to the manager."

He nodded. "He was seen arriving and checking in, as well as throughout the evening. There's a book that records the arrival and departure times of members, and the manager checked it for me. He even asked around and many of the members claimed to have seen him. According to the register, Warrington was there from nine-forty-five and didn't leave until just after midnight. He couldn't have come back to the house and ordered tea at ten."

It was so frustrating. I felt as though we were so close and yet a wall had been thrown up, blocking us, and I could see no way around, over or through it.

CHAPTER 15

"*M*r. Warrington *must* have killed her," I said. "I'm sure of it. But someone else returned to order the tea."

"Drummond," Harry said. "Warrington killed her at the time of the argument, then unlocked the drawing room window so that Drummond could get inside when Warrington was safely at his club, making himself visible to all and sundry."

"Mr. Drummond pretended to be Isobel to make it appear as though she was still alive at ten past ten," I added.

It made sense. Indeed, it was entirely logical. But it didn't seem quite right to me. Mr. Drummond had seemed genuinely shocked to be accused of her murder. I'd got the feeling he hadn't been involved at all.

But I couldn't rely on instinct. I'd be laughed out of Scotland Yard if I told them I had a feeling Mr. Drummond was innocent. I must only deal with known facts.

I gave Harry a flat smile. "What do we do now? We have no proof."

"I have to tell my father what we learned today. He never believed the vagrant story and has been on the verge of bringing it up with his superiors. Our information might give him the leverage he needs to force the case to be re-examined."

He was right. It was time for Scotland Yard to take over and find the definitive evidence that we couldn't.

"I'll stop by your office tomorrow and see how you fared," I said.

With a heavy sigh, he tilted his head back and searched the clouds. "Cleo...I..."

I narrowed my gaze. "Go on."

"I prefer it if you don't come to my office anymore."

I bristled. "I'll telephone your parents' house then."

"No. I'll update Uncle Alfred and he can pass on any news to you at the hotel."

"This is because of my uncle's warning, isn't it?" I threw my hands in the air and walked off. I didn't get far. I turned back and strode up to him. "I didn't expect *you* to bow to my uncle's ridiculous demands."

He lifted a hand to my shoulder, only to drop it before touching me. He crossed his arms. "Cleo, your present situation is reliant on his goodwill. If you break his rules, there'll be consequences."

"Let me worry about those consequences."

"I will, if they don't concern me. But he has specifically forbidden you from seeing me, and that makes it my concern."

"I can handle my uncle."

"Cleo—"

"*Harry.*"

He pressed his lips together. I waited, but he didn't say anything further. He simply looked at me with eyes full of pity. It only made my blood boil more. I didn't want his pity. I didn't want anyone's pity.

I wanted his acknowledgement that I could fight my own battle. But I wasn't going to get it. He was too gentlemanly to let me face a battle alone, even one that was not his to fight.

And that only made me more frustrated because a gentleman's honor was unbreakable.

"Well then," I said stiffly. "Goodbye." I turned and walked away. There was nothing more to say. It was the end of our friendship. He'd made that very clear.

"I don't want to part in anger," he called after me.

"Then you shouldn't have angered me."

There was no response and I refused to turn around and see if he had left or was still watching me. By the time I arrived at the hotel, my temper had cooled and I was beginning to think clearly again. Unfortunately, I didn't like my thoughts. Harry was right. We shouldn't have parted in anger. It wasn't fair to him when he was doing what he thought was the right thing.

I considered telephoning him, but he was on his way to Scotland Yard, and his office didn't have a telephone anyway. Besides, his entire point was that I shouldn't contact him anymore. All communication must be stopped if I was to keep on my uncle's good side.

This was entirely Uncle Ronald's fault. Yet there was little I could do about it.

What I really needed was some time with Harmony. Her direct, no-nonsense manner would clear my head and steady my frayed nerves. But she must have finished her duties for the day because I couldn't find her.

I returned to the foyer where Mr. Hobart broke away from the porters he was addressing to speak to me. He seemed in earnest. Surely Harry didn't have word from Scotland Yard already. He must have only just arrived there himself.

"Peter said you'd returned." Mr. Hobart nodded towards the front desk where Peter was checking in two women dressed in furs. They were Americans, going by their accent.

"Is this about my uncle again?" I asked.

"No." He glanced around. "I received a message from my brother this morning. Apparently you'd asked him to look into the beneficiaries of Mrs. Warrington's will. He has an answer for you."

My breath caught in my throat. What if we'd got it all wrong? What if Mr. Trickelbank had a motive after all? "Go on."

"Her husband gets all of it."

It took a moment for the implications to sink in. If Mr. Warrington got it all, then Mr. Trickelbank had no motive and Mr. Warrington was now a very rich man. He could spend his wife's money without answering to her, or to anyone.

"Thank you, Mr. Hobart. Thank you very much. I'm now certain we're on the right path."

His kind face creased with his smile. "I'm so pleased to hear it. I knew you and Harry would solve it."

"The problem is, we have no proof and our suspect has an alibi."

He patted my arm. "I'm sure you'll solve the puzzle, as long as you work together."

I managed to smile, but doubted it was convincing. Fortunately he was distracted before he got a chance to ask me what was wrong. He spotted my uncle emerging from the lift and joined him. They spoke briefly and even glanced towards me. I nodded a greeting at my uncle and he nodded back. Mr. Hobart gave me a small smile then followed my uncle back into the lift. I suspected Mr. Hobart had made sure Uncle Ronald saw me, to account for my presence in the hotel today. He really did think of everything.

If only he could think of a way to prove that Mr. Warrington was *not* at the club on Tuesday night, after all. Had he paid the manager to lie for him? Even if he had, there were other witnesses and he couldn't silence them all.

Goliath loped towards me, pulling an empty luggage trolley behind him. With one eye on the guests checking in at the counter, he greeted me. "You look troubled, Miss Fox. Is it the investigation?"

"In a way. You look better, not quite so tired."

He squared his shoulders. "I wasn't tired. I'm as strong as an ox."

"As stupid as one, too," came Frank's voice from behind me.

Goliath scowled at him. "Shouldn't you be on the door?"

"I'm having a short break. How is the case coming along, Miss Fox?"

"We've hit a blockage," I said. "I'm quite certain the husband murdered his wife, but he has an alibi." I explained how the coachman had driven Mr. Warrington to his club where the manager had signed him in and witnesses saw him.

"How can they be sure of the time they saw him?" Goliath asked. "I've seen gentlemen in the billiards room after they've downed a few drinks and they don't have much concept of the time, even with a clock in there."

Frank agreed. "Sometimes their wives have to retrieve them if they're heading out to a show."

Goliath drummed his fingers on the trolley. "Is it the Carlton Club on Pall Mall? That's where most of the Conservatives belong."

"The Alpine Club on Savile Row."

"Alpine Club, eh?" Frank grunted. "So he's a mountaineer. Explains how he was able to climb up the pipe."

Goliath's fingers continued to tap out a military beat on the trolley. "Savile Row is a fifteen minute journey by carriage from Kensington, maybe a little less if the traffic is light and the vehicle quick. It would take thirty minutes for a round trip."

"The timing fits," I said. "He left the house around nine-thirty, arrived at the club at nine-forty-five, and could have been back in the drawing room ordering tea at ten." The more I considered the theory, the more it made sense. But how to explain the manager seeing Mr. Warrington check in at nine-forty-five and not leave until midnight?

I watched Peter with the guests checking into the hotel in much the same way as Mr. Warrington would have checked into his club on the night of the murder. Peter wrote down the time in the book, followed by their details, then turned the book around for the guest to sign.

Good lord! That was it! "I know how he did it. I know how he checked into the club and didn't leave, yet was still able to order tea at ten in his own drawing room. You're right, Goliath. A fast vehicle was involved."

Goliath puffed out his chest.

"Did he pay the manager to sign him in at a different time?" Frank asked.

I shook my head. "The manager is innocent. Indeed, no one else colluded with Mr. Warrington. He did it all on his own."

I hurried upstairs to fetch my coat and gloves, and returned to the foyer, only to stop short upon seeing Uncle Ronald talking to two gentlemen. I hid out of sight for a few minutes then peered around the corner. The coast was clear.

With a quick scan of the foyer, I hurried across the tiles and left the hotel. It was a short walk to Savile Row. It would have taken me twice as long to go to Harry's office first so I didn't divert my course. Besides, he was probably still at Scotland Yard, or in transit. I didn't need to be accompanied anyway. I was not confronting a killer and there was no danger in confirming my theory.

The manager on duty at the Alpine Club was the same one I'd talked to on the day I'd first met Mr. Warrington here. He had reluctantly let me in that day, and now, he peered down his nose at me with the same snobbery he'd shown me then. In my experience, there were two ways of getting men to do what I wanted—through flirting or threats. Flirting wasn't going to work on the stony-faced manager, so threats it would have to be.

"My name is Cleopatra Fox."

"Yes. I recall."

"Then you'll remember that I work for Mr. Warrington, one of your members. I've been tasked by him to investigate the murder of his wife."

The manager's brows arched. "No, you haven't. There was another fellow here who insisted *he* is investigating the murder."

"We work together."

"Of course you do." The condescension dripping from his tone was as thick as jam.

"I need to see your book," I went on.

"Book?"

I indicated the open register on the desk. "You note down arrival and departure times in it. I need to see it to help prove a theory."

He slammed the book closed. "Your superior has already checked."

I gathered up all my patience, but it was wearing very thin. "He is my colleague, not my superior, and I am quite sure you didn't let him see the register himself. He merely asked you a question about it, and *you* checked. Isn't that right?"

He sniffed.

"You made a grave error in doing so, sir."

He bristled. "I simply read out the time of Mr. Warrington's arrival. How could I possible have gotten that wrong?"

"I'll fetch the detective inspector and tell him, shall I? I need to speak to him anyway."

The manager's face flushed and his nostrils flared. His temper would only be rising if he knew he couldn't win, otherwise he'd have a smug look about him.

It was time to press home my advantage. "You wouldn't want to be considered an accessory to murder, would you?"

He glared at me and I glared directly back. After a deep breath, he re-opened the book. "What do you want to know?"

"I need to see it myself."

He hesitated then turned the register around for me. I flipped back through the pages to Tuesday night and ran my finger down the column until I found Mr. Warrington's name. Beside it was his signature and the time of his arrival and then his departure. The arrival time was noted as 9:45PM, which fit with the time the coachman claimed he left his master here.

I then checked the line above and below, and closed the book. My heart thundered in my chest as I slid it back across the desk to the manager. "May I use your telephone?"

"No."

"But—"

"Miss Fox! What are you doing here?"

I spun around to see Mr. Warrington standing in the doorway, walking stick in hand. He removed his hat and coat and handed them to the doorman, but held onto the stick.

I breathed deeply in an attempt to tamp down my rising panic, but it didn't work. My stomach twisted into knots. "I was just following up on a clue."

His face froze. "Oh?"

"Is this woman working for you, sir?" the manager asked. "She claims she is investigating the murder of Mrs. Warrington, but I'm skeptical."

Mr. Warrington's gaze slid to the book. His Adam's apple bobbed with his swallow, but he had otherwise gone quite still.

A chill seeped through to my bones. He knew I'd discovered his secret.

"She no longer works for me."

If I needed confirmation that I was on the right path, that

was it. Panic must have set in for him, too, if he was denying our agreement to my face.

"I dismissed her for incompetence," he went on. "Have her thrown out." He signaled to the doorman

The doorman looked to the manager for approval. The manager nodded.

"I'll go voluntarily," I said.

I edged past the doorman, who looked keen to do his duty and make sure I left.

Mr. Warrington clicked his fingers at the manager. "Pass me the book."

"No!" I lunged towards the desk, but the doorman caught me around the waist. I kicked back at his shins, but my skirts tangled around my legs and lessened the impact. Pushing at his arm was just as useless.

Mr. Warrington clicked his fingers again. "The book!"

The manager frowned. "Sir? Why do you need it?"

"Just give me the bloody thing!"

"Don't give it to him," I begged. "He'll take it away and tear the relevant page out."

The manager eyed Mr. Warrington. "Would you, sir?"

"It's none of your business what I do with it. Give it to me."

I struggled to free myself from the doorman's grasp, but his arm was too tight around my waist. I even tried stomping on his toe, but he merely grunted without loosening his grip. I wished I'd brought an umbrella to stab him with, but it hadn't looked like rain when I left the hotel.

"The register is my responsibility, sir." The manager looked torn. I doubted he was used to disobeying the members.

"I don't bloody care," Mr. Warrington growled. "Your wages are paid by my fees."

The manager hugged the register to his chest.

Mr. Warrington raised his walking stick and struck the manager's shoulder. The manager cried out and dropped the book on the desk.

Mr. Warrington picked it up and calmly flipped through the pages. If he tore out the relevant page and destroyed it, there'd be no evidence, just my word to describe what I'd seen. It wouldn't be enough to convict him.

"Let me go, you fool!" I screeched. "That man is a murderer!"

The manager gawped at me. The doorman's grip loosened, but not enough for me to wriggle free. Mr. Warrington tucked the book under his arm and walked off. In one of the rooms back there would be a fireplace where he could burn the incriminating page.

"Stop him!" I cried. "Murderer! He killed his wife!"

"What?" The voice behind me sounded thin, but I recognized it.

"Mr. Drummond, please, you have to stop him. Stop Warrington. He killed her. Go! Before he burns the evidence. I'll explain later. Go!"

Mr. Warrington glanced over his shoulder. "Don't be a fool, Pierce. She's just another female suffering a bout of hysteria. You know what they're like."

Mr. Drummond passed a shaking hand over his mouth and jaw. He looked small, insignificant. I'd seen him take command when he'd ordered the photography assistant to hand over the negatives, but he clearly felt superior to the youth. Not here. Not with the man who supposedly loved him.

Mr. Warrington's smile was filled with contempt.

"If you're not guilty, why are you removing the register?" I asked.

His face hardened.

"Because you know it proves you weren't here when you say you were."

He clutched the book tighter.

"Did you do it?" Mr. Drummond's voice was still reedy and unsure. At least he was brave enough to pose the question.

Mr. Warrington merely sneered at him and walked off.

I pushed against the doorman's chest, but it was no use. "Mr. Drummond, please, stop him! I can prove he murdered her, but only if that page is still in the book."

Mr. Drummond pressed his lips together and raced after

him. "Release her!" he called back to the doorman. It would seem he'd rediscovered his bravery, at least with the staff.

The doorman let me go and ran after them.

"Women are not allowed in there!" the manager shouted.

I ignored him and pushed open the door that closed behind the men. The room beyond was a large sitting room with comfortable looking chairs and tables scattered throughout, covered with newspapers and books. The air was hazy with the smoke from cigars and pipes. Some of the gentlemen members had stood, while others looked on with interest or protested at the disturbance. Those who had seen me enter frowned in disapproval.

Mr. Warrington wound his way past the furniture, heading for the fireplace.

"Stop him!" I cried.

But only Mr. Drummond moved. The other members were either confused or not willing to take orders from a woman.

Mr. Drummond darted around tables, pushing them aside, knocking over a lamp as he tried to get to Mr. Warrington before he reached the fireplace.

He failed. Mr. Warrington opened the register and flipped to the page he needed, tearing it out.

Mr. Drummond lunged, but it was no use. Mr. Warrington threw the page into the fire. At the same time, he brought his walking stick down on Mr. Drummond's head. The crack reverberated around the sitting room, and Mr. Drummond collapsed on the floor, his eyes closed.

CHAPTER 16

A cacophony of voices erupted. Gentlemen shouted. Someone knelt at Mr. Drummond's side, while three more grabbed Mr. Warrington, holding his arms to stop him striking again. The stick was torn from his grip.

I noted all of this yet I kept my eyes on the page, its edges browning in the fireplace. It would catch alight at any moment. I fell to my knees on the hearth and plucked out the paper. I suffocated the flame that had taken hold of the corner with my gloved hand.

The paper was singed, but the relevant lines were legible. With a release of breath, I sat back on my haunches, and eyed Mr. Warrington.

He struggled against his captors—gentlemen who wouldn't obey a woman's order but drew the line at one of their own striking another member. Yet again, the English gentleman's code of honor was on display.

The manager and doorman stood in the doorway, looking somewhat dazed by proceedings. Thankfully, Mr. Drummond was regaining consciousness. Another member helped him to sit up, while a second assisted me to my feet.

I clutched the page to my chest. "Telephone Scotland Yard," I ordered the manager. "Tell them you have a suspect for the murder of Mrs. Warrington in custody and require urgent assistance." Whispers and murmurs of disbelief followed him out.

"You're a fool if you think they'll believe you," Mr. Warrington snarled at me.

"You're a fool if you think this little scene makes you look innocent." I smiled, pleased that I sounded braver than I felt.

Mr. Drummond held a bloodied handkerchief to his forehead as he stood on unsteady legs. A gentleman assisted him to an armchair where he sat, looking dazed. I sat on the chair next to him.

"You'll need to see a doctor," I said gently.

His eyes filled with tears.

"I'm sorry," I said and meant it. Sorry that he'd learned that his lover was a murderer. Sorry that he'd found out in such a dramatic fashion and in a public place in the presence of friends. "Thank you for your assistance."

He lifted his gaze to Mr. Warrington, being held by the doorman and a club member. Mr. Warrington glared back at us, his face thunderous. Murderous.

"Why?" Mr. Drummond whispered.

"To keep his secret," I said.

"*Our* secret, you mean."

"He had more to lose than you if it got out. Murdering her solved several problems for him. His secret would be safe, it killed her unborn baby too, and meant he inherited her fortune."

One of the gentlemen handed a glass of brandy to Mr. Drummond and another to me. It was far too early to be drinking, but I welcomed the burning sensation in my throat as I sipped. They say it steadied nerves, but one sip didn't do the trick. My nerves still vibrated like plucked violin strings. I took two more sips.

Mr. Drummond drained his glass and held it out for a refill. He blinked back tears but no longer looked at Mr. Warrington. He seemed unable to face him.

It took an eternity for the police to arrive, or so it felt. Detective Inspector Hobart came with another detective, the one who'd originally worked on the investigation and declared the vagrant was the killer. Harry arrived too, with two constables.

He crouched beside my chair. His eyes were filled with concern, but his jaw was hard. "Are you all right?"

"Fit as a fiddle. Thank you. Mr. Drummond needs to see a doctor, however."

The manager informed us he had telephoned for one.

Detective Inspector Hobart ordered the club members and staff to leave. Once they were gone, only the police remained, along with Mr. Warrington, Mr. Drummond, Harry and me. I was glad to see Hobart taking charge, and not the other detective. Indeed, he looked contrite and willing to let his more senior colleague take over.

"Miss Fox, I believe you have some evidence for us," Detective Inspector Hobart began. "Something that proves Warrington killed his wife."

I stood and winced as my knees protested. There must be bruises on them from when I landed on the marble hearth. Harry grasped me by the elbow.

"Cleo?"

"I'm fine, thank you." I handed his father the torn page. "Mr. Warrington removed this from the register." I indicated the book on a table.

The second detective picked it up and flipped through the pages until he came to the torn edge. "It's for the night of the murder," he said.

"Take a look at the time noted for Mr. Warrington's arrival," I said.

Detective Inspector Hobart glanced down the page. "Nine-forty-five. And?"

"And look at the line above it."

Harry peered over his father's shoulder. "It's an entry noting the arrival of a Captain Fanshaw." He swore under his breath. "If I'd seen this myself, I would have noticed. But the manager refused to let me look. How did you manage it?"

"I threatened him."

The second detective asked to see the page. He also swore, but louder than Harry. "Captain Fanshaw's time of arrival was five past ten."

"A full twenty minutes *after* Mr. Warrington," I added. "But if he arrived after Mr. Warrington, why does his name appear *above* it in the book? It should appear below. According to these entries, Captain Fanshaw arrived at ten-oh-five, Mr. Warrington at nine-forty-five, and a Sir Leonard

Lloyd at ten-thirty, in that order. Mr. Warrington's actual time of arrival must have been between ten-oh-five and ten-thirty."

"Did you bribe the manager to write an earlier time?" Harry asked Mr. Warrington.

Mr. Warrington pressed his lips into a thin line.

"I don't think he did," I said. "The handwriting is different. The way the five is written for the arrival time of nine-forty-five is different to the way it's written for Mr. Warrington's departure time of twelve-oh-five, as well as all of the other times that include a five. You can see the number was written without lifting the pen in all instances except for that one arrival time, where the five was written in two parts with a tiny gap between the strokes, the horizontal line at the top being separate from the rest. I think he distracted the manager and wrote the time down himself then signed it. The manager never bothered to check. I got the idea from watching Peter at the front desk of the hotel. He did the same. He never glanced at what the guest wrote when they signed in."

Mr. Drummond groaned. "How could you, Bertie?"

Mr. Warrington simply lifted his chin, but there was no defiance in his gaze now, only resignation.

"Talk me through that night," Detective Inspector Hobart said.

Mr. Warrington looked away, presenting us with his obstinate profile.

Harry recounted the events instead. "Warrington argued with his wife in the drawing room at nine, at which point he killed her."

Mr. Drummond made a choking sound then clutched at his throat.

"Warrington probably carries a small knife with him, as some men do. He killed her from behind as she sat in the wingback chair then unlocked the window."

"He would have avoided getting blood on himself if he did it from behind," Detective Inspector Hobart said.

"He made sure the chair was angled in such a way that someone standing at the door could not have seen her face. He then left through that door, made sure the servants saw him, and exited the house at about nine-thirty. The coachman took him to the club and will testify to the fact that it was nine-forty-five when they arrived. But if we question him again, I'm sure he'll tell us that he never actually saw Warrington *enter* the club. Instead of going inside, Warrington caught a cab back to the house. He climbed up the pipe and through the unlocked drawing room window. He rang for the butler and asked for tea, disguising his voice so that it sounded more feminine."

"For just a single word, it would have been easy to mistake him for Mrs. Warrington," I added.

"He waited until the butler returned with the tea. He didn't speak again, but merely pointed at the table where the butler left the tea before retreating. It was ten past ten at that point, perhaps a little before. Warrington then removed his wife's jewels and left the drawing room the same way he'd got in, through the window. He ran to the lane where he knew a vagrant had made his camp and tucked the jewels into his belongings. He took a cab back to the club, and entered for the first time that evening. He spoke to the manager and wrote his own time of entry in the book, noting it as nine-forty-five when in actuality it was more like twenty-five past ten."

Mr. Warrington snorted. "Anyone can write the incorrect time. It was a mistake. It means nothing, and it certainly won't hold up in court."

Detective Inspector Hobart nodded. "All true. But a little legwork will uncover the drivers who took you back to the house and picked you up again and brought you here." He looked to his junior colleague who quickly scrawled some notes in his notebook.

"You made sure you were seen by as many club members as possible in the hour and a half you were here," I said. "But I am quite sure none can pinpoint you as being here before ten-twenty-five with any certainty."

Detective Inspector Hobart signaled to the constables to escort Mr. Warrington from the club. "How unfortunate for you to employ the only private detectives in London with an ethical conscience. Anyone else would have overlooked your guilt and taken their money. Harry and Miss Fox couldn't let a murderer escape justice, even if that murderer was paying their fee."

Harry removed his hat and scrubbed his hand through his hair. "We almost let him get away with it. We even gave him the theory that he was the intended target, not his wife, and he faked his own stabbing because of it."

"But we worked it out in the end," I said.

He gave me a wan smile, but I suspected he was annoyed with himself for being so blind to the truth.

The constables marched Mr. Warrington between them to the door. As they passed him, Mr. Drummond caught his arm. "How could you? Isobel was your wife. You didn't have to love her, but you were duty bound to protect her."

Mr. Warrington's lip curled with his sneer. "You always were a sentimental fool, Pierce. Duty, honor, love…none of them matter if you don't have respect, and respect comes from power and money. If she had followed through on her threat and exposed me, I would have been finished."

"We would have got through it together," Mr. Drummond whispered through trembling lips.

"You're an even bigger fool than I thought if you believe that."

"Do you not love me? Did you ever?"

Mr. Warrington huffed a humorless laugh. "I enjoyed your company, I'll give you that. Goodbye, Pierce. Mind the scandal that's about to erupt. You wouldn't want to get caught up in it."

Mr. Drummond watched his lover being escorted from the room, his eyes full of unshed tears. I touched his arm, but he shook me off.

Harry and I followed the police outside to the pavement. The constables bundled Mr. Warrington into their waiting coach while the two detectives spoke to one another in hushed tones.

"I'll walk you home," Harry said to me.

It was broad daylight, but I didn't refuse his offer. I wanted his company.

His father broke away from his colleague and approached us. "Good work today. Both of you."

"Cleo did most of it," Harry said. "I should have insisted on seeing the register and not taken the manager at his word."

"It's not your fault," I said.

He didn't seem entirely convinced.

"You two make a good team," the inspector said.

"We're not a team," Harry cut in before I could agree. "In fact, our association ends after I walk Cleo back to the hotel."

His father's gaze flicked from Harry to me then back again. "If that's what you both want."

"It's how it must be."

Detective Inspector Hobart touched the brim of his hat. "Good day, Miss Fox. And thank you again."

I watched him climb into the carriage then headed off along Savile Row with Harry. "I'm sorry about earlier today. I lost my temper and I shouldn't have. The entire situation with my uncle is frustrating."

"We can agree on that, at least," he muttered.

We walked on in comfortable silence. The weather was mild for February and the walk quite pleasant. Or, rather, the companionship was pleasant. The traffic noise, smell of horse manure and overcast sky were certainly nothing worthy of note. Even so, neither of us hurried. A leisurely amble did us quite nicely.

"It's a shame we won't get paid," Harry said.

"There might not even be any publicity for us," I added. "I do hope you'll be all right."

"Financially? Of course. There are still several inquiries coming in for new clients, thanks to the publicity from the last case. Thanks to *you*, I should say."

"Are any of them for investigations that don't involve married men and women spying on their spouse?"

"One. A missing black and white cat named Coco. Last seen on her owner's front doorstep in Mayfair."

"Poor Coco. She could be anywhere by now."

"Don't feel sorry for the cat, feel sorry for me. The owner insisted I set aside the Warrington case and find her pet. She has come to the office every day, and even followed me home once. Now that she knows where I live, I might never be rid of her."

"She must be desperate to find it. I know some older folk whose pets replace their children once they grow up and leave home."

"She doesn't have children, grown or otherwise. She's only about twenty. Her chaperone escorts her."

"Twenty and unmarried? Now I do feel sorry for you."

He eyed me sideways. "I'm going to ignore your insinuation since you couldn't possibly think she'd want to hire me for any other reason than my reputation."

I laughed softly.

"That's better," he said.

I glanced up at him and caught him watching me with an intensity that was both unnerving and thrilling. He quickly looked away. "What's better?" I asked.

"You, smiling again. I don't like it when you're angry."

"I wasn't angry with you."

"I know, but..." He shrugged and left the sentence unfinished.

We were almost at the hotel when we met Victor emerging from the lane that led to the staff entrance. He didn't see us at first. He was looking down at the pavement, his hands in his pockets.

"Is something the matter?" I asked him.

"Afternoon, Miss Fox, Mr. Armitage. I was just thinking."

"Harmony will be pleased." My tease fell on deaf ears. He merely blinked at me. He was a hundred miles away. "What are you thinking about?"

"I wanted to get to the bottom of Chef's unhappiness over the new restaurant."

"Because it didn't make sense as to why he'd not want a larger venue?" Harry asked.

Victor nodded. "I thought about what you said, about him not being bothered to negotiate new agreements with suppliers. So I took it upon myself to speak to one of the suppliers who stopped by just now with a delivery. He said he'd have no problem increasing the order. He was very keen to keep doing business with the Mayfair, and especially glad to supply more fish."

"That's good news," I said.

Victor agreed. "So if all the suppliers are going to be as agreeable, why does the chef have a problem with expansion?"

"Extra paperwork?" Harry suggested.

"That's the thing. I just had a word with the chef, and offered to draw up new contracts for him, specifying the quantities and everything. The supplier I spoke to insisted the discount remain the same, as agreed, but that seemed like a reasonable request to me."

"I fail to see why this troubles you," I said.

"Because when I told the chef, he dismissed me."

I gasped. "He can't do that!"

"He can," both Victor and Harry said.

"Not without a good reason," I pointed out.

They both looked at me. They were right. The chef could hire and dismiss staff as he saw fit. He didn't need a reason. The kitchen was his domain and not even Mr. Hobart could overrule his decisions. The only one with any authority was my uncle.

"Let me sort this out," I said.

"Wait a moment." Harry glanced along the lane toward the staff entrance. "Tell me exactly what you told the chef."

Victor chewed on his lower lip as he tried to recall. "I said I spoke to our fishmonger when he brought around the delivery. Chef was furious. I thought he was going to slice me open like a leg of lamb. I tried to placate him by saying the supplier was real keen and there wasn't a problem, and when that didn't calm him down, I mentioned I'd take care of any extra paperwork. That's when he told me to get out and take my knives with me."

"So he didn't even like you speaking to the supplier in the first place," Harry said. "Does anyone other than the chef speak to them?"

"Only in passing if they happen to deliver goods themselves. No one but the chef discusses business." Victor shrugged. "Maybe Chef doesn't want anyone to know the hotel gets a thirty percent discount. Maybe he doesn't want chefs at other hotels to find out we get more than them."

"Thirty!" Harry shook his head. "Now it all makes sense. The contracts all stipulate *twenty* percent discount, not thirty."

Victor swore under his breath. "Chef's been pocketing the extra ten percent."

CHAPTER 17

*J*t was no wonder the chef had insisted on negotiating the contracts himself, and refused to let others discuss terms with the suppliers. He'd cheated the hotel out of the extra ten percent and kept it himself. He'd been doing it for years.

Harry gazed towards the hotel's front door where the doorman dressed in smart red jacket with brass buttons and rimless red hat opened the carriage door for a guest. "My uncle will be furious." .

"Mine will be apoplectic," I said. "We need to tell them. Come on. Both of you. We'll do it now."

Harry put up his hands. "You don't need me."

"But you worked it out. You should be there when we tell them."

"You also knew the contracts stated twenty percent. I remember telling you. I'm absolutely certain you worked it out at the same time as me." He shook Victor's hand and touched the brim of his hat in farewell.

"Harry," I snapped as he walked off. "You're missing an opportunity. My uncle will be pleased. It might be a way into his good graces."

He simply waved. He didn't even turn around. Why did he not want to please my uncle? It might go some way to helping Uncle Ronald agree that we could be friends again.

"Honestly," I muttered.

"Can I offer some advice, Miss Fox?"

"Please do. I don't understand men sometimes."

"Mr. Armitage knows it won't change Sir Ronald's opinion of him. Not in any way that counts."

"Nonsense. Of course it will. A little, at least."

"He also doesn't feel as though he's done anything to earn thanks."

"I disagree."

"You're not a Bainbridge, Miss Fox."

"Thank you. Finally someone acknowledges that."

"But you not being a Bainbridge means you don't know how things are for people *like* the Bainbridges. I don't know about Cambridge, but here staff have their place and they're never going to rise above it. That applies to former staff too." He nodded at the retreating figure of Harry about to be swallowed up by the pedestrian traffic.

I sighed. "The University is no different, although snobbery of the intellectual kind is rife there too. I have seen sons of shopkeepers and tradesmen rise in academia, however, although they are very few in number."

"I reckon it's rarer here. Even the hardest working hotel manager whose reputation for excellence extends across Europe won't be seen as anything more than an employee. He might mingle with princes in the foyer, but he can't sit down at the dinner table with them."

My heart sank like a leaden ball. He was right. My uncle's snobbery would never allow him to accept Harry as anything more than a former member of staff who lied about his criminal record. He would never allow us to be friends.

Victor and I entered the hotel through the front door since I was worried he'd be chased out by the knife-wielding chef if he was seen near the kitchen. The only reaction he received was from Frank who refused to let him in until I insisted. One or two guests stared, but that was all. None of the other front-of-house staff paid us any attention as we headed directly to Mr. Hobart's office. He wasn't there so I sent Goliath in search of him, and my uncle too.

Ten minutes later, they joined us. Victor repeated the conversation he'd had with the fishmonger, and Mr. Hobart immediately realized the chef was pocketing the ten percent difference.

He opened the filing cabinet drawer and flicked through the files. "He must have altered the copies of the contracts he gave to me." He pulled out a file and scanned the pages. "This copy definitely stipulates twenty percent."

Uncle Ronald accepted the file from Mr. Hobart. "It can be easily verified with the suppliers. Get onto it, Hobart. I want you to speak to every single food and beverage supplier and check the actual bulk purchasing discount against these copies. I'll speak to Chef about the fishmonger." He clapped Victor on the shoulder. "Good work, lad. You did well."

"It was Mr. Armitage who realized, sir."

I could have kissed Victor for mentioning Harry, saving me from doing it.

My uncle's brow plunged with his scowl. He turned an icy glare onto me. It would seem he suspected I was somehow involved after all. "What's he got to do with it?"

If I told him I'd been with Harry when we bumped into Victor, I'd be ordered not to leave the hotel without a chaperone in future.

Victor came to my rescue again. "I saw him outside, walking past, and he asked me why I looked troubled. I thought I'd just lost my job, and wasn't thinking Chef was duplicitous. I hope I didn't do anything wrong by the hotel."

Uncle Ronald grunted. "You shouldn't discuss hotel business with outsiders."

"He's hardly an outsider," I said. "Mr. Armitage cares about the Mayfair."

"Bah!"

"If this episode doesn't prove it, what will?"

He had the good grace not to comment further, but a scowl continued to score his forehead. Perhaps I should have left it there, but I could not.

"Perhaps you should consider paying him a fee as a means of thanking him, Uncle. As a private detective—"

"Pay him! I never engaged his services in the first place, why should I pay him anything?"

"Because he did you a good turn. One that will save the hotel money. He didn't have to point out the discrepancy to

Victor, but as a private detective, I imagine he couldn't let the chef get away with it. Paying him is only fair, and you are nothing if not fair, Uncle."

I wasn't sure appealing to his better nature would work, but it seemed coupling that with flattery did the trick. He gave a single nod and turned to Mr. Hobart. "See that your nephew receives a *nominal* amount."

"Yes, sir, and thank you, on Harry's behalf."

My uncle grunted and jerked open the door. He strode out of the office towards the foyer.

I blew out a breath. "That went well. Thank you, Victor."

"So, am I still employed?" he asked.

"You are," Mr. Hobart said. "I suspect we're going to need as many cooks as we can get. When Chef leaves, he'll take several with him. I suggest you take the rest of the day off, however, to avoid him. Sir Ronald won't dismiss him until after dinner."

"Who'll take his place?"

"That is a good question. But first things first." He returned to the filing cabinet and pulled out another file. "I have to speak to the suppliers in person. It'll take me all day tomorrow."

"Tomorrow's Sunday," I pointed out. "They won't be at work and nor should you."

"I'll be here. There's too much to do."

"Your job could be halved if Peter stepped into the role of assistant manager."

I thought he might dislike my interfering, but he actually smiled. "As a matter of fact, I was going to speak to him today. I was just discussing it with Sir Ronald when we were fetched to come here, and he agreed that Peter should be appointed assistant manager. He'll have a learning curve, of course, but he proved himself when he suggested one of the day porters move into the role of night porter. He even found a replacement to fill the daytime role."

"I'm so pleased to hear it."

"I'm not sure I would have given him due consideration if you hadn't been so convinced he had it in him, Miss Fox."

Victor and I left and headed for the staff parlor, collecting Goliath on the way. Frank and Peter remained at their stations, looking like puppies missing out on a treat. I'd hoped to find Harmony there. She sat in the corner, separate from the other maids, drinking tea and reading the latest novel I'd loaned her from the hotel library. The maids all stared at Victor. It would seem the gossip about his argument with the chef had reached them.

Harmony closed the book upon seeing us. "It's about time. I've been worried sick."

"You don't have to worry about me," Victor said as he poured cups of tea.

"Not you; Miss Fox."

Considering she didn't know I'd confronted Mr. Warrington at his club, she had no reason to worry about me. I suspected she'd been concerned for Victor, but didn't like admitting it.

I accepted a teacup from him. "You don't have to worry about me, either. Mr. Warrington has been arrested for the murder."

"Blimey," Goliath blurted out. "So you won't be earning your fee, Miss Fox?"

"I'm afraid not."

Victor perched on the edge of the table, cradling his cup of tea in both hands. Harmony watched him from beneath lowered lids. I suspected she was desperate to ask him questions about his argument with Chef, but didn't want to appear too interested.

I remained silent, concentrating on my tea. Victor did too, looking as though he didn't have a care in the world. His carefree manner was in stark contrast to Harmony's fidgeting. She couldn't sit still, and her thumb stroked the teacup handle as if trying to scrub off a speck.

In the end, it was Goliath who broke the silence. "Why is everyone looking at Vic?"

"Ain't you 'eard?" one of the other maids asked. "Chef dismissed him."

"Bloody hell," Goliath muttered. "What'd you do?"

Victor merely shrugged. "Told him his Hollandaise sauce is too runny."

Goliath and the maids stared at him, speechless. Harmony, however, didn't believe him. She arched her brows at me, requesting the truth. I merely shrugged. My uncle wouldn't want the staff knowing he'd been cheated by the chef, and I would respect his wish for discretion.

I finished my tea then returned to my room to put my feet up and read a book until dinner. I planned to eat in my room alone, but a message from my aunt arrived, requesting my presence along with Flossy's in her suite.

Despite the informality, I knew my aunt would expect me to wear something moderately elegant, so I changed into an evening dress of black silk with gray diamonds embroidered on the sleeves and a panel of chiffon covering my decolletage. She greeted me in her sitting room, taking both my hands in hers, and gave a nod of approval for my choice of outfit.

"You look pretty, Cleo, even when you're not trying."

"You flatter me, Aunt, but Flossy is the true beauty in this room." My cousin did look lovely in violet velvet with buttercup yellow swirls embroidered across the bodice and hem. Unlike me, she dressed as formally as she would if we were dining with guests in the restaurant.

We ordered our meals through the brass speaking tube which ran all the way to the kitchen. At the other end, a junior cook would write our order down and pass it on to the chef and his cooks. Tomorrow, the kitchen would be in chaos without its leader, but tonight, all would be as it had been, and we could be assured our meals would arrive in a timely manner.

Aunt Lilian had made sure to sit beside me on the sofa, and she now took my hand in her trembling one. She regarded me through bloodshot eyes. "Cleo, what *did* you say to Edward Caldicott during dinner on Wednesday night?"

I glanced at Flossy but she was no help. She looked as confused as me. "I don't recall. Why?"

"He's leaving on his Grand Tour after all."

"Good for him. I'm glad he decided not to abandon his travel plans."

Her fingers tightened around mine. "He was all set *not* to go when he thought—" She cut herself off and nibbled her lower lip.

"When he thought what?" When she tried to let go of my hand, I placed my other one over hers, trapping it. "When he thought I was interested in him? Considering I never gave him any reason to hope, he should not have altered his plans."

"You seemed to enjoy his company."

"I do, on occasion. But it's a great leap from enjoying a man's company to hoping there could be something more than friendship."

"Is it?" She turned to face me fully, taking a few moments to gather her thoughts. I allowed her the time, even though I didn't want to hear what she had to say. I knew I wouldn't like it. "Cleo, Edward is a fine young man with prospects. He comes from a good family and is even quite handsome. There is no gossip about him, nasty or otherwise, and nobody can think of a reason not to like him."

It was the blandest endorsement any fellow had ever received, and I almost laughed. I refrained, however, not wanting to disrespect my aunt. When she wasn't under the influence of her tonic, her mind became addled.

"He is a fine man," I agreed. "But it would be cruel to give him hope that we could be more than friends."

She clicked her tongue and withdrew her hand. "I know you *say* you won't marry, but that's because you haven't seen enough of the world. You don't know how it is for spinsters. While you're young and pretty, the world is a wonderful place. But as you age and your friends marry, they move on. Life will become terribly lonely if you don't have a husband and children to share it with."

"Except heiresses," Flossy said. "Everyone wants to be friends with an heiress. They don't have to marry if they don't wish to."

"Cleo is not an heiress."

Her words dropped like bombs, followed by a silence so dense it rang in my ears. My aunt and cousin knew that I should have been an heiress, if my grandparents hadn't excluded my mother from their will.

"Nor do I wish to be," I said cheerfully. "I wouldn't want people to be my friend simply because I was wealthy. Now, who would like to play cards while we wait for dinner?"

* * *

AFTER ATTENDING church with my aunt and cousin the following morning, I was stopped by Mr. Hobart in the foyer. He waited for Flossy and Aunt Lilian to be out of earshot before he pressed an envelope into my hand.

"I meant to take this home with me last night and give it to Harry at dinner but forgot," he said. "It's Sir Ronald's payment. Would you mind taking it to him this afternoon? I'm too busy. He said he'll be going into his office after lunch."

I was about to tell him Harry didn't want to see me anymore, but changed my mind. Just because Harry was worried about what my uncle would do didn't mean I had to give in too. I was concerned, of course, but I was also determined to maintain our friendship. We would simply have to careful never to be seen together.

I ate sandwiches with my family in my aunt and uncle's suite. It was not our usual Sunday lunch affair, but the chef had been dismissed after last night's shift so only a little more than half of the cooks had come in this morning. The dining room was closed to encourage guests to eat a light luncheon in their rooms or dine elsewhere. My uncle assured us the remaining cooks could be relied upon to make sure dinner was up to the usual standards of the Mayfair, but from the worried look on Floyd's face, I had doubts.

I made my excuses after lunch and retired to my room where I waited a suitable period of time before sneaking out. The foyer was quiet, but I couldn't avoid the staff on duty. I ordered Goliath and Frank not to tell my family I'd gone out if asked, then hurried off towards Soho.

Harry was in his office, reading correspondence. His coat, jacket and hat hung on the coat stand by the door, and his tie was a little crooked. I resisted the urge to straighten it.

His gaze narrowed upon seeing me. "I thought I made it clear you weren't to come here again."

"You did, and I chose to ignore you."

"That's not wise."

"Wisdom has nothing to do with it." I sat and withdrew the envelope of money from my bag. "My uncle is being unreasonable, so I've decided to do as I please. I'll be discreet, of course. It's in no one's best interests to antagonize him." I slid the envelope across the desk towards him.

"Because you'll lose your allowance," he said flatly. "Why is Sir Ronald paying you an allowance anyway? What happened to your mother's inheritance?" The moment it was said, he regretted it. "I'm sorry, that was rude of me. It's none of my business. It seems I've grown used to interrogating suspects and forgot who you were."

"It's all right. I don't mind telling you." To my surprise, it was the truth. I wanted him to know. "There was no inheritance. My maternal grandparents didn't like my mother's choice of husband so they cut her off. Aunt Lilian inherited their entire fortune. When I came to live here, I learned that my uncle had been paying me a small allowance ever since my parents died."

Harry rubbed his finger over his lower lip as he regarded me, his gaze assessing. Or, rather, reassessing. My admission had just challenged every assumption he'd made about me.

My pride wouldn't allow me to tell him that my paternal grandparents had refused to accept more and that without the little we had received, we would have been destitute. I couldn't bring myself to tell Harry, or anyone, that everything I owned was thanks to my uncle's generosity. But I could see from the pity in his eyes that he knew.

I stood abruptly and indicated the envelope. "That's your fee for discovering the chef's deception."

He blinked slowly. "Fee?"

"I should go."

He beat me to the door, yet again. I ought to learn to quicken my pace when leaving his office. "Cleo, wait."

I looked up at him and fell into the dark pools of his eyes. "Yes?" I murmured.

"I..." He cleared his throat and shifted his focus to a point on the wall above my head. "I told my father how the photographer, Sharp, has been illegally selling pornographic photographs without obtaining the consent of the customer. He said he'd look into it and have the studio shut down if there's enough proof."

I blew out a measured breath and clutched my bag tightly in both hands. "Good."

He dragged his hand through his hair and over the back of his neck. I wasn't sure if he had more to say, so I waited. He rested his hand on the doorknob but didn't open the door.

"Cleo…"

"Yes?"

"Goodbye."

"No, Harry, it's not goodbye. How can it be when we're partners?"

His features relaxed into a smile. My heart warmed to see it. "Partners? Last time I checked, your name wasn't on the door."

"Give it time." I glanced pointedly at the doorknob.

He opened the door and I left. "Don't come knocking on my door anymore," he called after me. "I won't let you in."

I glanced over my shoulder to see him leaning a shoulder against the doorframe, his head almost skimming the top. His lips tilted with his crooked smile. He looked more handsome in that casual pose, dressed in his shirt and waistcoat, than any man had a right to be.

"I always just walk in anyway."

He laughed lightly. "You're unbelievable."

"Thank you. You're quite unbelievable yourself."

Available 7th June 2022 :
MURDER AT THE DRESSMAKER'S SALON
The 4th Cleopatra Fox Mystery

A MESSAGE FROM THE AUTHOR

I hope you enjoyed reading MURDER INN THE DRAWING ROOM as much as I enjoyed writing it. As an independent author, getting the word out about my book is vital to its success, so if you liked this book please consider telling your friends and writing a review at the store where you purchased it. If you would like to be contacted when I release a new book, subscribe to my newsletter at http://cjarcher.com/contact-cj/newsletter/. You will only be contacted when I have a new book out.

ALSO BY C.J. ARCHER

SERIES WITH 2 OR MORE BOOKS

Cleopatra Fox Mysteries

After The Rift

Glass and Steele

The Ministry of Curiosities Series

The Emily Chambers Spirit Medium Trilogy

The 1st Freak House Trilogy

The 2nd Freak House Trilogy

The 3rd Freak House Trilogy

The Assassins Guild Series

Lord Hawkesbury's Players Series

Witch Born

SINGLE TITLES NOT IN A SERIES

Courting His Countess

Surrender

Redemption

The Mercenary's Price

ABOUT THE AUTHOR

C.J. Archer has loved history and books for as long as she can remember and feels fortunate that she found a way to combine the two. She spent her early childhood in the dramatic beauty of outback Queensland, Australia, but now lives in suburban Melbourne with her husband, two children and a mischievous black & white cat named Coco.

Subscribe to C.J.'s newsletter through her website to be notified when she releases a new book, as well as get access to exclusive content and subscriber-only giveaways. Her website also contains up to date details on all her books: http://cjarcher.com She loves to hear from readers. You can contact her through email cj@cjarcher.com or follow her on social media to get the latest updates on her books:

- facebook.com/CJArcherAuthorPage
- twitter.com/cj_archer
- instagram.com/authorcjarcher
- pinterest.com/cjarcher
- bookbub.com/authors/c-j-archer

CPSIA information can be obtained
at www.ICGtesting.com
Printed in the USA
LVHW031341181121
703498LV00001B/1

9 781922 554093